Exit Sherlock Holmes

Exit Sherlock Holmes

The Great Detective's Final Days

Robert Lee Hall

CHARLES SCRIBNER'S SONS
NEW YORK

Library of Congress Cataloging in Publication Data

Hall, Robert Lee.
    Exit Sherlock Holmes.

    I. Title.
PZ4.H17885Ex   [PS3558.A3739]   813'.5'4   76–56152
ISBN 0–684–14849–8

1 3 5 7 9 11 13 15 17 19 H/C 20 18 16 14 12 10 8 6 4 2

Printed in the United States of America

Acknowledgments

Thanks to the Ramona Street Regulars: Ruth, Marcia, Sewall, Marilyn, Jules, Spike, Jim, Kirsten, Charlene, Minuha, Millie, Grant, Myron, Gregg; thanks to Jean for correcting my prepositions; special thanks to guru Ray for showing me how to light a scene. Thanks to Pat for believing in me and to Thea for being Thea. Thanks to Dean and Shirley Dickensheet for reading the manuscript of an unknown writer and to Jacques Barzun for close attention. Thanks to my mother and dad for their help; thanks to Brian Hall for being my enthusiastic partisan. Thanks to Arthur Conan Doyle for that marvelously obsessive character, Sherlock Holmes, and for Watson, who wondered at the great detective's powers.

For my father

Preface

In February 1975 I received a registered letter from Murray, Murray, and Murray, solicitors of New Court, London, E.C. 4, announcing that Emily Percy Hall, my grandmother, had died peacefully in her sleep at Middlesex Hospital at the age of seventy-six. I had not seen her since my childhood, when my parents emigrated to the United States, so she is little more than a wan, vaguely smiling figure in old photographs. Nevertheless, according to the eldest Murray's letter, as her only grandchild I was sole heir to her estate—little of monetary value but one item of special interest: a battered tin dispatch box with a famous name painted on its lid, *John H. Watson, M.D.*

In that box were numerous heretofore unpublished cases of Sherlock Holmes.

Emily Hall, it seemed, had been the goddaughter of John Watson's second wife and thus, through that relationship, had come into possession of the box. Neither Violet Watson nor my grandmother seems to have opened it—little wonder; it is squat, gray, and unpromising. It was discovered, with other dusty, disused items, on a high shelf in a closet in my grandmother's flat in Belgravia. It had once, when Watson was alive, been thought important enough to be kept in the vaults of Cox and Company, Charing Cross; now it, and its contents, belong to me.

The following manuscript was the longest of thirty-two records of Sherlock Holmes' cases in the box. The other cases will be released to scholars and devotees in due time. The present work was in a yellowing envelope on top of the other papers, no doubt the last item placed in the box, and consisted of 346 sheets of ordinary unruled bond paper, numbered and covered on one side with the firm, legible hand of John Watson. So incredible is it that at first I thought it must be a hoax or fraud.

I have since changed my mind. Dr. Watson was not given to games; surely he wrote this in good faith, believing every word. Is it then a product of his senile mind? No. Although written when he was seventy-eight, the narrative is straightforward and lucid, and if Watson had fantasized he would not have created this, which is beyond his range and temperament, in no matter what state his old brain may have been.

There are two remaining possibilities. One is that the "secret" of the tale is just another invention of Sherlock Holmes' fertile mind—but if so, to what purpose? The other is that the story is true.

The answer appears to be hidden in the past—or perhaps in the future.

Each reader must form his own opinion.

Exit Sherlock Holmes

Prologue

L O N D O N   H A S   C H A N G E D; the world has changed. Hansom cabs no longer rattle through the rain, nor does the sea-coal flame upon the hearth in the sitting room at Baker Street, where once I was privileged to take my well-won ease with the best and wisest man whom I have ever known.

These are my thoughts as I sit, propped up by two great pillows in bed in my third-floor room at Bart's, looking down upon the snarled traffic on Little Britain where it curves to become King Edward Street. Double-decker red omnibuses spew their exhaust into the air, as do the black boxlike taxicabs and other motorcars which have replaced horse-drawn vehicles on London's thoroughfares. As my old friend predicted it would, the world has changed indeed.

It is 1930.

Bart's: the hospital of St. Bartholomew the Great. Its history is ancient and hallowed. Tradition holds that it was founded in 1123 by the jester of King Henry I, Rahere, who had caught malaria during a pilgrimage to Rome and vowed to establish a church in London should he recover. God spared him and in return he is supposed to have founded St. Bartholomew the

Great, to which was attached a hospital, the first charitable institution in London. However, Bart's is notable to me not because of this ancient history, nor because I practiced here as a young medical student, nor because I lie now in one of its beds; but because it was here in 1881, in a chemical laboratory crowded with bottles, retorts, and Bunsen burners with their flickering blue flames, that young Stamford introduced me to Sherlock Holmes.

"You have been in Afghanistan, I perceive," said the detective, astonishing me for the first time with his deductive powers. He grasped my hand in his quick, firm manner. Thus was our association begun.

Sister Milbank, full-bosomed, rubicund, smelling of antiseptic and violets, brings me the pen and paper I have asked her for. Her starched nurse's uniform crackles as she leans over to tuck in the blanket which I have allowed to stray. She adjusts the table tray so I may have a more comfortable surface upon which to write.

"Another Sherlock Holmes adventure, Dr. Watson?" asks she, dimpling.

"Yes," I tell her.

She does not know what to reply, for Sherlock Holmes, though famous, is a man of another century, remote from her modern concerns. She flashes a smile of cheery professional approval, scuffs briskly out of my room on her rubber-soled shoes, and closes the door.

I break the seal upon the package of paper and open it. The glare of early autumn light cascades from my window over the stack of blank white sheets. I take up my pen.

At long last I am about to reveal the secret which Sherlock Holmes kept hidden until the conclusion of his final adventure.

1

I RECALL my old friend saying to me one evening, while we sat as we so often did on either side of the fire in our lodgings on Baker Street, "My dear fellow, life is infinitely stranger than anything which the mind of man could invent." A smile whose meaning I thought I knew crossed his lips as he spoke. It was only at the conclusion of the final adventure which I was to share with him that the true significance of these words flashed into my brain, for that adventure, the most bizarre and shocking of any of our exploits together, revealed at long last the secret which Sherlock Holmes had hidden for years behind his reticent manner. I had assumed that his silence about his origins and relations was the result of a fine tact, but it proved instead to be but one more of his famous games, a convenient and necessary disguise. Sherlock Holmes was both more and less than he appeared, and yet—I thank God—he remained to the last my dear and loyal friend.

I feel trepidation as I begin, for who will believe what I am about to set down? Indeed there are moments when I doubt it myself. Then, the figure of my old friend rises in my mind, tall, lean, and upright, representing the finest impulses of

mankind, and I wonder that I doubt. Sherlock Holmes deceived me in many things, but in the end he told the truth.

For Holmes the affair began even before our fortuitous
meeting at Bart's in 1881, but I was not drawn into it until
nearly a quarter of a century later, on a dank evening in 1903.
During the intervening years I had shared the great detective's exploits, recording many of them for the delight and
amazement of an adoring public. On Tuesday, October 11,
1903, I received a note in Holmes' precise but eccentric hand
stating that it was imperative he see me that evening at eight.
Such a summons could not be denied, so, after returning home
from my Gloucester Road office to change my clothes and dine
with my wife, Violet, I begged her leave and took a hansom
the short distance from Queen Anne Street to the familiar
lodgings in Mrs. Hudson's house. I confess that my interest was
aroused, for a similar note had brought me round only a month
before to participate in the singular case of the "Creeping
Man," which had taken Holmes and myself for some days to
the university town of Camford. Since then, however, being
occupied by my re-established Kensington practice and a
pleasant if predictable domestic life, I had neither seen nor
heard from him. I had assumed that my friend was taken up
by his own scientific and criminological pursuits, but was glad
now that he once more wished to have me with him on some
new case.

A word about our relationship in those days is in order. I had
married again, this second time to the former Miss Violet
Hunter, the chestnut-haired governess whom Holmes and I
had aided in solving the mystery at the Copper Beeches in
1889. Holmes was pleased to say that I had "deserted him for
a wife," but in fact I remained loyal to him and was ever ready
to help him however I could. After so many years of association I was a habit to him, like the violin, the shag tobacco, the
index books wherein he kept his files of press cuttings about
criminal cases. (Fortunately there was one habit he had ended,
that of cocaine addiction, and with it the career of the late
Professor James Moriarty; my chronicle of that adventure had

appeared just ten years before in the *Strand Magazine.*) And so I was answering the detective's call as I had always done, ready to lend an ear or to bring along my old service revolver if a chase or a perilous entrapment should be in order.

My hansom drew up at 221B Baker Street. I alighted and paid the cabman. I pulled my scarf tighter about my throat; the night air was bitterly cold, and a yellowish fog was spreading up from the glistening cobblestones, almost obscuring the houses across the way and turning the streetlamps into attenuated spectral silhouettes. I glanced up toward Holmes' rooms. There was a dim light in his bow window, but the shades were drawn and no movement could be seen within. I entered the house to be met in the front hall by Mrs. Hudson, our landlady of many years. I was surprised to find her wringing her hands.

"Oh, Dr. Watson," she moaned. "It is terrible news!"

I was alarmed at once. "What is it?" I demanded.

Mrs. Hudson refused to answer. "Mr. Holmes must tell you himself," was all she would say, sputtering near tears.

I went upstairs at once.

Holmes merely waved an arm at me as I entered the familiar sitting room. He was seated by the fire in his voluminous chair with his knees drawn up, puffing at his black and oily clay pipe, the companion to his ruminative moods. Obviously one of these moods was upon him now, and I followed his lead in not speaking; I seated myself opposite him to wait. Usually in these fits (brought about by a dearth of interesting cases), which might be punctuated with cries of despair at the criminal world's lack of imagination, he donned his old purple dressing gown and slouched by the fire silently or scraped mournfully on his violin. This evening neither violin nor dressing gown was in sight. In fact I was a little surprised to see Holmes clothed in walking boots and sturdy tweeds, as if he were a country gentleman about to take a vigorous day's walk across the moors, perhaps with a fowling piece under his arm for some impromptu shooting. I wondered what strenuous engagement had caused him to get himself up like this, and wondered too at the drawn shades, and why the only illumination aside from the fire came from a single oil lamp, turned low, on the table beside him.

For the rest, the room was much as always—untidy, with Holmes' formidable row of scrapbooks and reference books bulging from their cases, the acid-stained, deal-topped table littered with the paraphernalia of experiments in the chemical corner, in another corner the spirit case and gasogene, and, within Holmes' reach, the pipe rack, the scuttle where he kept his cigars, and the Persian slipper with the tobacco in the toe.

After some moments my friend looked deliberately at his watch, then gazed at me and began as he often did in mid-thought: "I have long been convinced, Watson, that there is no completely evil persona, just as there is no totally good one. Humanity is a sad amalgam of conflicting impulses which struggle against one another until in maturity they strike a balance. This alliance, however uneasy, defines the human being. The tendency is different in each of us, in some leaning toward the base, in others the lofty, but in none of us does one side completely obscure the other—in almost none of us, I should say."

With this qualification he slouched lower in his chair as if to bank his fires. His intense eyes continued to burn abstractedly behind narrowed lids. I was anxious to discover the news which Mrs. Hudson had denied me, but I was afraid that Holmes was about to fall into another silence. I said, half jokingly, "You mean to say that even you, Sherlock Holmes, who expend all your energies in combating crime—that you harbor evil potentialities?"

Holmes blinked. "In spite of the rather naïve modern notion of the perfectibility of human nature, I do, as we all do. Even the best of us are capable of much which would shatter our fine notions of ourselves."

"But you with an evil counterpart within? Ridiculous!"

To my surprise Holmes started. He sat bolt upright, and his keen gray eyes were instantly alert, searching my face. At last he smiled ironically. "Watson, at times you are extraordinary and make me realize that not only I possess the gift for perfect intuition."

This unexpected compliment pleased me greatly.

Holmes leaned forward, pressing his fingertips together in his characteristic manner. *"An evil counterpart,"* he repeated. "You have hit the very phrase, for it is he who plagues me, though he is not within myself. No, he is free and roams the world still, plotting destruction after his own mad fashion. It is he who has caused my ruminations on the delicate balance within the human soul."

"Who is the man?"

Holmes hesitated while regarding me steadily, as if measuring me for the revelation to come. "He is none other than the Napoleon of crime," he said at last.

I was astonished to hear the ominous and all-too-familiar phrase. Could this be the news to which Mrs. Hudson had alluded?

"Moriarty?" I exclaimed in disbelief.

"I speak of none other."

"But Holmes, you yourself killed him! You described most vividly to me how you thrust him over the precipice at Reichenbach and watched him fall into those terrible waters!"

At the thought, I could not avoid my own giddy memory of that tremendous Alpine abyss, lined by coal-black rock, into which the long sweep of green water hurls itself to become a hissing caldron. It was there I had believed that Holmes and his archenemy, Professor James Moriarty, had discharged their final duty to one another fourteen years before in a terrible, lonely struggle from which only one had emerged victorious.

Holmes looked grimmer than I had ever seen him. "The fact remains, Watson, that Moriarty is alive, however he's managed it. It may be that only the sacrifice of my life will rid the world of him for good. Decidedly I am the only man capable of dealing with him. His reappearance is fate's message to me that I cannot escape its toils!" He rose and began to pace, moving like a caged panther. I noticed that he kept the lamp between himself and the window, so that no shadow fell upon its drawn shades. "Watson, I should have realized that fact. I felt in the grip of fate then as we, Moriarty and I, equal in power, struggled locked in one another's arms, eye to eye, at the edge of those falls. I felt then that there could be but one conclusion: that I could not let him be, nor he me, and that we must topple together. I cannot describe my sense of triumph when I realized that I had slipped through his grasp, heard him scream, saw him kick madly, clawing at the air to no avail. When he fell and I watched him disappear into those churning waters, I felt a great relief—for more reasons than I have told you, old friend, or than I intend you to know . . ."

I felt a pang. "I hope you can trust me, Holmes."

He stopped pacing to smile at me, kindly but with a touch of regret. "It is not a matter of trust, Watson, but one of protection. I shield you from a truth too strange for you or any man of this century." He gripped my shoulder reassuringly. "And so the old dilemma remains: Moriarty. This I can promise you —that if it proves to be the final problem indeed, I shall make every attempt to explain it all to you before my end. I hope the faith you have had in me all these years will continue, and that you will believe me."

"I shall!" I averred with feeling, never realizing how great a leap of the imagination it would take to keep that promise. "But how have you learned of Moriarty? What is his latest plot? Where has he been all these years?"

"One question at a time."

Holmes glanced at his watch, sat down, and leaned forward on the edge of his chair. His aquiline features showed concern but no trace of fear. I saw that the impending adventure had roused him and that he was eager for it to begin, to be matching wits with the one enemy worthy of his talents.

"Watson, my foe has been lying low these past fourteen years, plotting, recouping his losses, re-forming his diabolical organization. I have deduced his return not by any direct knowledge but from irrefutable circumstantial evidence. You know my methods. Be sure of it: Moriarty is back. His latest plot? It is directed against me. All his moves converge upon me in some fashion or other. That is why I must begin to make my offensive moves. I have known Moriarty for many years, from childhood in fact. The expression on your face tells me you are surprised at the news. Well, it is true. At one time we were as close as two human beings can be, but at a certain juncture I thrust him from me. Since then he has trailed my steps. At first I sought to avoid him, then to counter him blow by blow. Many of those seemingly unconnected cases which you have chronicled so aptly—if romantically—were darkened by his shadow. Only I recognized it behind a just-closed door or round a distant street corner, wreathed in a dense London fog. Now I see it again. It is unavoidable."

A faraway stare came into his eyes, as if he were seeing beyond the walls of 221B Baker Street, beyond England even, to some distant but inner landscape where a deep mystery was mapped.

"I see Moriarty everywhere now. He is near, he is my shadow. He dogs my every move. The end will not be long in coming."

"He should have perished at Reichenbach!" I asserted.

"It is a pity he did not," Holmes replied, with a strange, sad smile.

"And what will you do?"

Holmes' introspective moment vanished. At once he was again the Holmes I knew, all determination and energy.

"Disappear! I have done it before; I shall do it again. Beekeeping on the Sussex Downs seems a plausible reason. In fact I have a villa there. It has been mine these past few months, an excellent place, the result of much searching. It is upon the southern slope of the downs, commanding a great view of the Channel, and there is a splendid beach extending for miles. I have often threatened my retirement of late. Only the bungling of Scotland Yard has kept me from it. Now it shall come true. You shall publicize it, Watson, in your inimitable manner."

"Of course," said I.

"But be vague, Watson, be vague."

"As you wish. It is truly amazing that Moriarty has returned. Mrs. Hudson had reason indeed to wring her hands."

Holmes' eyes opened wide. "Surely she did not mention him?"

"No. She said only that there was bad news, and that I must hear it from your lips."

"Then things are as they should be. She knows nothing of Moriarty's return and should not be told. No one besides myself is to know of it, save you. The loyal Mrs. Hudson believes only that I mean to retire at last, and that I leave tonight. I am touched that she is so moved by my departure."

"You leave tonight?" I was taken aback at his precipitateness.

He leaned over to tap his pipe upon the grate.

"I am afraid it must be so. There is no time to lose. You will have observed the drawn shades, the dim light. It would be an extremely lucky bullet which could find its mark through a drawn shade, and Moriarty does not trust to chance. I invited you here, in fact, only to say good-bye. Do not look so distressed, dear fellow. I hope it is not the last time we shall see one another, though I am embarking on my fate. Unfortunately I must act alone, but you may help in some small matters, if you will. Mrs. Hudson has my instructions. Until we meet again . . ." We rose and he gripped my hand in his powerful fingers. His thin lips smiled, and his piercing eyes looked hard into mine for an instant. As he released my hand he murmured, "Take care—and keep watch."

Then, drawing on his cloth cap and flinging his traveling cloak about his frame, he was gone, leaving me stunned and pondering.

2

I SPENT the next week carrying out what brief duties Holmes had charged me with. He had already spoken to Mrs. Hudson of his intentions, though not of their true purpose. She believed only that he meant to carry out his long-planned retirement—to keep bees, to farm, to write some monographs on cherished subjects.

When Holmes planned a ruse or set a trap to snare a criminal, he was thorough. He was a master of disguise, and now that he meant to disguise his whereabouts he took full steps: our old lodgings were to be let; Mrs. Hudson and I were to pack all his possessions and send them by rail to Eastbourne to be picked up. I had no doubt that when we had fulfilled our task and his belongings reached Eastbourne they would vanish utterly. I still recall the rainy autumn afternoon when for the last time I saw Holmes' rooms as they had been for twenty-two years, during which time I was privileged to share his adventures and act as his Boswell. Mrs. Hudson was sniffling in a corner as she held his violin tenderly; I myself fought a lump in my throat as I packed his voluminous scientific notes.

During the following days I wrote some brief notices to the

papers and to my publisher, announcing Holmes' retirement, that he wished to vanish from the limelight, and that his whereabouts were to remain unknown. Naturally I had as well to speak to my agent, Dr. A. C. Doyle; therefore I took myself one afternoon to No. 2, Devonshire Place, near Harley Street, where he kept offices.

Doyle's handsome walrus moustache quivered with regret at the news that Holmes had decided to retire at the height of his powers, but he implored me not to stop writing my narratives, which the public, grown used to glimpses of the great man, could not do without every few months. "It would be a shame, Dr. Watson, ever to deprive them of their hero. He is such an example!"

Holmes had not required that I should cease writing about him; in fact I had his permission to set down details of many of the cases I had shared with him. (A series of them, later to be collected under the title *The Return of Sherlock Holmes,* had just begun its run in the *Strand.*) And so I relented. It is a promise I have kept to this day.

Newspaper reporters were no less importunate than Dr. Doyle, but to their requests for information I had to say no. One lean impertinent redheaded fellow badgered me persistently, offering me a handsome sum for a personal interview with Holmes if only I would arrange it. To this I could only reply with the truth: that I did not know where Holmes was and that if I had known I would still not betray my friend's commands for any amount of money. Soon even this disagreeable fellow, seeing my firmness, desisted, and all was calm. Too calm.

In truth I was rather at sea as to what, if anything, I should do next, without further instructions from Holmes. The "few small tasks" were the packing and shipping of his goods; these I had done. True, there had been a note as well, posted the day after his departure with a look of haste about its writing, but when I tore it open in the privacy of my study it offered no new information nor asked me to do anything significant; it begged me to be patient and of good cheer, and again cautioned me to keep the name Moriarty to myself. Its only note-worthy feature was an injunction to make certain that any orders from Holmes were genuine and not a trick of his enemy ("You must hear my voice and see my figure, Watson"). Holmes' signature completed the note; there was nothing more.

And so I waited.

During those long days, in which autumn changed to bleak winter and Londoners wrapped themselves snugly in scarves and heavy coats, I ruminated often over the startling fact of Professor Moriarty's survival and the intriguing information that he and Holmes had been associated in their youth. How far back, I wondered, and in what connection? Were they schoolmates? Boy rivals? Holmes had never shown the slightest romantic interest in women; his fascination with Irene Adler had seemed to me of a purely intellectual kind. Yet could Moriarty and he have been rivals for the affection of some woman? That was as far afield as my speculations took me, but, alas, they had to remain mere speculations. I had not Holmes' gift for arriving at completed vistas from mere glimpses, and glimpses were all I had ever obtained of his early life and relations. I had often endeavored with little success to break through the reticence which he showed about all that concerned him personally. As the length of his absence grew, made ominous by the tenor of our last interview, I wished I had pursued my inquiries into his past with more vigor, for I realized that if I should ever require help on his behalf I should not know to whom to turn.

Another difficulty under which I labored was the vow of silence Holmes had imposed upon me. I knew that Moriarty had somehow survived the encounter at Reichenbach; I knew that Holmes had not retired but was invisibly plotting his own countermoves against his enemy. This knowledge weighed upon me day after day, and I badly wanted to share it with someone, to have at least a sounding board to test my rampant speculations, but I could not speak of it, not even to my wife. More than once I woke her by my tossing in the grip of feverish nightmares. At the center of my visions, like a foul spider at the center of a web, was James Moriarty.

Moriarty—how little I really knew of him, though enough to make me fear for Holmes' safety. Holmes had mentioned his name occasionally during our early association, but it was not until Porlock's letter early in 1888, which began the adventure I was to chronicle as "The Valley of Fear," that he enlarged upon the dread theme: "Moriarty is the greatest schemer on Earth, the organizer of every deviltry, the controlling brain of the underworld which can make or mar the destiny of nations." And yet, Holmes went on to explain, this same man was immune to suspicion, a respected mathematics professor in fact, and the celebrated author of a brilliant treatise on the binomial theorem as well as of *The Dynamics of an Asteroid,* a book of rarefied scientific scholarship much ahead of its time.

And then, in April 1891, Holmes had surprised me by appearing suddenly one evening in my consulting room. I had somewhat lost touch with him; newspaper accounts and two recent letters had led me to believe him to be still in France working on matters of importance to the French government. He looked gaunt and harassed; I asked about his health. His answer was that he was on the edge of closing his case against James Moriarty.

"I have ensnared him in a net not unlike those sticky webs in which he has entrapped many a poor victim of his own," Holmes had told me. "It is my most cunning achievement. It only remains for a few final strings to be drawn before the devil is caught. Even now, though he walks the streets and had the effrontery to threaten me this very morning in my rooms should I refuse to let him alone, he cannot work free. The net I have cast will draw about him without my presence in England; therefore I think it wise to flee to the Continent for a few days until the creature ceases his struggles. Will you come with me?"

My wife being absent, I consented.

But Moriarty had slipped away—though many of his confederates had been taken and his organization smashed—and it was on that fateful journey which took the detective and me, hotly pursued by the enraged Moriarty, to Canterbury, cross-country to Newhaven, over the Channel to Dieppe, thence to Brussels, Strasbourg, and Geneva, and finally by way of Inter-laken to Meiringen, that Holmes and his enemy had met, fought, and presumably both plunged to their deaths at Rei-chenbach Falls. Three years later, to my amazement and joy, Holmes had returned. Now Moriarty, inexplicably, was once more in our midst, again at his infamous work, and the strug-gle was joined anew.

And so the evil one haunted my dreams—a vague shadow of a figure. I had seen him but twice, neither time clearly. The first occasion was as a tall blurred scarecrow waving his fist furiously at the Continental Express carrying Holmes and me safely away from Victoria Station; the second was as a distant gaunt silhouette striding along the curving path which winds over the green-mantled shoulder of the Swiss hills to Reichen-bach, there to confront the one man who could halt his intri-cate schemes. I had to be content with Holmes' description of him: tall, pale, ascetic-looking, with hunched shoulders, a bulg-ing white cranium, deep-set narrow eyes, and a slow side-to-side oscillation of the head. That description alone was enough to terrify. It and my knowledge that Moriarty had re-formed his organization, whose aim was extortion, murder, and politi-cal blackmail, made me tremble at the thought that, being Holmes' closest friend, I was the logical source of information about his movements. I could not think that Moriarty believed his antagonist had retired. I would be the next object of the evildoer's sinister attentions.

Yet weeks went by and I heard nothing, nor did anything dire materialize out of the footsteps I frequently imagined dogged mine along London's foggy streets at night. I re-mained ignorant of everything except that the most danger-ous criminal and the foremost champion of law of their gener-ation stalked one another. I could not help reflecting how alike they were in every way—two single-minded geniuses, with but one difference to distinguish them forever: one was dedicated to the destruction of all that was good, the other to preserving and protecting it. I began at last to wonder if somewhere, unknown to me or the world, Holmes and Moriarty had already met, fought, and Holmes had met his match. At that thought a sense of sorrow, rage, and frustration overwhelmed me.

During this time of waiting I occupied myself with watching the newspapers for signs of Moriarty's activity. Holmes had been able to combine the seemingly insignificant details of day-by-day crimes in the seething London metropolis—petty thefts, wanton assaults, purposeless outrages—into a connected image of Moriarty's far-flung activities. I found plenty of crime reported in the dailies, much of it without reason, but when it came to understanding it as the work of one malignant controlling brain I was at a loss. Yet, studying the papers as never before, I learned how much depravity existed beneath the civilized veneer of our city, and I discovered many a crime, baffling to the police, which might well have been the handiwork of such as Moriarty.

I had not heard a word from Sherlock Holmes for six weeks when I had two unexpected visitors, familiar faces, who brought home to me the seriousness of the detective's absence. They were Inspectors Gregson and Lestrade of Scotland Yard, who appeared in my consulting rooms one crisp afternoon. I had known these men almost as long as I had known Holmes. When I first met them in the course of the Lauriston Gardens mystery, which developed into the famous *Study in Scarlet,* they had been smug, quick to jump to conclusions, and inclined to pooh-pooh his opinions, even when they sought them out; but they had mellowed over the years and regularly consulted Holmes, with a due appreciation of his powers.

"I'll come to the point, Dr. Watson," Tobias Gregson said to me after the briefest of preliminary greetings. His once-flaxen hair now almost all white, his long face looking old and tired, he said, "We badly want the help of Mr. Sherlock Holmes." He seemed as dour and earnest as I had ever seen him, and his associate's ferretlike countenance was no less solemn. Both men's eyes showed want of sleep and the lines about their mouths were grim.

Knowing that I must eventually confess my helplessness, I felt rather sorry for them, but I did not lose the opportunity of obtaining some information first. "What kind of help?" I asked as innocently as I dared.

"The usual kind, doctor. We have a large number of unexplained crimes on our hands of late. Separately they do not seem to have much purpose. We suspect a connection among them but can't make heads or tails of the cases and hoped Mr. Holmes would help us out."

"Can you describe these crimes to me?" I suggested. I felt a trifle embarrassed to be pressing my advantage so obviously.

Gregson glanced toward his colleague then back at me.

"Of course there's no objection to letting you know, doctor," Lestrade spoke up, "seeing that you are a trusted friend of Mr. Holmes, but we would rather wait until we can give him the details face to face. We can tell you that it's a pretty serious business, with possible international complications. There are stolen documents, traffic in diplomatic and military secrets, and the bribing and blackmailing of officials. Not the sort of thing that gets into the papers—a good deal too serious for that. Whitehall is breathing down our necks to make something of it soon, but whoever has organized it is too clever for us. We run into a blank wall at every turn. Naturally we hoped Mr. Holmes might consent to give us a hand. This sort of thing is right in his line."

I saw that my question had raised the poor fellow's hopes, so I confessed my ignorance of Holmes' whereabouts.

"So it's true, then," Gregson said. His face fell still further.

"Yes. In any case," I added, "I know Sherlock Holmes is bent on permanent retirement. From now on I'm afraid you will have to do without his services altogether."

This came as a decided blow. Bidding me good-bye, the two men went out, looking as dejected as sparrows in a cold wind.

The interview had turned out more satisfactorily for me

than for them. I had learned that there was an increase in crime coinciding with Holmes' supposed retirement. Moriarty, emboldened by the retreat of the only man who could checkmate him, was apparently taking larger strides. I wondered at his goal.

Nothing more of this, for good or ill, interrupted my next two weeks of waiting. Habit and nostalgia more than once directed my steps out of their way toward Baker Street. The sight of a lamp burning bright in the upper rooms at 221B reminded me of times past, of a sometimes perilous but far more stimulating life than I now led, and brought home to me how privileged I was to have been his friend. Now the light above was not a beacon to adventure, heralding the cry, "Come, Watson, the game is afoot!" but the commonplace sign of occupation—for Mrs. Hudson had let her upper rooms to a young actor soon after Holmes' vacating them.

"He is a pleasant young man," she confided to me one afternoon when I stopped round to see her. "But," she added after a moment, "I miss the peculiar visitors at odd hours." I took this as her tribute to Holmes.

On the eleventh of December, Thursday, my wife left for a week's holiday in Kent. Like myself, she had no relations living, but she had many friends. She had received an invitation from one of them, the young woman who had been her ward when she entered the profession of governess in 1885. This young woman, now Mrs. Percy, had two babies; Violet was their godmother. Extremely fond of children (I always thought it a pity she had had none of her own), Violet looked forward to seeing these two bright curly-haired dears, and had informed me in her brisk manner that for a week I must do without her company. We had been married less than a year, and this was to be our longest separation, but I agreed to her plan.

I delivered her with her considerable luggage to London Bridge Station in the morning. The whistles blew; the doors of the carriages banged shut. Violet leaned her bright face, freckled like a plover's egg, out of the window to peck at my cheek.

"You will keep well, won't you, old dear? Why don't you take the train to your friend's farm on the South Downs for the weekend? I am certain that Mr. Holmes would be glad to see you. Yes, I wish you would go. You have been so dour since he left London!" She drew in her head as the train set off.

If only it were as easy as that, I thought.

Her departure was, in fact, the prelude to my great adventure. Standing in the noisy station, watching her train pull out, I could not know that I was soon to hear from Holmes in a most mystifying way.

Late in the afternoon of the following day, Friday, I was preparing to leave my surgery, having ministered to my last patient of the week, when there came a vigorous rapping at my door and a familiar youthful voice crying, "Dr. Watson, Dr. Watson!"

I jumped up from my chair, but before I had a chance to open the door it was flung wide, and Billy, Sherlock Holmes' sometime page, tumbled into my consulting room, out of breath, red-cheeked from the cold, and full of an excitement I was sure came from something more than the impending Christmas season.

Billy had been employed by Holmes to run errands and carry out those quotidian tasks that the detective, absorbed in unraveling crime, had no time to perform for himself. The wise fresh-faced lad had also helped a little to fill the gap of isolation surrounding Holmes after I had left him. From Mrs. Hudson I knew that Holmes had taken leave of Billy as he had of us both. I was therefore alarmed at seeing him so unexpectedly now, and in such a flurry.

"Sherlock Holmes!" were the next words Billy gasped. He waved a crumpled piece of paper at me as he gulped air into his lungs.

"Holmes?" I repeated, my heart pounding. "Calm yourself, Billy. What of Holmes?"

I forced the boy to sit down. His bright eyes popping, he thrust the piece of paper into my hand.

"Read this!" he panted.

The paper was wadded into a ball. As his breathing came back to normal, he watched me unfold it. The message was characteristically terse and uncommunicative: *Watson, come at once.* It was signed *Sherlock Holmes.*

I read the words over several times. I was familiar enough with Holmes' handwriting after our long years of association to be sure it was no forgery—but what did it mean? Come where?

I turned to Billy. "Where did you get this?" I demanded.

"Mr. Holmes gave it to me."

"What—Holmes himself? You saw him?"

"Plain as day. Well—plain as night—not a quarter of an hour ago. It was already dark and very foggy, but he stopped right in the lamplight where I could see him plain. I'm sure it was him. He was wearing the old ulster I know so well and his cloth cap. It was on the King's Road. I go by there every day round about now. He must 'a been waiting for me. He was in an awful hurry. He didn't say a word, just jumped out of the fog—scared me something fierce!—stared at me hard, pushed this here in my hand, looked round as if he might 'a been followed, and made off so fast I didn't have no chance for a word, I was so took aback." Billy looked at me quizzically. "Is Mr. Holmes in trouble?"

"I can't answer that, Billy." I forced an encouraging look. "But we know no one is better able to take care of himself, don't we?"

The boy grinned. "I should say so. Still, it's very odd. When I last saw Mr. Holmes he told me he was holing up on his farm. Do you think he's back on a case in secret?"

"Perhaps," I said. "Can't you remember anything else—some other detail?"

"No. It was just as I told you. The minute I read the note I ran straight here. That was right, wasn't it? You'll know what to do?"

"Of course," said I, hoping I sounded confident. "Now you must get home."

"Yes." Billy pulled his cap upon his tousled head. "Tell Mr.

Holmes how I do miss working for him. He knows if he wants me, I'll drop everything and be ready."

The boy's eager loyalty touched me. "I will tell him, Billy. Good night."

"Good night." He waved an arm and left, his footsteps clattering down my stairs.

I walked behind my desk and sat with the strange paper before me. It seemed to be asking for help, and I was glad Billy was gone, for he would have read on my face that I had no idea on earth how to answer it.

3

I SAT for fully an hour. Normally a moderate user of tobacco, I anxiously smoked two pipes and a cigarette, but they
did not help. At the end of that hour the obstinate scrap of
paper still refused to testify to anything save my inadequacy
at knowing how to interpret it. I was sure that it spoke eloquently, but *Watson, come at once* was all I heard, and I could
not act because I did not know where to go. Holmes must have
meant more, there must be some other direction, I reasoned,
but I could not find it. Pressed as he may have been on that
shadowy street—perhaps within a footstep of Moriarty's grasp
or that of one of his numerous henchmen—if he had time to
scribble this, his quick brain must have added more, trusting
to me to understand it. But a few dozen square inches of paper
and six words were all that I could see.

At last I stood to stretch my legs. It was seven o'clock. A
glance out my window showed me that it was dark outside.
The clip-clop of cabs and carriages, the cries of a late newsven-
dor, the singsong lilt of a harmonium player in a nearby pub,
the distant wail of a train whistle were all that interfered with
my ponderings—these and the muffled heartbeat of London,
of which all sounds were a part.

I turned to stare with a sense of angry frustration at the paper under the lamplight. In my helpless state I could not avoid comparing my befuddlement with Sherlock Holmes' keen mind and deductive skill. From clues that baffled Scotland Yard he was almost invariably able to reconstruct the plan of any crime and an image of its perpetrator. I, the police, the world seemed babes compared to him! I had never ceased to wonder at his extraordinary knowledge. "Genius, Watson," he had told me once, "is an infinite capacity for taking pains." As a doctor I had sometimes wondered what he might have done for humanity in another field—medicine or biology. He might have been another Pasteur or Lister or Erlich, or deduced the logic of nature with the skill of a Darwin. I had wondered too what had caused him to set his footsteps so doggedly on the trail of crime. For now, however, I could only wish I had his skill to solve the riddle of that damnable paper.

I snatched it up from my desk. For the tenth time I held it to the light for its watermark. There was none. I sniffed at it for the odor of perfume or tobacco or any suggestive scent and smelled only my own faint cologne and the Arcadia Mixture, my blend. I even lit a candle and passed the message gently over its flame, as I had seen Holmes do when checking for secret writing, but succeeded only in crisping the edges of the precious paper. In frustration I crumpled it again and hurled it to the floor, where it rolled out of sight under a chair.

At once an idea struck me. It was very simple yet persuasive: the answer might not be in the paper at all!

Though he had possessed a telephone for some few years, Holmes was not fond of the instrument; he much preferred written messages and telegrams. I had often received such messages before, delivered by Billy. When Holmes had asked to see me but had not specified the place, I had always known where; for twenty-two years *where* had been Baker Street.

I was convinced. I struck my hand into my palm with a cry, bent and scrabbled under the chair to retrieve the cryptic note. I spread it urgently before me upon my desk. There was no other clue; Holmes' lack of explanation must mean that our old rendezvous, the scene of so many dangers and triumphs, was to be revitalized by our meeting there again! I thrilled at the thought; the scent of adventure bloomed in my nostrils as I made myself ready to set out instantly.

Throwing on my coat and switching off the lights, I had my hand to the door to dash away when I halted. The sudden remembrance of Holmes' last command made me hesitate. In my eagerness to act I had forgotten: I was to do nothing without being absolutely sure my orders came from him. I stood in the darkened room, light from the hall falling through the glass pane across my puzzled face. Suspicion overwhelmed me. Might this be a trick? And yet Billy, whose position with Holmes had been nearly as intimate as mine, had testified that it was certainly my friend who had accosted him. Holmes had glanced about as if he were followed and then had fled. Had he feared to betray his presence by even a whisper?

I hung fire over these new considerations.

Yet it seemed perfectly possible that at that crucial moment Holmes had simply been unable to appear to me in person and had chosen the nearest expedient. I made a decision: I could trust to Billy for the "figure" of Holmes' command; the handwriting on the note, unmistakably Sherlock's own, would stand for his "voice." I would go to Baker Street!

I stepped out into one of those unpleasant yellowish mists that blanket London in winter, transforming houses, vehicles, people into grotesquely looming shapes. I was glad I had not a fanciful disposition, glad of a sure destination and the reunion with my friend to occupy my thoughts, and glad to find a hansom so readily as I did. One pulled up just as I emerged from my door, its driver swathed to the eyes against the cold. I gave him my instructions as I stepped aboard. "Right you are, sir!" he barked crisply and urged his mare into the traffic.

The roadways were congested with other cabs, carriages, trams, and lorries moving cautiously along. Their lamps loomed like yellow cat's-eyes through the mist; dark forms darted among them at intersections. It took fully forty-five minutes to reach Baker Street through the miasmatic night.

I stepped down and paid my driver. Out of old habit I

glanced up. No light shone from the rooms where the actor resided; no doubt the young man was even now upon the stage. I walked to the door and rang the bell.

Mrs. Hudson was delighted, if surprised, to see me. "Come in, doctor. How pleasant! But on such a night—you should not have ventured out."

I stepped from the cold into the warmth of the familiar entranceway, feeling a sinking sensation at her words. "Is Mr. Holmes not here, then?" I said.

This startled her more than my arrival. "Mr. Holmes? Why, no sir. I have not seen him since that last day. Did you expect him here?"

I did not know how to answer. Suddenly I knew that I had made a great error, that I had misinterpreted Holmes' message utterly, and worse, that I had failed my friend.

"I did receive a message of sorts," I confessed, unable to hide my embarrassment and confusion. "I seem to have mistaken it."

Mrs. Hudson passed easily over my chagrin. "Well, I should be glad to see Mr. Sherlock Holmes myself. Not a word from him have I heard." She looked hurt at that. "But I suppose he is very busy in his new life. Have a cup of tea with me?"

She led me into her comfortable parlor. Rather than use the basement rooms, she had set up in her ground-floor flat a small kitchen which had been perfectly adequate to her needs, those of Holmes, and mine when I too had lodged here. Her maid and cook, when she had employed them, had shared a room off the entrance hall opposite hers. Mrs. Hudson disappeared into her kitchen to emerge some moments later with a tray of tea and biscuits. She poured us each a steaming cup, then settled herself opposite me.

"Now tell me, what is your news from Mr. Holmes?"

I hesitated. "I must confess I do not know," I admitted.

She looked concerned. "Is there some new mystery?"

Mrs. Hudson was a discreet and unassuming woman, and firmly loyal to Sherlock Holmes. She was now past sixty. Her iron-gray hair was tucked into a bun at the back of her head;

she had a matronly but still pleasing figure over which she
wore, this evening, a plain green housedress covered by her
spotless white apron. She sat before me, teacup poised in one
hand, gazing at me with concerned but understanding eyes.
One of the great regrets of my long career as Sherlock Holmes'
biographer is that I never drew a fuller portrait of her nor gave
her the credit she deserved. She was often the buffer between
Holmes and his callers; she was his housekeeper and landlady
and a kind of mother to him as well. She had served him
faithfully. If Holmes had allowed me to publish the facts in the
singular case of the bishop's brass candlesticks, in which her
wise action helped him to avert a great ecclesiastical scandal,
she would have been praised and noticed by the public. Now
her insight and the calmness with which she expressed it were
infinitely comforting to me.

"A new mystery! Indeed there is, Mrs. Hudson," I said with
perhaps less discretion than she would have shown in my
place.

"Is it a secret, doctor?"

My hesitation in responding was even briefer than before.
Holmes had often used me as a sounding board for his ideas.
I had learned over the past two months how important such
a person was. I badly needed a listener and there was no one
better suited than Mrs. Hudson. I trusted her completely.

"I have received a note," I began. I gave the details, not
mentioning Moriarty. I explained that I felt an urgency about
the matter and that my coming to her had been on a hunch,
apparently false.

Her reaction was peculiar. She looked very grim indeed, yet
at the same time as though rapid thoughts were passing
through her brain. She put down her teacup and sat twisting
her hands in her lap for a long moment, not looking at me.

"You think it is serious?" she asked at last.

"I do."

"I don't know, I don't know," she muttered, looking away
again, struggling with some inner decision.

I was thoroughly puzzled by her unexpected behavior,

which had almost something of guilt mixed up in it. "Anything you can tell me, Mrs. Hudson," I urged.

"Well, you see, I have no definite instructions on this from Mr. Holmes now, and it is a prohibition from so long ago . . ."

"A prohibition?"

"Yes. I was not to tell a soul of it—not even yourself."

I was astonished. "Of what?"

She thought again, then came to a decision. "There seems now to be some emergency. I thought there was something strange about Mr. Holmes' leaving, especially as in a way he didn't leave for good, but I didn't want to pry into his affairs. I just took his explanation as always. Your thought about his note is sensible, doctor. There is danger, and he may very well have meant you to come here. We cannot know for certain of course, but I think we must take the chance that though he is not present he means you to be. Perhaps you are to act alone; perhaps something has held him back." She suggested this fearfully. "Anyhow with him missing you'll have to be in charge, so you must know that Mr. Holmes did not take all his things when he departed. In fact he left a great deal behind. It may give you a clue."

"Didn't take everything?" I echoed. "But his rooms were emptied. I saw every last scrap packed and shipped myself."

"Those were not his only rooms."

This simple statement amazed me more than her admission of a secret prohibition.

"But there are no more rooms in the house!" I protested.

"There is the basement," she said quietly.

Involuntarily I looked toward the door leading off her parlor to the lower floor, a door which I realized I had never seen opened.

The story of the house I knew well. Mrs. Hudson had come into it after her husband's death by means of a legacy to him from a wealthy aunt. The house had been the scene of that aunt's early married life. She had kept servants; as was customary their quarters and work area—sleep rooms, kitchen, pantry, and washroom—were below. The two upper floors were the family sector. When the house had fallen to her at her husband's death, Mrs. Hudson had taken the ground floor for herself and after some alterations had put the upper floor out to let. Holmes and I, short of money at the time and needing to share rooms, had snapped them up. Never in the course of living there had I given a thought to the basement rooms, supposing them closed for convenience or used only for storage.

"Dr. Watson," Mrs. Hudson went on, biting her lip, "Mr. Holmes kept those rooms all these years without your knowledge."

I tried to grasp this. "From the beginning?"

"Yes. He came round to see me alone after you had looked at the upper floor together. He asked me about the old servants' quarters. Did I mean to use them myself, he wanted to know. I told him that I hadn't thought about it. He asked me if I would be willing to rent them to him as well, and he offered a very reasonable sum, so I said yes. 'But wait,' he said, 'there are conditions.' He explained that he wanted complete privacy, that he was a kind of scientist and that he would be bringing in chemicals and electrical equipment and such, and that he wanted to use the place as a sort of laboratory for his work. He promised me that he would do nothing dangerous, and I believed him, so I agreed again. 'There is one thing more,' he added. 'I would appreciate it if no one knew of our arrangement except you and me—not even Dr. Watson.' His explanation was that that would safeguard his valuable equipment, and when I came to understand that he was a detective I understood his need even better.

"Well, I am a woman of my word, and no one has heard of this to this day. It is only the seriousness of the matter that makes me tell it—and just to you, doctor, who have known him for so long. I hope you believe me when I say that since the time of his taking over the rooms I have not ventured into them, as he asked me not to do so. I don't know what he has been about down there. I have seen him carry in some strange-looking pieces of equipment by the old tradesmen's entrance, but he was always secretive about his traffic. He was very quiet when he worked; I had never a cause to complain. He became so famous—especially after your descriptions of his cases were published—that I guessed he was doing important detective work where no one would disturb him. I came to think nothing of his being there. He surprised me a little by asking to leave his things below when he retired. 'I may need them again at some time,' he told me. Naturally I agreed; I was happy that my house could continue to be a convenience for him. A draft from Lloyd's for the rent has arrived regularly ever since.

"Now you know it all, Dr. Watson. I didn't like to keep a secret from you that was under your nose, so to speak, but I had to respect Mr. Holmes' wishes."

"Of course," I said. "I understand."

In fact I was considerably relieved. The news of secret rooms had startled me, but the explanation was perfectly logical, so much so that I did not feel at all the victim of a deception, as Mrs. Hudson seemed to think I might; rather that Holmes' unknown laboratory had been a necessity for his work and that his keeping it a secret from me was a matter of protection rather than mistrust. Secretiveness was a part of him, so it did not surprise me to encounter one more aspect of it. It was probably an extension of his reticence about his origins and background. He needed to protect his private self. My understanding of that humanized him for me.

I put down my cup and stood, anxious to lose no more time. "May I see those rooms now?" I asked.

"I think it is time you did, doctor."

Mrs. Hudson rose promptly and removed a ring of keys from her apron pocket. She walked to the door that led below and placed the key in the lock. She had some difficulty in turning it, but at last it yielded with a rasping sound. "I have not opened this door in many years," she explained as she drew it back, creaking upon its hinges. "Dear me, it is very rusty!"

I peered into the dark stairwell. Cool, musty air wafted up to my nostrils. Nothing was visible below.

"Have you a light?" I asked.

Mrs. Hudson left and returned with an oil lamp. "There is an electric light below. Mr. Holmes installed it himself. You will have to search for the switch." She stepped back as I took the lamp from her and placed my foot down upon the first step. "I will leave you to your investigations," she said, ever discreet. "If you need me, please call."

"Thank you, Mrs. Hudson."

Holding the lamp aloft, I descended into Sherlock Holmes' secret laboratory.

4

I HELD onto the handrail as I descended. I began to detect the acrid odor of chemicals mingled with the dank air. Midway down the stairwell I paused to hold my hand near the lamplight; my fingers were covered with grime. Moving on, I looked down to notice that as they stepped my feet raised clouds of dust from the disused carpet. Holmes had always been slovenly about his rooms. When we had lodged together it had been the greatest exasperation to me to live with his clutter—particularly with the boxes of papers relating to his cases and to the general history of crime which he studied so assiduously. Often these scraps were piled three feet deep in the corners of our sitting room. It had been only with the greatest patience and effort that I, needing a modicum of order in my life, had ever persuaded him to file them away, so it did not surprise me to find that these steps, which had not been used in more than two decades, seemed never to have been cleaned once in that time.

I reached the bottom level and held my lamp as high as I could. It projected a ghostly illumination. Ahead was a short passageway with a door at its end, two doors in the left wall,

and one in the right. All the doors gaped open and looked as
if they had stood so for some time. Since Holmes had been the
sole occupant of these apartments there had apparently been
no reason to shut off any of the rooms. There was no furniture
in the passageway. I could discover no light switch.

Feeling peculiarly like the investigator of a newly opened
tomb, I moved to the end of the hall to the farthest door. As
I had guessed, it led into the washroom, where clothes were
once laundered by the servants. There was evidence that
Holmes had occasionally used the tap in this room for water
which he would have needed in the course of almost any
chemical experiment, and there were a few empty reagent
bottles sitting on the floor and on rickety shelves, but little else
of interest. There seemed no reason to linger, so, retracing my
steps, I came to the two doors which had been on my left.

These gave onto rooms which must have been servants'
quarters. I passed through the nearest open door to find myself
in a medium-sized room containing an electric lamp on an end
table and, next to it, an upholstered chair worn with much
sitting. There were various dottles and plugs of dried tobacco
arranged on the table, further evidence of Holmes' peculiar
habits. The lamp was placed so that anyone sitting in the chair
would have a good reading light, and that was clearly the
purpose of this part of the hideaway. The most remarkable
feature of the room stretched around me on fully three sides:
makeshift shelves reaching to ceiling height and groaning so
heavily with volumes of all shapes and sizes that they appeared ready to collapse inward at any moment. On the floor
was a threadbare Persian rug; stacked everywhere on this
were more books, so that to cross the room I had to pick my
way carefully from place to place. I did not wish to disturb this
seeming disarray—I knew that Holmes would carry a perfect
map of it inside his head and could lay his hand on any volume
at a moment's notice—so I hopped and slid my way carefully
to the end table, placed my oil lamp on the floor beside it, and
switched on the electric light. I began a systematic examination of Holmes' books, hoping they might give me a clue as to
the purpose of his hideaway.

What I found was an extraordinary collection of scientific volumes—though not of the sort I would have expected. Most of Holmes' shelf space in the apartment upstairs had been given over to criminal studies, but I could discover not one such work here. Instead there were copies of the classics of science—the writings of Newton, Lavoisier, James Watt, and others—as well as the latest scientific books and journals. The science of physics was the most thoroughly covered, in both theoretical aspects and practical applications. In that field Holmes must have amassed one of the best private collections in London. I examined titles and authors carefully, particularly those of the most recent publications which I assumed would have interested him most. The names of Ernest Rutherford and J. J. Thompson stood out. I was intensely curious about the content of these books, with such lengthy titles as Thompson's *Elements of the Mathematical Theory of Electricity and Magnetism,* but I could not carry the books with me to examine at my leisure. On the back of a card, therefore, I scribbled some of the more intriguing titles for later reference. It seemed the sort of thing which Holmes in my place would have done.

Less well represented were the chemical sciences, though they too made a strong showing. On the biological and geological sciences there were surprisingly few volumes—puzzling, considering how Holmes' diverse though variable knowledge of those studies had aided him in his detective work. It suggested to me that his efforts below had been directed toward some aim other than that of bringing criminals to justice, but I was in no position to guess what that might be.

Lastly there were some works decidedly out of place in that rigidly scientific company. They were what might be called sensational literature, of which Holmes' knowledge was already immense (he knew every detail of every horror perpetrated in the last century), but these were strictly of a genre I would have thought inapplicable to his work—namely, the supernatural. I thumbed through several examples, most of them lurid and melodramatic, appealing to gullible natures, and found stories of ghosts, poltergeists, clairvoyancy, mysteri-

ous disappearances. Unlike me, Holmes was a highly imaginative soul; oddities had always appealed to him, though usually
only as an excuse for unraveling the strange warp into commonplace threads. Were these volumes his diversion, a game
he played to relax his mind between bouts of intensive study?
If they were something more, I could not guess it.

I turned to go. As I bent to retrieve my lamp I saw a small
octavo volume lying open by the side of Holmes' chair, perhaps the last book he had perused before his departure. Curious, I bent and picked it up. Its title, not fitting into the catego-
ries of the other books, surprised me: *Stage Ways and Means.*
Excitedly I thumbed through its pages. Here at last might be
a comprehensible clue.

The book proved to be a manual for designers of theatrical
settings and effects. A quick perusal showed that it was divided
into two parts. The first section told how to construct stage
settings of various kinds and how to produce special theatrical
effects—floods, tempests, lightning, and so on. The second half
contained stage diagrams of most of the theatres in London,
from the variety houses to the grand West End establishments
such as Wyndham's or Her Majesty's. For each theatre there
was a list of its equipment and devices for producing the spectacles described in the first half. One could refer to the book
to find out what any particular theatre offered in the way of
space, lighting, and equipment. I examined the page at which
the book had been left open. As I might have expected, it was
devoted to diagrams and descriptions not of a palace of culture
but of a common though well-known Surreyside music hall,
the Pavilion. I could imagine Holmes quite at home there,
wandering in seedy disguise among the habitués, observing
keenly, making mental notes of the habits of the lower orders
for use in some future case.

I was sure that this book, so out of place yet recently read,
had some special significance for him. Thrusting it into my
coat pocket for later notice, I switched off the electric light,
took up my lamp, and went to the next room.

Not much was to be discovered there. It was somewhat

smaller than the library, lit by an unshaded light bulb in the ceiling which I switched on by a dangling cord. There were scraps of wood and pasteboard on the floor, apparently remnants of packing cases of chemicals, piping, electrical equipment. Aside from these the most interesting features of the otherwise unfurnished room were several steamer trunks arranged against one wall and a cracked and stained full-length mirror. The trunks were unlocked, and I opened them. They were crammed with costumes of various sorts, including a selection of women's clothing, and I surmised at once that here was a cache of Holmes' extraordinary series of disguises by which he baffled the criminal world. I even found the wrinkled trousers and jacket of the old bookseller whose personality Holmes had donned on his return to London via Lhasa, Mecca, Khartoum, and Montpellier nine years before. It brought back my joy at learning that my friend had not perished with Moriarty at Reichenbach. It reminded me of the urgency of my present task.

Rearranging the costumes as they had been and switching off the light, I crossed the hall and passed into the last, uninvestigated, room. My lamp sketchily revealed what lay before me: a crowded space at least four times the size of the largest of the other three rooms. Near the door to my left was the gleam of an electric switch. I touched it and the space was flooded with bright light.

Here was a laboratory indeed! The room itself must once have been the kitchen, but all that remained of it was a large stove and oven in one corner, kept no doubt to heat chemical reactions. The rest was a maze of tables on which were heaped the remnants of old experiments along with his latest work—what seemed endless lengths of glass tubing, flasks, test tubes, retort bottles, rubber stoppers, electrical wires, Bunsen burners, metal pipes leading all about, at some points springing overhead like grotesque stick figures—all attached to gauges and machines whose purpose was impossible to read. Bottled gas and soldering and welding equipment were against one wall. They must have been used in fashioning some of the machines, which looked decidedly hand-built. There were at least three kilns too, of varying sizes and purposes, for enamel work and for making high-fire ceramic pieces, special insulators perhaps. There was a large drafting table to my right heaped with papers, complicated engineering diagrams of which I could make no sense, and the floor nearby was littered with crumpled balls of paper and broken pencils, testimony to frustration in some grand experiment—but what? Compared to this, Holmes' activities in the old chemical corner upstairs had been useful but limited.

I believed now, looking about me, that I had underestimated my friend's energies. To have carried on this as well as crime-fighting was an extraordinary achievement. Had I mistaken his purpose as well? Was his real work here? Or was this part of the magnum opus he had hinted at occasionally, his intention to write a *Whole Art of Detection* some day? Perhaps he meant to conclude that work by revealing a revolutionary new procedure, a criminal-catching machine for which this was the rough model.

It was an odd speculation, but I understood at once what had suggested it. For, confusing as was the array of equipment before me, it had a kind of logic. Straight ahead, through a narrow and jumbled aisle, was the unmistakable center of the puzzle: a cleared space wherein rested a cubical cage, reminiscent of a circus cage, made of silvery wire mesh. It was perhaps six feet square and might have held one or two medium-sized animals or—I did not know what delivered the idea into my head—men. It was connected by wires and gauges to all the rest, which radiated out from it like the spokes of a twisted wheel, giving the impression that the disarray of the laboratory was in reality one machine which served the cage. It was strange to contemplate, truly fantastical, like something that Mr. H. G. Wells or the Frenchman Jules Verne might have invented, or perhaps like the apparatus whereby Dr. Frankenstein infused life into his monster. I was more confused than ever. I had come seeking the solution to a mystery and had succeeded only in enlarging it by my efforts.

The mysterious cage drew me. I made my way along the jumbled aisle to reach it. When I had done so I saw at once that it could not be made for confinement of any sort, for a few blows would surely have bent the thin bright wires which wove in and out to form its sides. I saw too that the thing was a complete cube; the mesh, with its inch-square interstices, curved to cover the floor as well. But it was also obviously more than an object of contemplation. It was meant to be entered, for the side facing me was hinged and latched. I tried the latch. It was not locked, and the side swung easily, silently, and invitingly open. I was moved to step into the thing. I had just placed my foot upon its floor when a noise halted my experimentation. I heard the muffled but urgent rapping of a hand upon a door.

I confess that I jumped. Who had caused the sound? It came again, sharply. I withdrew my foot from the cage and looked across the room. Heavy boards were nailed at three places along the wall from which the rapping originated, and I realized that they covered the windows onto the basement-level area at the front of the house. Someone was there, outside, knocking to get in.

Had my interpretation of Holmes' message been correct after all? Was it he who rapped so urgently at the door?

I experienced a thrill both of joy and of trepidation, joy at the possibility of seeing my friend again after so long an absence, trepidation at . . . I knew not what. Stepping carefully over and around pipes and wires, I came to the boarded-over wall. I found the door. Its single glass pane had been painted black and a heavy wire screen was screwed on the inside. A double series of bolts and a large steel bar, all of which could have been released from the outside with the proper keys, held the door fast. It was a fortresslike arrangement and brought home to me how much Holmes felt he needed to protect his experiments.

The rapping came again. So great was my desire to see Holmes, to hear the story of his two months' absence, to know if Moriarty was defeated, to have the new mystery of the laboratory explained, that impulsively I reached toward the latch, wanting to free the door, fling it wide, and greet my old friend. But I did not unlock it. My voice shook as I called out, "Who is there?"

There was a pause; then, "Watson!"

It was the voice of Sherlock Holmes.

"Open the door, Watson!" it came again, commanding.

Hurriedly I worked the locks, raised the bar, pulled the door back. I peered into the darkness. A man's figure in a long cloak loomed there, but his face was obscure, falling outside the range of the light from the door. My heart was pounding.

Why did he not use his keys? I wondered.

He stood outside for a moment. I searched the dark blur that was his face. He seemed to be looking not at me but beyond into the room.

"I am alone, Holmes," I assured him.

He came forward a step. I was relieved to see the light fall across the familiar features, though still he did not glance at me. Trailing wisps of fog, he brushed past me into the room.

"Shut the door," he said.

The unfamiliar imperiousness of his tone chilled me, but I did as ordered, fastening the locks and the bar firmly in place. When I turned, his back was to me. He was surveying the room, his head turning slowly back and forth as if to make certain that everything was still in its place.

"I am very glad to see you," I said eagerly. "I did not understand your message, but made the best of it I could. I hope I have acted correctly."

"Not understand?" Holmes said, turning at last. "You seem to have done very well, considering."

His look was directed at me now, and the light from one of the ceiling lamps fell brightly upon his face. My already uncertain sense of relief was undermined by doubt. Holmes' lips were smiling, but it was a smile I had never seen before. It seemed to mock me unpleasantly.

"I hope I shall always serve you well," I said uneasily.

"I hope so too, doctor," he replied.

There was an alteration in the voice too. His first words had been in the familiar cadence and timbre, but these were spoken more softly and with great precision, and they had an insinuating edge.

Holmes shrugged off his long gray traveling cloak. He held himself oddly. In fact his upright stance seemed to change before my eyes to something lower, as if a furtive tightness about his back made him hunch forward. His head dipped notably, then moved to one side—as if to see me better I thought—but immediately it slid to the other side and continued to move thus, back and forth, in a kind of slow, strange palsy. All the while his eyes glittered as the mocking smile expanded upon his lips.

"What is wrong, Holmes?" I asked, thoroughly alarmed. "Why do you look at me like that?"

"Can you not guess, doctor?"

The smile broadened still more. It was, I think, the ugliest smile I have ever seen, cruel, capable of joy only at human discomfort. Yellow teeth appeared from behind those lips, and a sudden burst of maniacal laughter rattled from the throat and echoed round the laboratory.

I drew back in horror. At once I knew that this could not be Sherlock Holmes. Never would he have behaved so with me. It was some ghastly charade of which I was the victim, a sinister piece of playacting.

And then it struck me—the hunched shoulders, the oscillating head, the reptilian manner!

The laughter stopped abruptly. "I see the light of knowledge in your eyes, doctor. Yes, you are perfectly correct. Allow me to introduce myself: I am Professor James Moriarty."

5

I WAS STUNNED. I stepped back until I felt against my shoulders the door which I had just bolted. If it had been open I might have fled from the man's mad assertion.

Yet I believed him instantly, in spite of his perverse resemblance to my friend, for which I had no explanation. It was not mere words that convinced me, though he spoke, as Holmes had described, in even, almost whispered tones carrying a conviction of terrible sincerity which a mere bully could never have produced; it was instead his whole manner which spoke the truth. In his presence I felt a kind of horror, a sense of evil I had never experienced before—not from Colonel Sebastian Moran nor Dr. Grimesby Roylott nor Charles Augustus Milverton, nor any other monster it had been my displeasure to encounter in my adventures with Sherlock Holmes. Professor Moriarty exuded an aura which was the antithesis of the detective's. Both had authority, but Moriarty's was the authority of evil, as if he were the last word in evil. Well I understood why Holmes had labeled him "the Napoleon of crime." This man, I felt, was capable of dominating the world, and if he could not dominate it, of destroying it. The man who could produce such an effect of corruption must be Moriarty.

As if I did not exist he turned and began exploring the laboratory. In this action he displayed a contemptuous confidence that I would not flee. There was good reason for it: he had struck me helpless with amazement. Yet I wanted to act, to counter him in some way. I cursed myself that I had not brought along my old service revolver, the companion of so many hair's-breadth escapes and captures with Holmes. Lacking it, I thought of rapidly throwing the bolts of the door and rushing out, or of dashing toward the hall up into Mrs. Hudson's apartment. I wanted to cry a warning that evil had invaded this London borough. These were powerful impulses, gone in an instant. Moriarty was right in his instinctive assessment: I was paralyzed at the knowledge that I would never complete any such actions. I must await his command.

He went rapidly up and down every aisle, moving with the oily grace of a snake, undulating around every obstacle. He was careful to touch nothing with his hands, but he paused often, and I heard an occasional chuckle.

"Very good," he said once, "better than I had hoped."

His deep-set eyes gleamed as they darted here and there.

I realized that his initial survey of the room had been a taking-in of what was new to him. Yet his manner of closer examination suggested that it was not entirely mysterious, that he recognized or understood at least part of it. Holmes had praised his enemy's powers highly: "a genius, a philosopher, an abstract thinker with a brain of the first order, equal to my own." No doubt in that concatenation of wires and rheostats and chemical bottles which had so baffled me, Moriarty's perverse genius had traced a connection and a purpose.

At last he finished his exploration. Seeing him bear down upon me along the narrow aisle was to be startled anew. His resemblance to Sherlock Holmes was uncanny! The tall height, but for his bent back, was perfect; the thin frame, the features—they were Holmes' to a tee. And yet they had all gone wrong; they were distorted by personality. In Holmes the height, wiry build, and features—hawklike nose, square chin—produced the effect of purposeful dignity. In Moriarty they were altered into something low and disreputable, and I could only assume that it was some terrible psychological force which had worked such damage. The effect was as if Sherlock Holmes' face had rotted and his noble stance had been perverted by the habits of a furtive, calculating nature. I recalled Holmes' description of Moriarty: pale skin, round shoulders, puckered eyes, protruding face quivering from side to side. At the time the description had revolted me. Seeing the creature in person, how much more appalled was I!

Holmes knew what he was describing at the time—and yet no word to me of the resemblance. What was I to make of that? And what was I to make of Moriarty's peculiar ability to draw himself up into the very image of Holmes—enough to fool me and, I realized suddenly, enough to fool Billy.

"You sent that message!" I blurted out.

Moriarty smiled his gloating smile again. He had come within five feet of me and stood easily, regarding me with leering eyes.

"Another light dawns. Marvelous! And yet rather too late, doctor. I perceive you have not learned much from your friend Sherlock Holmes."

He spoke the name with bitter irony.

"But the handwriting," I said, caught up in my own discovery.

"Really, doctor, you are too naïve. A simple forgery. Can you look at this"—he pulled himself upright, pirouetted, his face coming round in the fantastic Holmes-mask once more—"can you look at this and believe me incapable of Holmes' handwriting as well? There are many kinds of imitation; I am a master of them all." He allowed his face to fall back into the Moriarty sneer.

"I must concede you points as a dissembler," I said ruefully.

"Do you recall a redheaded journalist?" He imitated a wheedling tone.

I started.

"Ah! Your surprise tells me that you do. He was one of my

guises to get information. Don't fancy you thwarted me in that game by cleverness. We both know it was obstinacy and ignorance. And the cabman who brought you here tonight—was I not good at that? So, your expression tells me you are becoming immune to my revelations. Still, I fancy no real cabman in London could have gotten you across town more quickly than I in that fog. When I do a thing, doctor, I do it thoroughly. Don't think that your beloved Sherlock Holmes is the only man who can pretend."

"I daresay he is not. And what is it that you pretend to tonight?"

He laughed again, a raucous, high-pitched whine.

"A show of spirit! How delightful! Well, for one thing, I pretend to be amused by you. You make that easy for me, doctor. But why am I here? I think I shall serve you better than your friend, who has left you very much in the dark, if I am not mistaken. I know that is so, because I heard every word of your conversation with Mrs. Hudson—a sharp ear, a convenient window, and a dark night are the ruin of secrets. Holmes has misdirected both of you greatly. Well, that is his choice—and I understand it. Oh yes, I understand Sherlock Holmes very well; no one in the world understands him better than I. But I cannot sympathize. Not to trust his nearest friends! That is not ethical. It shows a want of form."

I had overcome my first shock enough to make some observations about Moriarty and to analyze my reactions to him. His voice continued low and soft, belying the mockery and veiled threats which he sent my way. Holmes had been right about that voice: it represented power—not the power of brute thundering force, but subtle intellect, supreme control. Moriarty's hissing tones suggested I was no better than an insect, beneath notice. His narrowed eyes pierced my soul and found it shallow; his pitying expression proclaimed my foolishness. It was an act of bravery to keep my eyes upon that face, whose changes bordered upon the obscene.

"The note," he went on, "was meant to get you to lead me to Sherlock Holmes. I am an avid reader of your writings, Dr.

Watson. I greet each new adventure with eager anticipation. The collected works are one of my studies, and I have expended much oil on them in the past. (I have figured in them more often than you might guess. For example it was I who masterminded the assassinations in 'The Five Orange Pips' and my organization which carried them out.) You may be surprised that I am in the main flattered by your portrait of me, via Holmes, in the very interesting but erroneously titled 'Final Problem.' I do Holmes the credit of not underestimating him when I confess that in this—which will surely be the final problem for him if I have my way—I have until now been baffled by his intentions. I believed that you, his closest friend and biographer, must know where he was and that with the proper stimulus would lead me to him so I might satisfy my curiosity, but I discover that you are as ignorant as I about where he has gone. But this"—he flung his arm wide to take in the laboratory—"this is better, doctor, far better. From it I have read his intentions; I know the end Holmes has in mind for me and shall act accordingly. Tut, tut, doctor; you have served your master very ill in your haste."

This was a bitter pill to swallow, but I stood up to it.

"And what do you read here?" I asked defiantly.

"Ah, you would be a dangerous man if you knew that—a peril to both Holmes and myself. If you could but imagine, doctor!"

He threw his head back in a kind of horrible ecstasy until the cords on his white neck stood out.

"But you are such a stodgy fellow, an idolator with no imagination. Worshiping Sherlock Holmes all these years, worshiping a fool, a weakling! I am by far a fitter object of worship. I know how to reward a man, how to amuse him."

He smiled slyly. A rack of empty test tubes stood on the counter by his side.

"For example—watch!" he commanded.

He took three of the test tubes in his left hand. Abruptly he flung the hand up and one, two, all three of them arced over his head. Startled, I expected to hear the crash of splintering glass, but instead he caught the tubes one by one in his right hand, tossed them again singly back into the left, and sent them flying once more. He was juggling the glass cylinders! I stared, no doubt looking extremely foolish. He watched my face and shook with his wheezing laugh, his pale face almost flushing at his delight, for he was enjoying his own performance.

Appalled as I was, I could not help appreciating it myself. The effortless skill with which he juggled was masterly. A hand snaked out of the moving configuration of glass to snatch another test tube from the rack. Then there were four tumbling overhead, suddenly five, then six. Moriarty's effort appeared no greater. He gave each a little twist and the test tubes began individually to whirl like little crystal dervishes in the air, but the thin fingers still caught them unerringly and sent them whirling again. I became almost mesmerized by the glinting things as they rose higher and higher toward the ceiling.

Then as suddenly as it had begun it was over. Moriarty caught and held all six test tubes in one hand. With a flourish he replaced them in the rack.

"What, no applause? You are a very unappreciative audience, doctor. But I forget—you are used to the higher realms of crime-solving. Base tricks do not impress you. Perhaps if you knew the truth about Sherlock Holmes you would not be so impressed by him. Yet we were speaking of other things before my diversion." He waved an arm grandly at the scene behind him. "This laboratory! I never guessed that it existed, and yet it is perfect, daringly near the mark and first-rate. No matter. I see it now, and it tells me much. Thank you again."

He bowed slightly to me, then looked at his watch.

"I have work to do, but I owe you who have revealed so much another moment at least. Any questions, doctor?"

I was furious at his offhand manner.

"I thought you always worked through confederates to save your skin. I am surprised you are not doing so now."

Immediately I regretted my words, but Moriarty only smiled.

"You must know Polonius' old saying about discretion and valor. I admit it is more than a bromide to me. But in the present matter I trust no one but myself. Now, it is Holmes and I. We must have this out face to face; nothing else will do. On that I know we are agreed."

"You should have perished at Reichenbach!" I exclaimed.

"Once I have Sherlock Holmes out of the way and can bring my plans to a successful conclusion I am sure the world will heartily concur with you. It was a great mistake for your friend to assume, when I disappeared over the ledge into those awful mists, that I was dead. It was uncharacteristic carelessness on his part. He knew I was his equal in the Eastern art of baritsu, which teaches one how to fall as well as fight. As it was I broke my left leg in three places, my left arm in two, and cracked several ribs, not to mention numerous bruises. But I was alive on that rocky outcrop to which I was swept out of his sight by the torrent, and that was what mattered. If he had picked his way downstream he would have found me helpless and could have finished the job. But he did not do so. I have often wondered about that. Perhaps he did not wish to know. Perhaps he did not want to join the struggle again. Look at this face, doctor. Its peculiarity cannot have escaped you. Imagine what it must mean for Sherlock Holmes to confront it, to know that he must destroy it or be destroyed himself."

Moriarty's fingers, the very image of the detective's in fact, came up to stroke the face, and a faraway look came into his eyes.

"It would be like killing one's own self," he said.

His hands dropped and he was the leering reptile again.

"No such sentiment for me, however! Holmes is full of it; I have none. It sets us against one another implacably; one of us must die!"

I controlled my revulsion. Not wanting to waste another question, I asked immediately, "How did you come to look so much like Holmes?" Only one possibility had occurred to me. "Are you brothers?"

Moriarty looked at me appraisingly.

"You are thinking, doctor. Good. It raises my regard for you. Brothers? We are closer than brothers—and farther apart than any two beings can be. Are you religious? It is a moral difference, if you will, or so Sherlock Holmes would have it. He is insufferable! And that absurd name! But so he chooses to call himself, and it is only slightly more ridiculous than James Moriarty. Both are useful and would play well on a bill together, don't you agree? High drama!"

He looked very smug at this, as if he had scored a great point.

I had no satisfaction from the answer. He used my questions to confound me. Still, aware that I might never escape to use it but hoping nonetheless to learn something that might help Holmes, I tried to get him to speak about the laboratory.

"I am heartily sorry to have led you here to learn things you may use against my friend," I said.

"Your friend, *your friend!* This grows tiresome, doctor. But yes, you are right." He turned and began stalking along the aisles again. "You have made a great blunder. This is the very lair of my enemy. He has fled, but his great work remains to me. I would never have expected him capable of it. I did not guess his game. What a piece of nerve even to attempt it. And to think that he may have succeeded! God, he is a formidable opponent. Life will be smoother but less interesting when I have snuffed him out."

He had reached the center of the room, the focus of the many-armed apparatus, the silvery wire cube which had reminded me of a circus cage. He stroked his hand along the mesh of one side and looked the thing up and down, his face suffused with smoldering emotion.

"I have seen this before and never thought to see it again," he said almost inaudibly, seeming to forget my presence. "The rest is new; the rest is Holmes' extraordinary reconstruction, his grand achievement, but this—this is my old friend, yet my enemy now . . ."

I had left the side of the cage open. Suddenly Moriarty swung his body through it and into the enclosure. He thrust

his fingers into the mesh, rattled it, peered out with a grimace
that might have made me pity a prisoner in such a place,
crouched, bobbed and wove his head, thrashed his body about
so that I was reminded of an angry ape. His face was full of
barely controlled fury. The cage was distorted by his thrash-
ing.

He shouted to me: "I have been here too, doctor, inside
these wires! So long ago. Damn Holmes! He shall never get me
here again!"

This exclamation was a screech, making me certain that his
usual low tones were but an instrument as much under control
as his body. Now something had gone wrong. The control
vanished and what came forth was very like the petulant howl
of a child—or a madman. This was what lay beneath the wily
surface!

Moriarty seemed to go berserk. Abruptly he leaped from
the cage and began flailing wantonly at every object within
reach, smashing and destroying. He rushed down the aisles,
overturning bottles, sweeping glassware and electrical equipment to the floor, cutting his bare hands but ignoring the
blood which streamed from them. I stared as he shouted and
grunted, his face distorted into a livid mask in which no trace
of Sherlock Holmes remained, no trace of civilization at all,
only an insane will to destroy. I knew that if I stepped in his
way he would break me like a stick.

His mad destructive binge went on and on. When there
seemed no more that could be smashed or disarranged with
his bare hands he picked up an iron bar and commenced
anew, striking furiously at the already ruined equipment as if
he would pound it through the floor.

Last of all, with his most terrible fury, he attacked the cage,
reducing it to a crumpled mass of metal wires.

When he was finished he stood in the center of the litter to
survey his achievement. He was hunched lower than ever
before, his long arms hanging at his side, almost touching the
ground. All was silence except for his ragged breathing, which
continued until I thought I must cry out with the agony of
waiting for his next move.

He moved, but not in my direction. From here and there in the wasteland of ruin arose hissing sounds, the result of spilled caustic agents eating at wood and metal. Moriarty wished to hasten this new kind of destruction. Near the door was a tin of turpentine. He rushed to it, unscrewed its top, and began splashing the contents about.

"Nothing shall remain of this!" he rasped.

When the tin was empty he tossed it upon the debris and picked up my still-burning oil lamp.

My throat ached with the need to cry out, my body agonized with paralyzed motion; I remained as immobile as stone as I watched Moriarty toss the lamp into the wreckage. Its glass chimney shattered, and the room exploded into flames.

6

I WAS CONSCIOUS of intense heat, of rivulets of flame chasing about the room, of roaring and crackling, but these were nothing compared with the sensibility that Moriarty's eyes, which seemed brighter and more terrifying than any fire, were now turned upon me. In them I saw the present holocaust reflected by a yellow flickering, but there was a deeper flame below the glinting surface, a threatening quality of mind, a promise of total destruction for mankind. Nevertheless the wantonness of Moriarty's present act against my friend's property made me lose my fear of him.

"You devil!" I cried above the roar of the blaze.

He crouched low before me, the smoke and flames framing him so he seemed truly the incarnation of Beelzebub in the pits of hell.

Beelzebub smiled.

Without thinking I leaped upon him. My fingers barely clawed at his coat when he turned aside my attack with a single effortless blow that toppled me to the floor. The wind was knocked out of me, but I scrambled to my feet and glared at him.

"Devil?" he repeated with a snarl. He placed his hands upon his hips and wheezed out another of his snide laughs. "That is very good, doctor. So appropriate. Holmes would not disagree with you, for he is a very angel. But the war between heaven and hell goes on. Its outcome is by no means certain."

He flung a hand toward the rising destruction behind him. "I rather think I have won this skirmish!"

Smoke began to fill my eyes, and I coughed. Moriarty threw on his cloak and wrapped its collar about his mouth and nose. Through it I heard his voice a final time.

"Save yourself, doctor! Save yourself! For I shall do no more tonight. After all you are not my enemy. Tell Sherlock Holmes of this when you see him. Tell him his plans are thwarted. I shall never go where he wishes to take me!"

With these words he flew to the door. The bolts were free, the iron bar loosed and flung backward in an instant. In another instant he was gone, and shortly I heard the clip-clop of the hansom in which he had carried me here disappearing down Baker Street at a gallop.

I heard voices calling. "Dr. Watson! Oh, doctor!"

It was Mrs. Hudson's frantic cry from above, echoing down the inner stairway. By now the smoke must be upstairs, and she could not have mistaken the crackling sound beneath her floor. Too, the horrendous noise of Moriarty's destruction of the laboratory must have aroused her.

"My God, what's wrong? Dr. Watson!" she cried again.

I heard another voice, a man's, and I thought I knew it though I could not place it: "Dr. Watson, can you hear us?"

It too came from above.

I was dizzy and sick from the smoke, and nearly blind. "I am all right," I shouted. "Call the fire brigade! Get out of the house to save yourselves!"

By now I could not see even the door, which was only paces away. I staggered in its direction but tripped over some piece of debris on the floor and fell headlong. I struggled to rise, but a fit of coughing overwhelmed me again. The acrid stench of smoke filled my nose and throat and lungs, burned my eyes, seemed even to cloud my brain. I was aware that I was losing consciousness and that if I were to save myself it must be now. But my body, overcome by paroxysms of choking and drenched in sweat by the almost unbearable heat, could only flail about helplessly. I had lost all sense of direction and, had I been left to my own devices, might as well have rolled into the flames as toward the door and safety.

Just as I felt myself blacking out, strong hands lifted me and propelled me toward cooler air.

"This way, Dr. Watson," said the familiar voice which I had heard from upstairs.

I felt the door jamb brush my shoulder; then the foggy night air enveloped me. Never had I welcomed it before, but my arms went out now in a kind of embrace, and my parched throat gasped to take it in. I leaned against the bricked wall of the area, panting. My eyes began to clear. It was obvious that the cold air rushing into the laboratory must only be feeding the blaze. I saw a slim vigorous figure before me, no doubt that of the man who had saved me. He pulled the door shut with a bang.

"That will damp the flames somewhat," he said briskly, turning to me. "I have shut the upper door as well, and Mrs. Hudson is safely out. Perhaps she has the firemen on their way already. Let us hope so. I have a personal stake in seeing this blaze out before too much damage is done."

It was too dark and my eyesight still too much impaired to make out the features of my rescuer, but I was now convinced that I knew him. I could not speak. He took my arm and led me up the stairs to the sidewalk. Already a small crowd had gathered, and along the street the running footsteps of others could be heard. Cries of "Fire!" and gasps of awe grew louder. Carriage traffic began to bunch up and then to halt. Neighbors flung wide their windows and front doors, lighting up the scene. They peered out anxiously at the growing crowd and the billows of smoke that now issued from the basement of 221B Baker Street.

There was a commotion and a clanging of bells. Around the

corner of the Marylebone Road careered one fire wagon, then another, the great white horses that drew them wild-eyed and heaving in their traces. I thanked God that help was here so soon. The wagons' rapid arrival gave me hope for the house which held so many memories.

I was beginning to feel very much myself again and surprisingly little the worse for wear. My vision had cleared. I saw that my rescuer standing by my side was a young man, strangely familiar, though I still could not identify him. He proved himself as able an organizer as savior. At the first sight of the speeding wagons he dashed into the crowd and soon parted it with a few sharp commands. With upraised arms he held it back as the wagons raced to a halt before the house. I fell back with the crowd to watch. The firemen unrolled their hoses and soon had floods of water gushing over the iron railing into the basement.

A moment later I caught sight of Mrs. Hudson in the throng opposite me. She appeared unharmed, but her tear-streaked face, lit by the flickering flames, was tense with concern for the house, and she wrung her hands in a piteous manner as she watched each move of the firemen intently. The young man had stepped near her. Separated from them by the mad rush of the firefighters, I watched as he leaned close to comfort her. The commotion of the crowd and the shouts of the firemen were such that I could not hear what passed between them, but her expression told me clearly that she knew him and was relieved to see him, that she was even more relieved by the encouraging words he spoke to her gently for a moment. At last he pointed across to where I stood. I was touched by the sudden joyous light that came into her eyes.

She waved and I waved back in turn, trying to encourage her with my look. My own hope was borne out when I turned back to the house. Huge billows of greasy smoke still boiled up from its depths, but there was little sign of flames. It appeared that the house would be saved.

When that hope became a certainty and the strenuous efforts of the firemen had calmed, the young man walked

across to me. The crowd was thinning, and the fog and blackness which had been dispelled momentarily by the light and
heat of the conflagration were closing in again. Soon the scene
would be deserted, leaving only the acrid-smelling odor of
burned wood to testify to the drama that had enlivened Baker
Street this night.

Mrs. Hudson stood nearby with two policemen. I could hear
their words: they were trying to combine kindness with duty,
comforting her indulgently while asking the necessary question: how had the blaze begun? Glancing covertly at me, Mrs.
Hudson earned my eternal gratitude by her next act. She took
full advantage of her position as a distraught woman to become helplessly hysterical. She drew forth a handkerchief and
wailed into it in a most uncharacteristic way—this from the
woman who had manipulated the wax head of Holmes fashioned by Oscar Meunier of Grenoble, when that head, silhouetted against the bow window of 221B Baker Street, was about
to be exploded by Colonel Sebastian Moran's deadly air gun.
She did not know, she sobbed; she could not think, she could
not speak! She waved her hands about madly and swayed this
way and that. It was an admirable performance with enough
real feeling to make it convincing.

The talents of women! I thought. It was a pity that Holmes
had fully appreciated the talents of only one.

The police were routed. Reluctantly they retreated, leaving
Mrs. Hudson to the arms of neighbors who led her off, but not
before I sent a discreet nod of appreciation her way. Of course
I knew that this might be just a reprieve, that some witness
might have seen the young man lead me out of the laboratory.
The police made up in persistence what they lacked in insight;
they would surely be back, but for now at least I did not have
to explain my presence in the basement of 221B Baker Street.

Standing next to me, the young man leaned close to say
confidentially, "A remarkable woman, that—though I can remember when she and I lost no love between us. Yes, I used
to upset her greatly."

"How?" I asked.

I searched his smiling face. He looked not more than twenty-five—handsome, with finely cut features and dramatically flaring nostrils. His blond hair was cut rather long in a dashing style, enhancing the jaunty quality which was the immediate effect of his presence. He had the confident air of being the master of any situation, a D'Artagnan-like insouciance. He had certainly rescued me with cool-headed efficiency. Why did he seem familiar?

"Do you not recognize me, Dr. Watson?" He thrust out his hand frankly and announced with a toss of his head and a certainty of being known: "I am Frederick Wigmore."

I had never heard the name in my life, but I put out my hand. He shook it warmly as if we were old friends meeting after years. His smile was frank, but a touch of mischief twinkled in his blue eyes.

"Frederick Wigmore?" I repeated, bewildered. "I do not believe . . ."

"I am Mrs. Hudson's new lodger."

"The actor?"

"Yes, thanks to Mr. Holmes. It was he who suggested that I apply for the vacancy. I have the rooms you and he used to share, though I knew them well before I moved into them. I was in them many times in years past without ever dreaming that they would be mine some day."

"I was aware Mrs. Hudson's new lodger was an actor," I conceded, "but I am certain she did not introduce us. You are familiar with Holmes' old rooms, you say? I do seem to know you somehow."

"As well you should, doctor. I am Wiggins, late of the Baker Street Irregulars!"

I stared at him. It had been more than a dozen years since I had last seen towheaded young Wiggins. Then he had been perhaps twelve, the leader of the band of street Arabs whom Holmes had employed to discover what the police could not. They had been introduced to me during the course of our very first investigation together. It had been the revelation to my already reeling mind of just one more disconcerting side to

Holmes' eccentric practices. Six dirty little scoundrels, Wiggins among them, had clattered boldly up the stairs and tumbled into our rooms. Mrs. Hudson, tolerant as she was, had never grown used to them. I well remember her cries of disgust.

"There's more work to be got out of one of those little beggars than out of a dozen of the force," Holmes had explained. "The mere sight of an official-looking person seals men's lips. These youngsters, however, go everywhere and hear everything. They are as sharp as needles, too; all they want is organization."

The young man before me, now grown, had been introduced as "my dirty little lieutenant, Wiggins." Now he was dressed like a dandy. He had been the leader and spokesman for the Baker Street Irregular division, and though I had not dealt directly with him myself I remembered his shrewd ways. That he had become this confident young actor did not surprise me in the least. What did surprise me was that he had turned up after all these years to drag me out of a blazing inferno and that he was living in Sherlock Holmes' old rooms.

"Wiggins!" I exclaimed at last, when my mulling of these facts had loosened my tongue. "I am heartily glad to see you." I gripped his hand warmly a second time. "I won't apologize for not recognizing you. You are much changed—for the better."

He laughed gaily and took my arm. We walked to the pavement in front of Mrs. Hudson's house. Most of the crowd were gone now. The formerly boarded windows and door of the basement were black gaping holes where the brigade had chopped its way in. A gash of sooty gray scarred the front of the house, pools of grimy water lay all about, and a faint dying hiss could still be heard in the air.

"Yes, I have come a long way from my urchin days when I performed for Sherlock Holmes for a shilling," my young savior said as we stood surveying the damage. "Now I perform for a decent salary. I am quite successful, you know, the rising star —no longer Wiggins, but Frederick Wigmore in lights. It is amazing what a change of name can do. Please don't tell Mrs. Hudson who I really am; she could not bear it. But will you believe that I miss the old days sometimes? There was the excitement of the hunt, and, then, Mr. Holmes took great care of us boys. Did you know that?"

"I am discovering many things about him of which I knew nothing," I replied somewhat ruefully.

Wiggins appeared not to notice. "Mr. Holmes seemed to consider helping us his duty," he went on in a reminiscing way. "He could not have been more strict or prompt in our care if he'd been a penitent working out a sin by good works. He found homes for as many of the boys as possible. He was moved by our unfortunate situation."

"I never thought of him as sentimental," I said.

Wiggins turned to me with surprise. There was a hint of reproach in his look as well.

"That you of all people should say that! It was not sentiment but kindness."

I flushed with chagrin. "I am sorry, Wiggins. This night has been very trying for me."

"I understand."

Wiggins did not look at all tired himself, but rather invigorated by his exertions. His dress, too, was miraculously unaffected by being near the fire. His white shirtfront showed not a smudge of soot; his elegantly cut frock coat with velvet lapels was immaculate. We walked to the front door of the house. His step beside mine was light; he might have been returning from a night on the town none the worse for wear.

"Mrs. Hudson appears to have been well taken care of by her neighbors," he observed. "I imagine that officialdom will descend upon us soon enough to discern the why and how of the matter. Until they do I think I shall use my time to see how my rooms have fared. I hope I can sleep in them tonight. By the way, when the police come back tomorrow I shall say nothing of finding you in the basement—unless of course you wish me to. I was there long enough to observe some very peculiar things which I did not understand, and I certainly cannot explain why I saw a cabman fleeing down the street, lashing his horse unmercifully, when I looked out of my window at the first whiff of smoke."

My opinion of Wiggins—I could not think of him as Frederick Wigmore—rose. His offhand manner hid a keenly observant mind and shrewd nature. My own brain was in a whirl and I did not want to think about being questioned by the police, so I appreciated his discretion, useless as it might prove in the long run. I offered no explanation of what he had seen in the laboratory, nor did he seem to expect any. He would surely form his own theories.

"I have forgotten to thank you for saving my life," I said.

"It was nothing. I am only happy to have come straight home after the show tonight so that I was here to help you and Mrs. Hudson. You do look all in! Shall I call you a cab?"

"No thank you. I can manage that myself." And I shall scrutinize the cabman very closely, I added to myself.

Wiggins stepped upon the porch.

"Remember that I am at your service, Dr. Watson, for whatever you may need me, but especially if this matter concerns Mr. Holmes and wants my talents, such as they are. Do call upon me."

He held out his hand again and I shook it.

"In any case I hope that we shall see one another soon," he added warmly.

"I hope so too, Wiggins. In fact you can answer a question now before we part. You puzzled me when you said that you had become an actor thanks to Sherlock Holmes. How did that come about?"

"Oh, it's easily explained." He seated himself casually on the area railing. "I told you that he helped us boys—found us places to sleep instead of doorways, made us go to school even when we were inclined for the streets and only fidgeted in schoolroom forms. But he knew the value of instruction, knew when to give us our head as well, let us follow our inclinations when it came time. One boy, Harry Best, who began as a pickpocket—he could clean out even Mr. Holmes—is now a politician." Wiggins laughed. "An honest one, I mean. Another's on his way to becoming a barrister's clerk, still another owns a greengrocer's shop on the Brompton Road—all thanks to Mr. Holmes. As for 'Wiggins'—he wanted to be an actor. I think Mr. Holmes took a special interest in me for that. The theatre was the closest thing to his heart, after detecting of course. He loved the stage. He caught me more than once when I had skipped school for a music hall matinee. My tastes in theatre were not so grand then, and I still love the acrobats and singers and clowns. I would sneak in by tricks I had learned from the detective himself, though he never intended any of us to use them that way. The limelight and music and magic of those places fairly captivated me, and I'm sure that Mr. Holmes discovered me as much by the happy glow of my cheeks that gave me away as by anything else. He would be there in some disguise, following a criminal trail I thought at first, though I think now he often came just to watch. An old cripple or some gruff drunk or a skinny bank clerk out on a lark would sidle up to me, and it would be Mr. Holmes.

" 'Wiggins,' he would say quietly in his own voice, and I would start with shame. 'Wiggins, there is time enough for this. You shall have your day as an actor if you wish. I promise it. For now, you must be in school!'

"So away I would scamper, glad to get off with only a warning. But he proved true to his word, as I knew he would. I had the best acting training when I needed it, some from his own hand."

"Holmes himself taught you?"

"A few things. You have seen him in disguise. The world lost a great actor when he chose to be a detective, don't you think? He would have been a wonder on the stage!"

"I daresay."

"Well, that explains it, I think. Now I've a good part in Mr. George Edwardes' latest musical production, and it looks to be a hit, so I can afford these rooms for a while."

We were alone on the street. The fire wagons had gone moments before; the traffic on Baker Street was sparse. I glanced at my watch. It was midnight. The drama of an hour past had given way to this cold, nearly deserted setting.

"You were going in to see if any damage had been done to your rooms," I reminded Wiggins.

"Yes. I'll leave you now. But wait, doctor. You look a bit glum. Let me show you something to cheer you up before you go—a free performance. You shall have an exclusive front-row stall, compliments of Frederick Wigmore!"

With that he leaped forward like Puck, grinning from ear to ear at the thought of showing off for me. I was charmed by his enjoyment.

"A trick from the repertoire of the great Sherlock Holmes himself!" he announced, bowing low.

He jumped to the curb, bent, and scooped up several pebbles from the roadway. With an impish grin he tossed them one by one into the air and while his feet danced a jig on the sidewalk juggled them artfully before my eyes.

7

THIN DECEMBER SUNLIGHT slanted through my bedroom window to awaken me about nine A.M. the next day. Upon saying good-bye to Wiggins, I had found a safe cab home and, limp and weary, befogged in mind and fatigued in body, had fallen into bed immediately after climbing my stairs, there to lie comalike through the night. I arose. I felt none the worse for the strenuous events of the previous evening and was anxious to begin work. Whereas Saturdays usually imposed the burden of deciding how to fill them, this one had its agenda ready-made. I had much to ponder, and it was with a sense of labors to perform and duties to be fulfilled that I washed and dressed quickly and went downstairs to the breakfast room.

I made a simple breakfast of tea and toast and sat among the bric-a-brac of the room. I am a man of simple tastes and survived my bachelor times with just what would do. But, like my first wife, Violet had a fondness for things. And so the room was a tidy little whirlwind of objects upon shelves, of rugs upon rugs, and myriad indoor plants which tickled one's ear wherever one sat. They were tokens of my current placid married state, and so I tolerated them without complaint, the more so since Violet dusted and took entire care of them and I had to have no relationship with them other than as mute companions to my home hours. My reestablished Kensington practice could easily have afforded us a maid, but the stubborn thrift and sense of duty which Violet had acquired as a governess made her insist that she alone should care for our home and for me. I fended for myself in her absence.

I confess I missed her bustling presence in the kitchen that morning. She was a warm-hearted woman who tolerated my friendship with Sherlock Holmes, perhaps my most trying habit. In fact when the detective and I had extricated her from Jephro Rucastle's sinister game at the Copper Beeches fully ten years before, it had crossed my mind that her saucy independence might make her a good match for Holmes. But he had not shown the least interest in her other than as the subject of a diverting case. When she arrived in London eighteen months ago, once again a governess after some years as the head of a private school at Walsall, I renewed our acquaintance and took my own chance with her. We were married six months later.

Violet looked askance at my association with Holmes solely because it might lead me into dangerous waters—other than that, she admired him—and so she was probably quite happy that he had retired. (Her parting suggestion that I visit him had been the first of its kind.) On that Saturday morning I should have been grateful for the diversion of her conversation but decided it was best after all that she was on holiday. Because of Holmes' prohibition not to speak of Moriarty, as well as my own wish not to upset her, I could hardly have recounted the previous night's episode, yet I would have been hard pressed to keep it in. Now all I could do was to mull it over as I drank my tea.

What a welter of impressions and facts there was to sort out! It fairly stumped me where to begin. One thing stood out above all: Moriarty—I had met him at last! And what a meeting! I understood now with creeping horror in what danger Holmes, indeed the entire world, might be from so ruthless a

creature. "There is no completely evil personality save one,"
my friend had said. I now understood his reference. Moriarty
had produced a sense of total corruption as if, as Holmes had
suggested, all finer impulses had been drained out of him,
leaving only the dry shell of evil. A devil indeed!

But there were other things to consider. I had known Moriarty was the world's foremost criminal brain, but now I had
discovered that he was more: in appearance somehow, inexplicably, he was Sherlock Holmes. The body, the hands, the features, the voice, the penmanship of my friend—possessed by
this fiend! How could it be?

I felt myself lost in a maze.

I attempted to apply Holmes' principles of logical deduction. My conclusion had been that the resemblance between
the two men was due to blood relationship—that they were,
in fact, identical twins. Holmes' admission that he had known
Moriarty in his youth seemed to bear out this explanation. Had
the emergence of Moriarty's evil tendencies been the reason
Holmes had parted from him? It seemed as if it might. I wondered what had been the exact nature of the crisis which had
perpetrated the split. I wondered, too, if remnants of broth-
erly feeling were the reason the detective had failed to make
sure of Moriarty's death at Reichenbach.

The idea that Holmes and Moriarty were sibling rivals en-
hanced the drama of their conflict. I saw the two antagonists
as representatives of good and evil, struggling over the fate of
the world. They were equally matched; Holmes himself had
told me so. When, a dozen years before, he and I were fleeing
Moriarty's pursuit, I had made the mistake, because of the
detective's elaborate precautions, of assuming that we must
have eluded his enemy's encircling net. I had so expressed
myself.

"My dear Watson," Holmes had responded gravely in re-
proof, "we will not have escaped him so easily. You evidently
did not realize my meaning when I said that he is quite on the
same intellectual plane as myself."

At another time Holmes had described Moriarty's methods:

"He does little himself. He sits motionless, like a spider at the center of its web. He only plans. But his agents are numerous and splendidly organized. Is there a crime to be done, documents to be abstracted, a house to be rifled, a man to be removed? The word is passed to the professor; the matter is organized and carried out. The agent may be apprehended. In that case money appears for his bail or his defense, but the central power which uses the agent is neither caught nor even suspected!"

Now I knew that Holmes' own brother was the elusive, perversely brilliant head of this organization.

But did I know it? I had arrived at my theory rather quickly, and Holmes had often warned me against haste: "It is the obvious that is most open to suspicion, my dear Watson, especially in matters of crime."

Was there anything else which might explain how Moriarty could look so much like my friend? There was—a sudden recollection of the cache of costumes which I had found in Holmes' secret rooms brought it to mind—playacting! Without arousing my suspicions, Moriarty had played a red-haired journalist and a cab driver. Obviously his skill at disguise and acting was as great as the detective's (another indication of how equally they were matched). Perhaps Moriarty's startling appearance had been a fiendishly clever display of makeup and mimicry—but to what purpose? If his resemblance to Holmes were a disguise, was it meant to confuse me in some way, to mislead? How, and why? Was it meant to undermine my trust in Holmes himself?

I realized I had wandered deeper into the maze.

I was suspicious of everything Moriarty had said to me; however, one phrase intrigued me. I had asked if he and Holmes were brothers. "We are closer than brothers," he had replied. If my first theory were wrong, did this answer contain a clue to the truth? Or was Moriarty toying with me?

The experience of being toyed with had been unpleasant, yet I had been fascinated too. While in the East, I had watched snakes fascinate their prey by languid movements before striking at and devouring them. I could now agree with

Holmes' description of Moriarty as "reptilian," yet for all Moriarty's grotesqueness there was also something fey about him; he danced with the truth just out of reach. Holmes too exhibited a sense of play, a sly wit; I had seen him toy with criminals and clients alike. (To give just one example, in the case of the Mazarin Stone, he had twitted the rude Lord Cantlemere by hiding, in the lord's own overcoat pocket, the gem which Cantlemere was desperate to recover.) But Moriarty's play was of a different order, motivated by cruelty. He would toy with anyone who stood in his way like a cat with a mouse, before destroying him utterly.

Recalling the blinding smoke and flames licking around me, I was glad Moriarty had not considered me dangerous enough to finish, though he had played with me indeed. Perhaps he was saving my end for a later amusement.

I had just begun contemplating the curious coincidence, forgotten until now, that Wiggins, the very man to save me from Moriarty's act of destruction, had entertained me as Moriarty had, by juggling, when there came a loud knocking at my front door. I started and glanced at the clock on the sideboard. It was nearly eleven. So far I had solved not one of the many problems raised by my previous evening's adventure, so it was almost with a sense of relief that I went to open the door, but I was not pleased at who was there: Inspector Athelney Jones, with his meaty fist raised for another impatient blow on my oak.

This was the descent of officialdom I had dreaded.

"Dr. Watson!" Jones beamed. He thrust out a fat hand. "May I come in? Thank you, thank you."

He swept roundly past me into the hall before I could speak. He had never been in my house before but occupied it familiarly, trailing a too-heavy lavender scent.

"Splendid, splendid," he declared, craning his burly neck. "Very nice, very cozy for you and Mrs. Watson, I should think. Is she about? No? Just as well—we can talk freely. I've been hard at work this morning, doctor. I am very warm from my labors, I can tell you."

He pulled forth a large handkerchief and mopped his brow.

I glimpsed the police carriage at the curb as I shut the door. Athelney Jones wheezed as if the trip from it to my doorstep had been a mountain climb. He took my elbow.

"It has been a long time, doctor, a long time."

Athelney Jones had not changed much since I had seen him last; he was perhaps a little stouter. Portly in his gray suit, red-faced, with a pair of small twinkling eyes peering out keenly from between puffy pouches, he was a Yard officer of considerable repute, much of it due to the genius of Sherlock Holmes, which Jones was ever loath to acknowledge. Jones had been involved with the detective and myself in various cases, often those of a sensational nature in which the public cry for justice was loud. He put himself in the way of such cases. He stood before the press and made pronouncements, gave assurances, puffed pompously on a cigar as he was photographed in his confident manner as if posing for a public monument. He theorized volubly, then ran to Sherlock Holmes when his patchwork ideas unraveled in his hands. Fortunately for him, Holmes had always been content to hide his candle under Inspector Jones' bushel. Like Gregson and Lestrade, Jones had from the beginning scoffed at Holmes' methods, but whereas the other two, decent enough fellows with modest talents in the detecting line, had over the years come round to a healthy respect for Holmes' work, Athelney Jones remained his scoffing self while still scurrying to Baker Street for help whenever he was stuck. I had always been a bit put out by his pretensions, though Holmes tolerated them, and I had rectified as many mistaken impressions in the public's mind as I could by telling the truth behind the solving of such cases as *The Sign of Four,* for which Athelney Jones originally got the credit.

I led Inspector Jones into my sitting room. His conversation still demonstrated his politician's conviction that saying a stupid thing often enough was sure to make it believed.

"Splendid, splendid!" he pronounced again, his cheery eyes roving about my far from splendid sitting room for the fifth time. He settled himself with a thud into the largest, softest chair in the room and periodically flicked his cigar in the direction of the nearby ashtray.

"Now down to brass tacks," he announced in a cozy way.

"Yes?" I said, almost my first word in the one-sided conversation.

He frowned and waved his cigar about impatiently. His florid features squashed themselves together even more than usual. "Come, come, doctor. You know what I wish to discuss —the fire at Baker Street."

"I was aware that there was a fire."

"A fire! It was a conflagration, doctor, and you were present!"

"Your facts are correct. I was certainly there. It was a terrible fire but fortunately brought under control in time. Neither Mrs. Hudson nor her lodger was harmed, I believe."

"Thank goodness! A bad business, a bad business. Well, I have as you say got my facts in hand. But theories are what we need, doctor, theories! Theories are what solve cases."

"I am certain that Sherlock Holmes would agree with you if he were here—though he always welcomed facts."

"What Sherlock Holmes did or did not welcome has nothing to do with this case. Too many facts, Dr. Watson, too many facts can be a policeman's undoing! My opinion is that Mr. Holmes set far too much store by them. Sniffing at carpets, scooping up cigarette ash, peering under hatbands—why it is very trying and takes time! We have not the time, Dr. Watson. One bold intuition will solve this riddle!"

I tried not to be provoked by Jones' egregious manner. "I take it you think some crime has been perpetrated, but I am not clear how I can help."

"Why, as a witness, of course—and as a friend of Sherlock Holmes. We have reason to believe that this fire was set deliberately and that it is connected in some way with him."

I was silent at this near hit.

"What took you to Baker Street last evening, Dr. Watson?"

My heart began to pound. "I was paying a visit to Mrs.

Hudson. As well as being my former landlady, she is an old friend."

"Quite so. So she said in my interview with her this morning. You discussed only general matters?"

I hesitated. "Yes." I appreciated anew Mrs. Hudson's quick wit and aplomb.

"You did not speak of Sherlock Holmes?"

"On the contrary. We spent some time as we always do in reminiscing about former days with him. They were exciting times."

Athelney Jones discharged an impatient flurry of ash upon my carpet. "Undoubtedly. And the fire. Naturally you were first alarmed, as you sat sipping tea, by the smell of smoke, and . . ."

I was thoroughly pleased to have Athelney Jones sketch in my answers along with his questions. It saved me a great deal of trouble.

". . . and of course we acted as anyone would," I supplied.

This general clue gave him his lead. "Of course. It must have been a fearful thing. It was Mrs. Hudson who ran to sound the alarm while you waited behind, just outside, with—what's his name?—Frederick Wigmore—an odd character. You did not notice a cabman hurrying away in his rig, I suppose."

"Why yes. I do recall the sudden clatter of hooves going rather fast. But it was so very dark and foggy before the fire had time to light up the street. I saw only the back of a hansom careering away."

"Just so, damn it! Several neighbors heard the cab, but no one got a good look at it. That cabman—or his passenger—is our culprit, make no mistake! But there is something else very peculiar about this case, doctor. Of course you did not know it, as Mrs. Hudson has explained, but Sherlock Holmes kept secret rooms below her apartment in Baker Street."

He made this revelation in the triumphant manner with which he was wont to announce to the press the latest developments in a case. I had no wish to disappoint him, and so acted surprise with all my might. No doubt my nervousness about how much else he had discovered lent credibility to my performance.

"There were several rooms below," he went on. "We went through them this morning—a filthy task, but one must put up with such things when one is a public servant. One of the rooms appeared to have been a library of sorts with scientific books and works on witchcraft—only partially burned. The other rooms were of no consequence that we could see except for the largest, which had been fitted out as a laboratory. By the evidence of an empty tin of turpentine the fire appears to have been set there deliberately. The place was a terrible shambles, and there seems no way to reconstruct its purpose. Do you know what scientific problems were preoccupying Sherlock Holmes?"

"No."

"I see, I see. Then only Holmes himself—and perhaps the culprit—can explain it now. Unfortunately for our investigation Holmes appears to have vanished for good. Why did he keep the rooms when he had retired, I wonder, and why would someone destroy them after he was gone?"

"It is a puzzle to me, Inspector Jones," I said. "You are the theorist."

"Just so, just so," he mused. "And I will surely come up with something!" He mopped his face with the handkerchief again. His usually cheery eyes had lost their luster.

"Crime has been so much more malignant than usual of late," he went on. "And it is no longer confined to the lower orders where one expects it to breed. Do you know that respected public officials have been bribed? None of this turmoil helps our relations with Germany or with any of the other continental powers. I tell you, it is very trying. There are currents going against us. Whitehall is on me very heavily, and this diversion does not help matters any. Your Sherlock Holmes has misguided ways, but I confess that I should like to speak with him on this." He looked at me hopefully. "You really do not know where he is?"

"No one would like to see him more than I, inspector. But

as you say, his ways are his own. He decided to disappear and has done it well."

"Just another mystery. The man is too efficient at times! Still, if you hear from him I should be glad of a word. And I will make sure that you are the first to know when I have settled this matter of the fire and the cabman, the very first."

With this show of confidence he rose and wheezed his way out the door, trailing his handkerchief in one pudgy fist like a dejected tail.

I had to sit down to recover. I went back to my sitting room and fell into the chair vacated by Athelney Jones. The mixed smell of tobacco and lavender filled the room, and his cigar ash lay about the floor to remind me that if I had not exactly lied to the police I had at least misrepresented the extent of my knowledge and withheld information. I realized that without thinking I had made a decision to follow Sherlock Holmes' instructions to the letter; I would not mention Moriarty's name to the police nor reveal the true reason for the detective's supposed retirement.

But this was beginning to pose problems which Holmes seemed not to have anticipated. Not only had I been drawn into a very unpleasant, not to say dangerous, situation, but as a result of it I now had more to hide than just what he had told me. I had found out about his secret laboratory; had examined the thing intact, which Athelney Jones had not. Most significantly I knew of Moriarty's devilish resemblance to Holmes and could have described it in detail for the police.

I chuckled. Would the pompous Inspector Athelney Jones have believed me had I done so? What "bold intuition" could account for that?

But there was in addition other information, clues, which I could have yielded up: the book on British stage design, for example, which I had not forgotten and which still reposed snugly in my overcoat pocket. There were the things Moriarty had said to me, full of hints and obfuscations but rich in material. And there were other matters which I hardly dared bring before myself as yet, but which nagged at me and seemed to connect with things I had wondered about for years. Young Frederick Wigmore was one of these.

The simultaneous pealing of church bells and clock chimes told me that it was noon and I'd so far accomplished nothing. But what was there to accomplish? I found that I was not relaxed, but sitting on the edge of my chair feeling—I was startled to realize it—an immense anger at Sherlock Holmes for placing me in this predicament and fencing me round with prohibitions. I was furious with my old friend! But then, perhaps my anger had answered the question of what I must do.

Holmes had kept secrets from me. How often I had attempted to draw aside the curtain of reticence which Holmes kept ever drawn about his privacy! He was a lonely island one could reach but was forbidden to explore. I had always felt frustrated by his distance, especially in one for whom I cared, but I was neither a snooper nor a gossip, so I had respected his unexpressed wish never to be pressed about his past.

That sacred past of his—what did I really know about it? I stood up abruptly, lit one of my own cigars to drive the odor of Athelney Jones' foul brand out of the air, and began to pace furiously, frowning, summing up in my mind what I could say for certain of the life of Sherlock Holmes before I had known him. There was surprisingly little, and I was shocked at myself to think that I had gone twenty-two years in friendship with the man, actually lived with him for seventeen of those years, absorbed and recorded the minutiae of his daily habits, yet knew so little of his all-important youth. About that, unlike most men, Holmes had not been given to anecdotes. Why not?

Who were his parents? I did not know their names. I had assumed them dead, and out of deference to his feelings had never asked him about them. Where was he born—county? town? I did not know. Where had he gone to school? I could give no name of a grammar school. I had assumed that he was a university student at one of the colleges at Camford in the fen country, but I could not name the college nor, now that I thought of it, could I recall Holmes ever saying definitely that his two university years were spent at Camford. Relations?

Here I was on somewhat firmer ground. I had met his brilliant brother, Mycroft, on two occasions, and a distant cousin, a young doctor named Verner, had bought my practice with Holmes' financial backing when I moved back in with the detective in the spring of 1894. (I had not discovered that Verner was a relation of Holmes' until some years after the purchase; I bought the practice back at the time of my second marriage from a doctor other than Verner, who had sold it to him and migrated to Canada.) Other than these two men, I had only vague references to go on about ancestral "country squires" and a grandmother who was the sister of Vernet, the French artist. In my present state it seemed very little.

Holmes had arrived in London in 1878 and had engaged modest rooms on Montague Street just round the corner from the British Museum. He pursued his own course of study at the museum and at St. Bartholomew's Hospital while trying to make a name for himself as a detective. His first case had been that of the Musgrave ritual, which I had transcribed and published; other cases from that time I knew only from passing references: the Tarleton murders, the case of Vamberry the wine merchant, the affair of the old Russian woman, and several more.

Early in 1881 at the Criterion Bar in Piccadilly I had run into young Stamford, who had been a dresser under me at Bart's. Considered unfit to continue campaigning with the Fifth Northumberland Fusiliers in the second Afghan war because of a bullet wound which had nearly cost me my life, I was back in London, living on eleven shillings and sixpence a day and looking to share lodgings to cut down on expenses. Stamford had offered to introduce me to a fellow, "a little queer in his ideas," who was also looking for a roommate. That fellow was Sherlock Holmes. On the following day we had engaged Mrs. Hudson's upper rooms at 221B Baker Street.

But how sketchy was my knowledge of Holmes' life before I met him! There must have been more to it than he had revealed. Beneath his meticulous ways lay a passionate nature. I had assumed that his devotion to criminal studies had completely absorbed these energies; now I knew differently. There had been a secret life. The elaborate machine in the now-destroyed laboratory told me so; Moriarty's maddening hints suggested it too.

No question, then: Sherlock Holmes had hidden much and had much to explain. That was the deepest source of my anger —that he had not confided more in me, had not rendered up the full confidence due to a loyal friend. And now, having been kept from the truth, I was placed in jeopardy, was most probably still in danger, as Mrs. Hudson and Wiggins might be too, as well as anyone who had associated with the detective.

For the first time since I had known him I questioned his instructions. Should I remain passive, stay out of the affair until I heard from him? It was a momentous consideration, and I hung fire over it for long moments, but at last felt a decision upon me and struck my fist into my palm.

"By God, I shall act!" I exclaimed.

As I stood there I felt in my shoulder the pang of the old Jezail bullet wound which I had sustained a quarter of a century before, the wound which had led indirectly to my association with Sherlock Holmes. It came as a sobering reminder that I had been often in the fray since then, even in the heart of civilized London, sometimes in circumstances more perilous than the murderous Ghazis of the Afghani plain had afforded, and that I was sure to be heading into the midst of it again. I was used to being guided by the great detective; now I was alone. It made me wonder at my audacity—but I would not hang back. I must resolve the mystery which I had seen at last, and I was determined that no considerations of danger would prevent me from pursuing my quarry who was, strangely, Sherlock Holmes himself.

8

I HAD DECIDED to take matters into my hands; how was I to carry out my intent? I knew that before acting I must be absolutely clear what I wanted to find out. That was the way Holmes had always proceeded, never making a move in any criminal case without first planning carefully. I must order my thoughts into a plan.

My study was stuffy with the warmth from the coal furnace, and my mind felt stuffy too. I started toward the lace-curtained window overlooking Queen Anne Street, intending to raise the sash for a moment to clear my head with a breath of cold air, but stopped halfway across the room. I had been indoors all morning; an outing would help to order my thoughts, and I owed a visit to Mrs. Hudson to see how she had fared since the disaster and to offer her my assistance. I decided to see her now; I would ponder my problem on the way.

Throwing on my coat and hat, and wrapping a woolen scarf about my throat, I went out to call a cab. Soon I was rattling toward Baker Street.

In one of my coat pockets was still the octavo volume on theatres which I had retrieved from Holmes' library; in the other I had slipped my Adams .450, fully loaded, which I vowed never to be without until this adventure was concluded.

My cabby turned left at Welbeck, then right onto Bentinck Street in the direction of Manchester Square. The trees there, and those I glimpsed in Portman Square as we turned toward Regent's Park, were rather dismal looking, with their black branches stripped bare by winter. In spite of the biting air the crowd of shoppers along Baker Street was large. Sparkling eyes, enhancing faces turned rosy with cold, gave evidence that the Christmas season was nearly upon us. Small children, bundled to the chin, were rolypoly gnomes; dragged along by their mothers, they peered wide-eyed into every shop window. The frail midwinter sun bathed this scene in a thin light.

Wrapped against the chill, I took only the barest note of the midday parade. I had already decided, by my responses to Athelney Jones, that I would not tell the police of Moriarty's return nor of Holmes' false retirement, nor would I ask them for help—unless I were in dire straits. It was only the detective's order to wait for his instructions before doing anything that I intended to disobey. Things had come to too fine a point for me to be able to keep that prohibition. My life had been threatened, Mrs. Hudson's and Wiggins' as well. Holmes might not have foreseen and accounted for this, but we were suddenly in the midst of danger nevertheless, and I could not sit still.

The great thing was to find Holmes—that would solve everything. But could I do what the wily Moriarty, with all his resources, had been unable to accomplish?

That question would be answered soon enough by my success or failure. I found myself thinking of something else, which blunted the edge of my anger at Holmes for leaving his friends in danger. Perhaps he had fully intended to contact me, to instruct me, to warn me even, but had been unable to do so because he himself was in danger, hard-pressed by Moriarty's organization. This seemed very likely; I could think of no other explanation for my friend's long silence. Wherever

he was, possibly far distant, he might have no idea that his
laboratory had been destroyed; if I did not reach him he would
never hear of it. I was the only person who could describe to
him the true and awful circumstances of its demise. From
what Moriarty had hinted, the secret rooms must have been
crucial to the detective's plan for stopping him. No doubt it
was a telling blow Moriarty had struck, and it further cooled
my anger at Holmes, making me more than ever determined
to proceed with a clear head henceforth. To think that I was
the dupe who had led the devil to his triumph. Moriarty's last
bragging cry to me had been to tell Holmes of his destructive
act. I intended to deliver this message, but I would give it as
a warning to take care.

By the time my cab's wheels scraped the curb in front of the
dreadfully blackened facade of 221B Baker Street I was clear
about the reasons for searching for Holmes. One of them was
to tell him of his enemy's fatal work in the laboratory; another
was to help Holmes if he were surrounded, imprisoned, or
otherwise unable to act—in short to offer the services of a
faithful friend as I had always done; the third was to solve the
riddle of the laboratory and thus, I hoped, of Sherlock Holmes'
secret life.

Descending from the cab I peered briefly over the railing
in front of the house. The police were still sifting among the
ruins of the laboratory. Through the gaping holes that had
been windows I glimpsed both Gregson and Lestrade among
the officers taking samples below. I pulled my head back
quickly so they would not see me. They were more acute than
Athelney Jones and would have questioned me far more
closely than he had. I wished them well; if they could find
anything to put them on the trail of Moriarty, well and good
—but they must do it without my help.

I approached the door of Mrs. Hudson's apartment. A young
officer standing nearby hailed me gruffly: "What is your business?" I explained that I was a friend of the landlady, a doctor,
and that I wished to see if Mrs. Hudson was well. Still gruff, but
yielding, the young policeman directed me to a house several
doors down toward Oxford Street where, he explained, Mrs.

Hudson had spent the night. He believed she would return to her own home later that afternoon.

I walked to the house he had indicated. A familiar face appeared at my ring, an old friend of Mrs. Hudson's: Mrs. Pickett, a cheerful lady with unruly hair, seven children, the heart of a saint, and the bellow of a fishwife. She greeted me effusively and showed me into her parlor, where I found Mrs. Hudson, looking none the worse for her ordeal, sitting before the remnants of a light lunch on a tray. I refused Mrs. Pickett's offer of tea, and she left us alone to dash off to her noisy brood, which could be heard tumbling about in the upper reaches of the house. I could see that Mrs. Hudson would be glad to get back to her quiet rooms, but neither she nor I allowed the muffled war whoops or the jiggling ceiling fixtures to interfere with our brief and sober conversation.

I had no chance to ask how she was before she inquired after my well-being. We exchanged reassurances. Then she asked about Sherlock Holmes.

"I do not know about Mr. Holmes," I told her.

She saw my caution. "You didn't see him then—or you cannot say. I understand, doctor. I do not know what happened below, but I didn't tell the police that you were there—or about the other person. I heard another voice—I couldn't help it—a mad voice that gave me chills. Yet I imagined I heard Mr. Holmes' voice as well. I don't pry, I don't want details if you can't give them, but I hope Mr. Holmes is well. Can you assure me of that at least?"

I could not. I decided to be honest but to ease the blow as best I could. "It is a serious business, Mrs. Hudson. Still, we know that Mr. Holmes has always been able to take care of himself. We must believe he will triumph."

She was as cheerful as possible at this. I thanked her for her discretion. Under the strained circumstances we said little else. Before parting I offered to help however I could. She thanked me but said that her solicitor, the police, and her friends and neighbors were taking good care of her. She was grateful to us all.

As I walked back past 221B Baker Street, Wiggins came

bounding out its front door. He appeared as jaunty and un-
flappable as at our last meeting and was dressed even more
like a dandy than before. A vivid yellow scarf with streaming
ends ornamented his neck.

"Doctor! I am very glad to see you." He pumped my arm,
then stood back to survey me drolly. "You are looking dour.
That will never do. I am unscathed, Mrs. Hudson is well taken
care of, and your eyebrows are not even singed. It is a matter
for rejoicing!" He beamed at me to punctuate this proof of the
rightness of the world.

I could not help smiling back, if not so broadly as he. We
began to walk along the street together. I inquired about the
state of his rooms. He explained that he had found them little
affected by the smoke, had put them right in a moment, and
had slept soundly through the night. Unfortunately Mrs. Hudson's rooms were rather gray from smoke, he said, and cinders
had burned holes in her curtains and an antimacassar or two,
but a band of neighbors were set to descend upon them that
afternoon to make the place spic and span again. Miraculously
no serious damage to the underpinnings of the building had
been done, so its ground and first stories were perfectly safe.

Wiggins glanced at his watch and began to dance off along
the pavement.

"I am sorry, doctor, but I must rush. I am off to a matinee
at one of those dreadful music halls I told you about. I am still
addicted, you see. It is all for fun, and I would not miss it for
the world! In truth there is a great deal to be learned from Mr.
Dan Leno and Mr. George Robey about my craft—though
some West End snobs would not acknowledge it. And I think
Marie Lloyd the equal of Melba!" He came back to me.
"Would you care to come along? You want cheering up. Please
say yes. It will be a great experience and will give you a first
look at the man who is sure to be the rage of London: The
Great Escott. I have not seen him myself, but my friends tell
me he is the most extraordinary magician in the world. They
say he makes even John Nevil Maskelyne look like a parlor
trickster. Do join me, doctor!"

Wiggins importuned me a moment more in this manner. I appreciated his kind motive but insisted that I could not go. I last glimpsed him waving an arm as he flew off down the street like a modern Ariel, the ends of his outrageous yellow scarf blowing about his shoulders. I envied his carefree manner. At that moment I would gladly have given up my duties for an hour with the Great Escott, if I could have been assured that Sherlock Holmes was safe.

I started to hail a cab, then dropped my arm. Without the plan which I had promised myself I would develop, I was in no hurry. I decided to return to Queen Anne Street on foot.

As I strolled south on Baker Street I knew the time had come to face up to my decision: I must become a detective, and alone, for there was no Sherlock Holmes to whisper clues into my ear and show me my mistakes. I did not feel wholly discouraged at the prospect of testing what I had learned from him. If he had not often praised my deductive powers, Holmes had at least conceded that I had an ability to observe. "I never get your limits, Watson," he had exclaimed once in the thick of a case. "There are unexplored possibilities about you." Now was my chance to live up to those possibilities. I had not my friend's brilliance of mind, but I had my own bulldog tenacity, and I intended to grip my mystery firmly to make it yield; I would worry it to the ground.

I planned to walk to my house via Marylebone High Street; therefore I first turned left onto Paddington Street. The afternoon air sharpened my thoughts. How could I locate Holmes? From what seemed at first an impossibly knotted problem appeared one or two threads at which I could begin.

There was Mrs. Hudson. I believed she knew nothing about the detective's present whereabouts, but, having known all these years about his secret rooms, she might remember some clue that could lead to him. I did not want to increase her anxiety, nor did I want to tell her of the return of Moriarty, much less about his resemblance to Holmes, but I decided that if need be I would question her.

Then there was Wiggins. I intended to cultivate that young

man's acquaintance. He had offered to help me, and he might
be able to supply clues from his early association with the
detective that would cast a light on where he had disappeared.
Holmes had apparently formed a special bond with Wiggins'
former gang, teaching them some of his own tricks of disguise
and subterfuge. What else might they have learned from him
—besides juggling? I intended to find out.

There was another reason I wished to get closer to the
young actor. His rather dandified look and offhand manner
was misleading; I had observed him in the thick of crisis and
seen that he was cool-headed and resourceful under stress, not
unlike Holmes himself. I could use those qualities. I did not
doubt his loyalty to Holmes and would not hesitate to tell him
the full story; Frederick Wigmore might be a potent ally.

At this point my ideas began to falter. Of other allies I could
not be certain. Of acquaintances Holmes had many; a verita-
ble parade of them had marched in and out of our rooms—
railway porters, mendicants, slipshod old women, furtive ped-
dlers, elegant gentlemen who turned out to be peers of the
realm. Holmes' pursuits took him into all strata of society, and
he cultivated useful persons of every social standing. But most
of these were unknown to me. Too, they were people he used
as tools of his trade, not intimates in whom he would have
confided. His solitary ways cut him off from me at the time I
needed him most—and when he might desperately need me.

Yet it is the obvious which so often escapes us—if we are not
Sherlock Holmes. Such was the case now. I turned right onto
Marylebone High Street and spent the distance to New Cav-
endish fruitlessly reviewing as many associations of Holmes as
I could, rejecting one after another, while a great ally, a man
of subtlety and power, utterly trustworthy and shrewder even
than Holmes himself, loomed before me as large as St. Paul's
and surely as ready to succor me. That man was the detective's
own brother, Mycroft. If there were anyone to turn to, it was
he.

When his name flashed into my mind I struck my forehead
with my palm. Of course, the logical choice! My very next
move must be in his direction.

I had met Mycroft Holmes but twice. The first instance had introduced to Sherlock Holmes the case of the Greek interpreter, one of the few cases whose explanation is still shrouded in mystery; the second had been exactly eight years ago, when the singular death of Cadogan West on the Underground was baffling Scotland Yard and alarming Whitehall. Sherlock Holmes had spoken to me of his brother rarely, but I knew Holmes thought highly of him and that Mycroft occasionally helped him in various ways. Mycroft had restored and kept the detective's rooms while Holmes was on the long hegira of 1891–94. Mycroft had once aided me too, though I did not know it at the time, when, disguised as a cabman, he had driven me to Victoria Station to meet Holmes for our flight from Moriarty in 1891.

Now, I hoped, he would help me again.

I recalled how startled I had been to learn that my friend had a brother. I had come to believe that Holmes was an orphan with no living relations. One summer evening in 1888 in the course of desultory conversation it had come out: there existed a man with better powers of observation and deduction than he, and that man was his brother, Mycroft. Holmes told me Mycroft was incapable of using his powers for detective work. This had seemed illogical, and I had protested, but the detective had cut me short.

"I said that he was my superior in observation and deduction. If the art of the detective began and ended in reasoning from an armchair, my brother would be the greatest agent that ever lived. But he has no ambition and no energy."

It turned out that Holmes occasionally consulted his brother about criminal matters and that Mycroft had indeed unraveled some cases—but only after Holmes had done the legwork and assembled all the pieces of the puzzle. Detective work was merely a dilettante's hobby for Mycroft, who did not like being up and about, interviewing and gathering clues. Though undoubtedly brilliant, he led a slothful life, more circumscribed than Holmes' own. Yet, dilettante though he be, I had seen examples enough of his reasoning in the Greek interpreter case to convince me that if anyone could puzzle out

Sherlock Holmes' whereabouts it was he.

There was only one place to find him, and that was at the
Diogenes Club. I thought of flagging a cab for Pall Mall at
once, but recalled that Mycroft Holmes never arrived at his
club before a quarter to five—and never after either. He
would be there from that precise time until exactly twenty to
eight. That was his daily routine, never broken.

It was now not quite three; I had two hours to wait. Therefore I continued home and in ten minutes was pulling off my
coat in my front hall. I made myself a sandwich, which I barely
touched for the excitement of anticipation filling me. I lit a
cigarette and dropped into an armchair in my study; none of
the room's familiar objects touched my consciousness, not
even Violet's palm frond, which waved over my head like an
exotic awning. The smoke from my cigarette curled upward
as I ruminated. My eyelids grew heavy.

Objects, seemingly illuminated by spotlights which picked
them out one by one, took form before me in a dark void.
There were chemical implements—Bunsen burners, retorts,
test tubes, labeled and stoppered bottles filled with phosphor-
ing liquids of vivid color. Torn from Sherlock Holmes' scrapbooks, and hanging motionless in the air with the rest, were
yellowed clippings of criminal cases. There were also books,
sober scientific volumes, and other rarer books on the occult
—the incunabula of superstition; there was a small octavo volume on stage design; a violin case and a violin, a Stradivarius;
pipes: a cherrywood and a black, oily clay; the familiar spirit
case and gasogene, and a hair-trigger pistol with a box of Boxer
cartridges hovering nearby; and there was clothing: waistcoats
and breeches and topcoats and boots, bodices and skirts, wigs
and hats of innumerable shapes, sizes, and colors; and a single
Persian slipper with tobacco dribbling out its toe.

Suddenly these objects began to move. They had been scattered aimlessly across the blackness, but now they marched
into the form of a great upright circle and began turning,
faster and faster, until they whirled at dizzying speed in the
void, the glassware glittering, the clothing gesticulating like

the severed parts of bodies, the books rustling their dry pages angrily like bat wings. And the violin!—the bow skittered of its own volition wildly across the strings to play a dissonant tune I had heard before when a depressed mood came upon my friend, Sherlock Holmes.

I grew aware that there was a fixed point in this madly circling vision, something or someone just outside its edge which did not move with it. Struggling against a frigid current of air, I drew nearer. Yes, it was a person, a man. He it was who caused the great wheel to move by grasping each object just before it fell to toss it up again into the circular stream. Nearer still I came until I stood not ten feet from him. The man wore a long gray traveling cloak and a close-fitting cloth cap, but the face was in darkness.

The clothing I recognized.

"Holmes!" I cried.

The long white hands continued to catch and toss the objects before they could fall, but the figure made no response. I called the name of my friend again. My voice sounded small and artificial, and I strained to make it louder, but it stuck in my throat, choking me.

Suddenly the face became clear. A spotlight had picked it out. It was indeed the face of my friend, lean and strong, with the piercing gray eyes I knew so well. They recognized me, and the thin lips began to smile.

I heard the sound of applause behind me. I turned to find that we were in a great dim auditorium and that beyond the blinding footlights at my back must be an audience, clapping more and more enthusiastically at the incredible feat which Holmes performed. I turned back to him—but his face had altered. The half smile had become Moriarty's sneer, and the erect body with firmly planted feet had begun to hunch over. The gray eyes now mocked me.

The applause at my back grew louder. There were whistles and cheers. The great wheel of objects was moving ever faster, the violin's screeching tune becoming more frantic. Again it was Holmes manipulating the huge whirling thing; then it was

Moriarty. Only the dexterous white hands remained the same, never faltering, never missing a move. But the face and posture alternated in a blur: Holmes . . . Moriarty . . . Holmes . . . Moriarty. The applause grew thunderous, drowning out the violin; the shouting verged on hysteria. Feet stamped and clamorous cries reached the stage, deafening me.

The huge wheel began to tilt and wobble. I could no longer perceive the Holmes-Moriarty creature; it was a gray smudge, dying and receding, leaving only the objects whirling over my head and the shrieks of the invisible crowd at my back. At last, with a roar, the thing crashed upon the stage to explode in white splinters of light and clouds of smoke. I sat bolt upright in my chair in the study, blinking at the winter light shining in through my west window and smelling the smoke from my cigarette, which had fallen upon the carpet and was burning a neat round hole therein.

9

FOR THE SECOND TIME that day I was in a hansom
cab maneuvering through the streets of the great city, this
time along Bond Street in the direction of St. James's Palace.
It was nearly five P.M., and Mycroft Holmes, unaware that I
was dashing to confront him, would just have pushed his portly
frame through the doors of the Diogenes Club for his unvary-
ing three hours. It was nearly dark, and lamps were coming on
along the street. Earlier the thin sunlight had given way
before clouds, and a cold drizzle fell, making the dark pavement glisten beneath the streetlights and carriage lamps. For-
ests of umbrellas were opened above the creaking horse-
drawn buses, whose sides were emblazoned with ads for Pear's
Soap and Guinness. In spite of the rain, crowds jostled along
the sidewalks. The December Saturday night seemed even
more filled with the gay spirit of approaching holidays than
the afternoon, and it would have taken weather more inclem-
ent than this to keep these Londoners indoors. They hurried
on to brighter and warmer scenes—to family and home fires,
to parties, to public houses, to dinner engagements, to the
theatre.

I rattled past them alone on the first leg of my quest for Sherlock Holmes.

As on my previous two journeys of the day my mind was reviewing its own parade of thoughts and images—particularly my unnerving dream of only an hour before. If that was what it meant to be an imaginative man, I wanted none of it! I had awakened in a cold sweat and was only now coming to terms with what the dream had suggested, that Sherlock Holmes and Professor James Moriarty were the same man. Of course they could not be literally the same; I rejected that completely. Yet the idea would not let me be. "Closer than any two beings," Moriarty had said . . .

"St. James's Palace, sir," my cabman called down to me.

I alighted and paid him, raising my umbrella over my head. I was at the corner of Marlborough gate. At my back were the imposing yet rather dismal gray walls of St. James's, glistening with moisture; I faced east toward Pall Mall. I had been to the Diogenes Club but once, when I had first been introduced to Mycroft, so I did not remember its exact address, only that it was some short distance from the Carlton. I was confident of finding it on foot, so I proceeded.

Club life has been an important feature in the daily existence of the moneyed Londoner from Addison's time onward, but never more so than now; and Pall Mall, that solemn array of fine houses in which the English gentleman goes through the solemn ceremony of enjoying himself, was the very center of club life in London. I was confronted with the row of imposing clubhouses. I walked past Marlborough House, the Oxford and Cambridge, the Automobile Club, the Reform, the Travellers, the Athenaeum, the United Services. It was near the dinner hour, and a multitude of carriages crowded against the curbs, discharging their dignified top-hatted passengers who brushed by me and into their club doors as if I did not exist. In the preoccupation of my search I ignored them as well.

At last I found the entrance to the Diogenes, rather less prepossessing than the rest and with hardly the stream of members flooding through its doors. This was no doubt due to

its character, which was most unusual. Sherlock Holmes had
described it as "the queerest club in London," and so I had
found it upon my sole visit—a society of misanthropes made
up of the most unsociable and unclubable men in town. The
diversity of London was reflected even in her clubs: here was
one for eccentrics. My friend had further informed me that his
brother was one of its founders. That fact I had taken as a
measure of the circumspection of this brother's highly unpub-
lic life.

I mounted the short flight of gray stone steps and pushed
through one of the tall double doors to arrive in the thickly
carpeted hall which I somehow remembered distinctly. Nothing seemed to have changed. The greenish pattern under my
feet bespoke reticent dignity; the damasked walls did the
same. Brass fixtures gleamed discreetly, and it was deathly
quiet throughout. No one prevented my entrance, nor did any
deferential club employee inquire my business or whose guest
I might be, or offer to take my hat, coat, and umbrella. There
was a conspicuous place for them to my left, an alcove with
spaces for garments and stands in which several dripping umbrellas already stood. I left my things there and walked past
upholstered chairs to the end of the hall. Through thick glass
paneling I glimpsed the large reading room in which the
members perused their papers and smoked, never speaking or
noticing one another under pain of fines and expulsion. It was
one of the rules of this odd place that communication, except
in the Stranger's Room, was strictly forbidden. Sherlock
Holmes had said that he found the contemplative atmosphere
here soothing at times, but I thought it stuffy and unnatural.
A fine for laughing, indeed!

I stood at the glass partition and searched for Mycroft
Holmes among the club members, who sat each in a private
shell of frowning concentration or silly ennui as if he had the
whole vast room of armchairs to himself. Occasionally another
member would arrive and pass by me into the room like a
phantom. When the door beside me was opened, so well-oiled
and hung that it made not a sound, not even the clink of a glass

or the flutter of a page came from the sepulchral inner sanc-
tum of the Diogenes Club. I was loath to enter there for fear
of making some terrible gaffe that would bring these men's
misanthropic wrath down upon my head, so it was well that
I was able to satisfy myself from outside that Mycroft Holmes
was nowhere within. His huge bulk would have been unmistakable.

But where was he, then? I began to grow uneasy. It was
forbidden to speak, so how was I to inquire for him, and from
whom? I looked about for a members' book in which he might
have signed his arrival but saw none. So unconventional was
the Diogenes Club that its members came and went with no
record, it appeared, and little service. There seemed but one
possibility, and that was the Stranger's Room, where Sherlock
Holmes had first introduced his brother to me. There alone in
all this peculiar fraternity was human intercourse permitted.
I walked in its direction.

The modest-sized Stranger's Room was as well appointed as
the hall and reading room, with thick rugs which made the air
seem peculiarly dead. There were a few armchairs and ash-
trays on stands scattered about, but little else in the room save
a single tall bookcase against one wall, packed with imposing
volumes in heavy leather bindings, decorative no doubt and
rarely touched save by the feather duster of a discreet morning maid. There was but one man present. Bent and old, he
stood smoking a long-stemmed pipe and holding the green
velvet curtains of the street window back with one hand as he
gazed out into the misty night.

The man turned slowly and dropped the curtain as I entered. How he had heard my footsteps I did not know. He was
excessively thin, his long limbs wrapped in a close-fitting gray
suit that hugged him like a sausage casing. The top of his head
was mottled and as bald as a bullet, but a cloudlike wreath of
wispy white hair floated about his ears. His sharp eyes regarded me with a curiosity which I could not interpret as
friendly.

I hesitated at the door, feeling very much the intruder on

a private meditation, but plucked up my courage and began to cross the room toward the old man. To my surprise he did not wait for me but met my advance halfway, scuttling spryly toward me like a quick old crab and bobbing up under my nose like a cork. He must once have been tall, but age had lowered his bald head to the level of my chin, and he had to cock his eyes upward to examine me. This he did ruthlessly.

"My name is Dr. John Watson," I mumbled, somewhat disconcerted by his stare. "I am looking for a particular member of your club."

The old man thrust out a gnarled hand.

"Bliss!" he ejaculated in a high voice like the crack of a whip.

I took his hand and had mine crunched in a bony grip for my trouble. I saw a spark of delight spring up in his eye. He released me before he had done much damage.

"I beg your pardon?" I said.

"Simon Bliss!" he replied impatiently.

I felt a great fool. It was obviously his name. "Oh," I responded, compounding my foolishness.

Simon Bliss continued to stare up at me sideways like a wary old parrot. At last he raised his pipe to puff at it again, only to discover that the bowl had gone cold.

"Damn!" he exclaimed, stamping his foot like a child. "You have made my pipe go out!"

He formed a deep scowl with his bushy white eyebrows as he struck a match. He sucked noisily at the pipe until puffs of smoke spurted from the corners of his mouth.

"Not a member, are you?" he demanded, his sharp eyes on my face again.

"No," I confessed.

"Rules!" He shook his pipe stem dangerously near my nose. "You must know our rules if you expect to get along here. Never ask questions—that is the first. And leave your fellow man strictly alone. Those are the precepts of the Diogenes Club."

He said this with the sternest look thus far, then began to chuckle softly, his face transformed into a wrinkled visage of

amusement. His laugh was a series of almost inaudible gasps.
He leaned close to me and nudged me hard in the ribs with
his elbow.

"Deuced unfriendly, don't you think?" He cackled some
more.

"I suppose it is," I replied, bewildered and beginning to be
annoyed by his changeable manner.

He ceased laughing and glanced about as if spies might be
present. "Oh, don't let anyone else hear you say that," he
whispered, rolling his eyes, "or you'll never become a member."

"That is not my intention!" I protested at once.

He tut-tutted. "Very wise of you." He sucked placidly at his
pipe in a resigned way. "I have been a member for many
years, and I have always regretted it. But I have a wife, you
see—a devil of a woman!" He glanced about again, as if to see
that she was not lurking behind a curtain. "She would not
tolerate any other sort of club." He sighed. "I would have
preferred one with billiards and a bit of life, but Hermione is
pleased only with this one, so I have remained with it. It is
after all a perfectly satisfactory escape. I come here for a pipe
and a spot of quiet thought whenever I can. But forgive me
—you were looking for someone?"

"Yes," I said, relieved that old Simon Bliss had at last come
round to my question. "I wish to speak to Mycroft Holmes."

Bliss squinted in puzzlement. "Mycroft Holmes? I do not
know the name."

It was my turn to look puzzled. "But I am certain he is a
member. It was admittedly several years ago, but I met him
in this very room, and I know that he has never changed clubs.
In fact he is here every evening from five to eight."

Bliss' expression became fixedly certain. "You must be mistaken. I am often here between those hours, and I do not know
a Mycroft Holmes."

"Oh, perhaps it is the nature of your club," I suggested
somewhat anxiously. "If you do not speak to one another,
naturally you will not learn one another's names. I know that
if I describe him to you . . ."

The old man waved a hand to cut me short and sucked ever more vigorously at his pipe. "No, no, Dr. Watson. Descriptions do not matter, for I know the name and face of every current member of the Diogenes Club, and Mycroft Holmes is not among them!"

Simon Bliss could not have alarmed me more if he had struck me. I wanted to protest, to demand proof, to believe that the old man was mistaken, or senile, or simply wished to rid himself of my presence. But in spite of his eccentric manner, I believed him. His sharp old eyes carried conviction.

He could not have failed to see the confusion on my face. "You see, doctor, I am the most peculiar member of this very peculiar club. I alone of all its members am interested in human life. I love to learn people's names and how they lead their lives. I love to exchange secrets. I love to gossip. In short, I am perfectly normal by any standards other than those of the Diogenes Club. Circumstances have placed me here, but I have learned to overcome them by playing my own little game in my declining years. It is quite a challenge and amuses me even more than if my club were one of those hearty pukka-sahib types which you may find anywhere else on Pall Mall. I search out secrets about my fellow clubmen in spite of their stuffy reticence. I play the detective in my quiet way and chuckle to myself at how I get past them. And believe me, doctor, many of these men have much to hide. It is not solely an antisocial nature which causes them to choose this particular haven. And so you have made a fortunate choice in him from whom you inquire about the Diogenes. I can tell you everything about the place—and Mycroft Holmes is not a member."

His wizened face relapsed into a placid confidence that the matter was settled. He continued to puff away at his pipe, waiting for some new subject to arise. It did not.

"I tell you, Mycroft Holmes was one of the founding members," I insisted.

Bliss snorted triumphantly. "Again you are mistaken; there are the names of the founders just over your head!"

The jabbing stem of his pipe directed my gaze to a brass

plaque above the door behind me. I turned to examine it. Its tarnished surface indicated that it had been there for years. Its wording proclaimed unmistakably that the three large names etched on it were those of its founders. None was Mycroft Holmes.

"Obviously you are mistaking either the man or the club," Bliss concluded curtly.

"But he is Sherlock Holmes' brother!" I blurted out.

"The famous detective? Yes, I have read a tale or two in *The Strand*. Do you mean you are *that* Dr. Watson? Oh dear, for that reason alone I wish that I could help you, but I do not see what this man's being Sherlock Holmes' brother has to do with it. In fact I did not know that Mr. Holmes had a brother at all."

"I am beginning to doubt it myself," I said, thoroughly downcast. "You are quite certain that Mycroft Holmes never belonged to the Diogenes Club?"

Another acerb puffing at the indefatigable pipe and a disappointed lowering of the brows. "No, no, doctor, I did not say so. He is not a member *now.*"

My heart leaped. "Then of course he was at one time. Are there old membership books? Might I see them?"

"That should pose no difficulty. It is highly irregular for even another member of the Diogenes Club to look into them, but they are perfectly accessible, and such prohibitions have never stopped me. Indeed, here those ledgers are my bible. Have you ever noticed how all the best things are highly irregular at one time or another? When they become regular it rather takes the spice out of them, don't you think?" Bliss wheezed a sly laugh and again nudged my ribs with his sharp elbow. "I shall bring the books."

He scuttled out the door.

Five minutes later we were sitting in two chairs pulled close together, examining a dusty volume.

"This is the very first ledger of membership and dues. You see?" He indicated the earliest entries. "Mycroft Holmes is not among them. Now let us trace the history of the Diogenes Club."

His hand began to move rapidly up and down the columns. He flipped page after page. Occasionally new names would appear and others be crossed off. It took several moments to reach the end of the first book.

"Hmmm—that takes us through 1876. Let us see what volume two reveals." Bliss brought up a second ledger from the stack on the floor beside him. His fingers raced through its years: "1877 . . . 1878 . . . '79." A third volume came up. ". . . 1880 . . . '81 . . ." Volume six began with 1888. Bliss' finger chased with undiminished fervor down the columns. I was nodding with disappointment and defeat when he stopped. "Doctor, I have found it."

My eyes blinked open. "Where?" I looked at the line he indicated. "Mycroft Holmes" was written there in modest letters. My eyes crossed the line to the date: September 1, 1888. I protested at once. "That cannot be! It is the very year and month of the Greek adventure!"

Bliss regarded me impatiently as he repacked his pipe from a tin of Embassy mixture. "I know nothing of any Greek adventure, but the authenticity of the entry is not to be doubted." I took the book onto my lap. He reached over to tap Mycroft's name with his pipe stem. "See, the dried ink matches the other entries perfectly. An observation worthy of your detective friend, don't you think?" His wrinkled lips smiled smugly as he struck a match to his pipe.

"But that was the very month I was introduced to Mycroft," I gasped. "And yet Sherlock Holmes led me to believe that his brother had been a member of your club for years."

"You seem to have been the victim of some joke," Bliss said coolly. He took the book from me. "Let us see how long this Mycroft was a member." He turned a single page. "Oh, this is very amusing! The Diogenes Club appears not to have agreed with your friend's brother very well, for he withdrew his membership in October, the very month following his initiation. That is a joke indeed!"

Bliss turned to wheeze at me with delight, but his expression altered at the sight of my face, which had surely blanched.

"My dear fellow! May I help you? A glass of brandy?"
My head was spinning. "Please!"

I had fallen back in my chair in a state of complete bewilderment, with a sense of awful and inexplicable betrayal suddenly rising about me and drowning all my trust in Sherlock Holmes. Not a scrap of wreckage could I see to cling to, and the deluge of feeling caused an actual roaring in my ears that made me think I would faint. I sat thus numbly, my arms dangling limply over the sides of the chair, until Bliss placed a glass of brandy to my lips a moment later. I felt the warm spirits course through my veins to steady my whirling thoughts.

Bliss seated himself by my side. He crossed his sticklike legs and sent curling puffs of smoke at the ceiling. "I do not understand your reaction, doctor. One cannot blame Mr. Mycroft Holmes for fleeing the Diogenes Club as soon as possible. He must have seen immediately that it was peculiar, and so he left as any man of sense—except myself—would have done."

"He is more than a man of sense!" I heard myself exclaim. "He is Sherlock Holmes' superior in analytic powers!"

Bliss kept his lips pursed in mid-puff. He turned his head slowly to look at me. "Indeed? Well, that is saying something, doctor, that is saying a great deal." He continued to regard me oddly. I guessed that he had decided I was as mad as any member of his club. His next words confirmed my thought: "I do not doubt you, of course. Are you quite certain that you would not like an application to join our fraternity? I would be most happy to bring your name up at our very next meeting."

I did not know whether he joked with me or not, but I found his frank stare, both pitying and amused, highly uncomfortable. It brought me to my senses and forced me to look at my assertion. It did sound foolish: *Mycroft Holmes is superior to his brother in analytic powers.* Mycroft might be the great detective's equal, though now I doubted even that, but superior? For years I had believed he was because Sherlock Holmes had said so. Now the assertion sounded fantastic. I had also believed that Mycroft Holmes was a founder of the Diogenes Club and could be found there every evening from five to eight. That was proved a patent lie.

I felt a quivering at the corners of my mouth. I downed the remainder of the brandy and heard, astonishingly, the sputter of my own laughter. It was rueful rather than amused, but it relieved me.

"There now, Dr. Watson," Bliss said with much satisfaction, "so you are a man of sense after all. Laughter is the surest sign of it. There are so many absurdities in the world. One must live with them. Why not be amused by the show? I have been constantly entertained by the pageant of life. And there is always something new—you, for instance, and your intriguing case."

"I have, as you say, a case," I admitted.

"You have certainly been misled in some way, though to what purpose I cannot guess. One thing is certain: you must mull this over. You have new facts; now you must fit them into your scheme. Is not that what the great detective would say? In fact you must confront him at once, since the mistake, or the deception, must have come from him."

"Unfortunately that is not possible, but I shall surely think things over. I have much to do in that way."

Simon Bliss, a chameleonlike character if ever I met one, now appeared very wise to me. He chuckled with pleasure, still with the bowl of his pipe clasped in one gnarled hand, its stem tucked firmly in a corner of his mouth. "My own eccentricities are mostly the result of indulging the privilege of old age, which has its conventions," he said. "Please ignore them. I hope yours is not a serious matter, only a misunderstanding. If it is more than that, do not rush to judge. You must consider the wonder of the invention, and that your Sherlock Holmes, who has the reputation of being a very good man indeed, would surely not have misled a friend maliciously and to no purpose."

It was good advice. I felt recovered enough to rise and did so. I did not want to take up more of old Bliss' time. He stood with me, his body bent beneath mine. He seemed to me now like some wonderful gnome. I shook his hand warmly; this time his grip was gentle. I thought I caught a wink in one eye.

"Thank you for your help," I said gratefully. "I shall remember your advice."

"Not at all, doctor. Do return and tell me how it all turns out. I would be happy to add the chronicle of our briefest member to the secret chapters of the Diogenes Club which I keep in this old brain of mine." He tapped his forehead once, then walked slowly back to his position by the window where he again drew aside the green velvet curtain and resumed his ruminative stance, puffing away as he reflected on the passing show of this dark wet evening.

I myself turned and, retreating through the still silent hall of the Diogenes Club, collected my hat, coat, and umbrella before rejoining that show on the street outside. Once I was there, with the hard wet pavement beneath my boots and the icy mist drifting about my ears, I realized how uncertain I was as to what part I was to play in the drama. As I began hesitantly to walk down Pall Mall, jostled by the clubmen scurrying to get in out of the rain, I remembered times past at Baker Street when my friend had chafed in frustration because no interesting mystery presented itself for his scrutiny.

What a perfect case this would have made for Sherlock Holmes, had he not been its object.

10

I WANDERED EAST along Pall Mall with no goal in mind. The rain had slowed to a drizzle. As Simon Bliss had suggested, I attempted to fit my new facts into some sort of scheme. It was an exceedingly difficult task.

I began with the facts themselves: Mycroft Holmes had not been a founder of the Diogenes Club; he had not been a member prior to my meeting him there in 1888; he was not there daily from a quarter to five to twenty to eight, because he had been a member for but a month, fifteen years ago. Sherlock Holmes had lied to me. Why? And why had his brother agreed to the deception?

Deceptions! The secret laboratory was a deception. Holmes' not telling me of Moriarty's strange resemblance to him was a deception.

How many others might there be?

Uncertain as I was of details, I felt that the scales had been lifted from my eyes and that I was beginning to glimpse outlines of the truth. It was painful, but I could not deny the awful half-formed vision before me. I knew that I had been misinformed, tricked, and perhaps used for a purpose to which I had

not given my consent. This much called all else into question.
I began to think about Sherlock Holmes as I had never thought
about him before; he seemed a smug villain to have so toyed
with me, a person apart, a man I did not know. For the first
time I stood outside my close relationship with him and saw
how fantastic he seemed.

His uncanny ability to find clues and, from them, to
deduce the solutions to knotty problems when perfectly able
men failed—it seemed like some gross fiction, and yet I had
seen it, indeed had recorded it, and I knew that he had the
power. Whence had Holmes derived it? Was he simply a genius? With my ordinary and admittedly rather stodgy nature,
I was in no position to judge, though I knew that genius
could seem like dangerous witchcraft. Yet for one man to
have done so much, to have turned detection into a science
single-handedly . . .

Of course he had done much more. He was the author of
numerous monographs: "Upon the Distinction between the
Ashes of the Various Tobaccos," "Upon the Tracing of Footsteps," "Upon the Influence of Trade upon the Form of the
Hand," "On the Typewriter and its Relation to Crime," "Of
Tattoo Marks," "On Secret Writing," "On the Surface Anatomy of the Human Ear," and others requiring much research
and energy before pen touched paper. He was an accomplished violinist and had written about music as well; his "On
the Polyphonic Motets of Lassus" was said by experts to be the
last word on the subject. He was a fencer, a boxer, a baritsu
expert. He was a consummate mimic and master of disguise.
His mind was an encyclopedia of arcane knowledge.

Could one man, even a genius, have done and known so
much?

And yet he had, patently he had. The deception was not in
his evident accomplishments, but it existed, and I began to see
its facets—the laboratory, the relationship to Moriarty, the lie
about Mycroft Holmes and the Diogenes Club—as parts of a
larger mystery.

The most painful stroke was that, wrack my brain as I did,

I could think of no explanation for the Diogenes Club charade other than deceiving me alone. Why had Holmes done such a thing to his loyal friend?

I found myself at the Regent Street intersection. I realized that I was the only man in sight with an umbrella up; the rain had ceased entirely. I folded my umbrella and tucked it under my arm, turning left and wandering up Regent Street in the direction of Piccadilly Circus, still pondering, paying little attention to my course, ignoring the pedestrians crowding the sidewalks about me, still trying to sort out my thoughts. I skirted the glittering expanse of Piccadilly, noting only that the rain had driven away the flower girls who usually spread their baskets and bouquets at the foot of the Eros statue. I angled onto Shaftesbury Avenue and realized that I was in the heart of theatre country. Behind me were the London Pavilion and the underground Criterion; I was strolling past the Lyric, the Apollo, the Shaftesbury, the Palace. The huge black street was rent with loud traffic and ablaze with lemon-colored light from pavement to rooftop. I thought of Sherlock Holmes' love of acting. I thought too of Wiggins and wondered in what play he was appearing, indeed if he might be putting on his makeup in one of the theatres I wandered past now. At Cambridge Circus I turned down Charing Cross Road and walked by the Garrick and Wyndham's to find myself at last in Leicester Square, dedicated almost entirely to musical comedy, though Shakespeare presided on his pedestal in the little park at the heart of it. The oriental minarets of the Alhambra, the more solid roofline of the Empire, and the baroque façade of Daly's stood lit up against the sky.

For the time being I had forgotten my goal of finding Sherlock Holmes. The question that nagged at my brain was: what larger necessity could explain all of the detective's deceptions and secrecy about his origins and relations? I tried to follow his example in thinking about the problem. He had always urged me not to theorize without facts. I felt that there was much more I must ascertain before I could make any intelligent guesses, but still I could not help my mind from scrambling

madly from speculation to speculation until it was thoroughly
exhausted and confused.

I made three turns about Leicester Square, then headed
south past Trafalgar Square to the Strand.

If anything, the Strand was more crowded with merrymakers than Piccadilly. Here there were restaurants, numerous
public houses, and more theatres. I passed under the arcade
of the Tivoli Theatre of Varieties and suddenly knew that I
must see Wiggins.

I stopped walking and was jostled to the edge of the pavement. The crowds surged by, chattering gaily. I examined my
impulsive feeling. Yes, he was the very man, perhaps the only
man. My presence near the West End theatres had made me
think of him, but it was his former friendship with Sherlock
Holmes and his quick thinking under stress that made me
believe I could trust him and that now, when I badly needed
a fresh point of view and a level head, he was the one soul to
whom I should turn.

Such was my need that I wanted to see him at once. But
where? Though I knew he was appearing somewhere in London in a play, I did not have the least idea at which theatre I
might find him. I glanced at my watch; seven thirty, and curtain time was eight. I pushed through the crowd to a news-
hawker at the corner of Adam Street and bought a copy of *The
Times*. I walked back to the Tivoli arcade and, out of the way
of the throng, opened my paper and thumbed rapidly to its
theatrical pages. I recalled that Wiggins had mentioned a
George Edwardes production. There were two of them pres-
ently in London, I discovered: one was the immensely successful *Country Girl* at Daly's, which had been playing for nearly
two years; the other was *The Orchid*, at the new Gaiety
Theatre at the corner of Aldwych and the Strand, not three
streets away. I was not up on theatre lore—the triviality of
theatrical gossip appalled me—but it was impossible not to
know the Gaiety Theatre or to be cognizant of Mr. George
Edwardes as the king of musical comedy—and of the reputation of his Gaiety Girls. They were said to be the prettiest

and wittiest young women in London, and the curb outside
the Gaiety stage door was crowded nightly with elegant
broughams and carriages. (It was there that so many young
peers of the realm lost their hearts and, in their parents' eyes,
debased their coronets.) In fact the Gaiety Theatre had been
much in the news recently. It had been sumptuously rebuilt
because of the widening of the Strand and had opened not two
months ago in no less a presence than King Edward himself
and his queen. That period corresponded to the time Wiggins
had occupied the upper floor at Baker Street; therefore, *The
Orchid* must be Wiggins' play. In my excited state I was inor-
dinately proud of this little deduction.

I stepped back into the stream of pedestrians and hurried
east up the Strand. The Gaiety's lights brightly spelled out *The
Orchid.* The crowds were thick at the side entrances. In front
a continuous stream of hansoms and four-wheelers came and
went, discharging passengers. I entered with them under the
dome of the theatre to find myself in a circular columniated
crush room. I paused for a moment to gaze at the parade of
beautiful women with enormous hats atop their padded hair,
bedizened with furs and ribbons, carrying feather boas or
parasols; and fashionable men who, having shed their great-
coats in the cloak room, stood about in pearl gray frock coats
and starched shirtfronts. The women wore jewels and trinkets
from Cartier's or Asprey's; many of them would have had their
portraits painted by the likes of John Singer Sargent. The fat
aroma of cigars and the heady scent of perfume flooded the
air.

There was now obviously no chance of seeing Wiggins before the performance, so I decided to attempt to book a stall.
First, however, I examined one of the numerous playbills. I
found the name of Frederick Wigmore opposite a character
called "Meakin," so I knew that I had chosen the right theatre.
To the left and right of the lobby, staircases led up to the grand
circle; the box office was beneath the left-hand staircase. Already there was a considerable line of late ticket buyers. I was
not dressed for the stalls, but that option was not open to me,

for when I had at last cleared the line only a very few gallery
seats remained. I purchased one and was shortly in the jam-
packed atmosphere of the "gods," where a good-natured
crowd sucked oranges and buzzed with anticipation as the
moment approached when the curtain would rise. I had time
to note in my program that the star of this musical entertainment was Miss Gertie Millar and that the songs were by Ivan
Caryll and Lionel Monckton before Mr. Caryll himself appeared to applause and struck up the overture.

The musical comedy was just what I needed. It was diverting and utterly inconsequential; its light melodies and silliness,
a far cry from the serious bowing of Sarasate and Neruda
which had filled so many of my evenings with Sherlock
Holmes at St. James's Hall, completely took my mind off my
dilemma. Wiggins was a surprise. I had expected him to play
a young man—his age and looks were admirably suited to
insouciant leading-man parts, I thought—but his Meakin
turned out to be an old man, the villain of the piece, and if I
had not known to look for my young friend under the fierce
makeup I would never have recognized him. In fact I thought
him the best thing in the play. Though old, Meakin was spry
and rascally, and Wiggins made the most of his villainy, upstag-
ing the pretty Miss Millar several times. He had three songs
and turned what was probably a fine strong tenor voice into
an amusingly wobbling device that sent the audience into
gales of laughter. He won much applause.

After the play I made my way out with the rest of the
audience. Their cheerful babble proclaimed that they were as
satisfied with the evening as I. In front of the theatre the
pavement was still wet, but the rain had not returned. A few
stars twinkled through scudding clouds turned a ghostly yellow by the moon.

I strolled round to the stage exit to wait for Wiggins to
emerge. Already several eager young men dressed in the
height of fashion hung about the exit, affecting boredom but
with the irrepressible spark of heartstruck youth in their eyes.
After a while the young ladies who had so delightfully deco-

rated Mr. Edwardes' stage began to appear. They were coy
and self-possessed and as pretty as I had heard them described.
They stepped into the carriages of the young men and were
swept off to suppers at the Trocadero in Piccadilly, the Ritz
(where their food would be touched with the genius of Es-
coffier), or Romano's just down the Strand.

At last I caught sight of Wiggins. All traces of Meakin had
been stripped from him, and I had to adjust to his dapper
appearance. Over his frock coat he wore a long Artois cloak
with a velvet collar, and he was just fitting a black top hat on
his head at a slightly rakish tilt. He was daringly without umbrella but carried a malacca stick. He was in vivacious conversation with three of the most beautiful of the Gaiety girls who
looked, from their fond smiles, as if they would gladly have
given up any engagement to spend the evening with him. At
once I wondered if indeed one of them might have been
waiting for him, but all three were greeted shortly by young
men who appraised Wiggins coolly before leading their prizes
away.

Wiggins spotted me and bounded over with a great expression of delight.

"You at the stage exit of the Gaiety!" he exclaimed. "Have
you an engagement with one of our soubrettes? And I've surprised you at it! Well, well, I shan't tell Mrs. Watson, but I am
astonished at you, doctor!"

He stood back and, leaning easily on his stick, grinned at me.

The relaxed mood which *The Orchid* had produced in me
was wearing off, and now that Wiggins was before me I was
anxious to speak to him about my difficulty. I came to the point
at once: "I must consult with you about Sherlock Holmes."

"Oho! And if it does not concern the mysterious fire at Baker
Street I will be surprised," replied he. "But come. We cannot
discuss serious matters in the street."

He took my arm and led me off peremptorily down the
Strand in the direction from which I had come.

As we pushed through the noisy bundled-up throng of after-
theatre merrymakers, I complimented him on his perform-

ance. I could see that he was pleased, for his cheeks, rosy with
the cold, grew even redder.

"Nothing to it, doctor." He brushed aside my compliment
in an offhand way, but his already airy step grew positively
breezy.

"There seemed a great deal to it to me," I protested,
"though I am only a theatre-going novice. You are possessed
of remarkable gifts."

At that Wiggins laughed and leaped suddenly into the thoroughfare, nimbly dodging carriages and twopenny omnibuses
as he dragged me after him.

"Gifts, doctor!" he exclaimed when we had reached the
opposite curb safely, myself breathlessly, and were proceeding along. "If only you knew. You have been associated far too
long with Sherlock Holmes, who makes the arduous appear
miraculous and rarely reveals his agonies. He has described his
results as 'elementary,' but do not be fooled. What is elementary to him is so only because he has taken the time to learn
his ABCs, and that in any art means great effort."

"You have worked at it then?" said I, willing to learn more
about the theatre from this engaging young man. To tell the
truth I was particularly interested in how Frederick Wigmore,
the rising young actor, had developed from that scruffy and
unpromising street urchin Wiggins.

We were between Bedford and Wellington streets. Wiggins
paused in mid-stride to gaze at me benignly. "There is no
subject more fascinating to me than my own history—but only
over a pint of ale would I consent to share it with anyone. And
here is the perfect spot. Come, while we drink you shall hear
of my apprenticeship."

With that he piloted me by the elbow through a particularly
clamorous knot of revelers into the Adelphi Bar, which lay just
at hand. I had not been in the Adelphi before and so gazed
about curiously. Its interior decor and architectural features
appeared somewhat overwrought to me, and it was crowded
with patrons who seemed, from the flavor of their conversation, the grandiloquence of their gestures, and the greasepaint

on their vests, all to have some connection with the stage. Many of them sported the unmistakable signs of the acting profession in astrakhan collars, unbarbered hair, and neckware of the *La Bohème* variety. Somehow Wiggins contrived to find for us a relatively isolated corner out of the way of the general hubbub. As we drank our ale, he reminisced.

"I did not begin as a child of gifts, you know," said he, "but the street is a strict and knowledgeable schoolmistress, if only you obey her rules. The audacious survive—they earn her grudging approbation—and the theatre is a form of public audacity, so I was well prepared for acting early on when I had my first love affair at the age of nine."

"At nine!" My eyebrows shot up.

"Just a footlight affair, doctor—with the Columbine of a children's pantomime at the Drury Lane Theatre. I had sneaked in, as you may have guessed. I sat entranced and tried to sneak back in several times afterward, but my mooning made me careless, and I never saw that particular Columbine again. But I began to watch for performances of mummers and musicians in the streets and to dodge into music halls when I could. Gradually my love of that painted doll of a performer, who had seemed magical to me, grew into a love of the magic of theatre itself, its limelight and movement and music and sound—which is achieved by much sweat and labor, as I have told you. The toil of learning how its effects are produced has not diminished my love for it.

"Since those early days I have performed for all sorts of reasons. I think what I enjoy most is fooling people into believing I am what I am not. I am sure that it is a legacy of the streets—and of my days with Sherlock Holmes. When a boy, I had to perform to survive. I succeeded and grew to enjoy stretching my talents. Now on the stage I can become another person. I can take the audience in, hold them, sway them with my tricks! And they pay me for it and insist on being fooled. It is an exhilarating thing, to be rewarded for showing off!"

Wiggins drank the last of his ale. He grinned at me and I felt the full force of his charm. This young man would go far, I thought. His "tricks," as he called them, would obtain more for him than the income of the finest gentleman of the land could ever buy. I was not certain that I approved of his impulsive want of seriousness, but his delight in life and in his profession was not faked, and it was that which saved him for me.

"You make acting sound very romantic indeed," I observed. "How much of an influence had Sherlock Holmes on your career?"

"Aha!" Wiggins exclaimed with a knowing look. "I thought we would come round to our old friend sooner or later. Well, he taught me street lore, and how to fool a copper and a crook alike, and he took me in hand, gave my life a shape which it badly needed. And he was the great model of my youth before Forbes-Robertson and Henry Irving became my lights. When he saw that my steps were set firmly on the theatrical path he gave me good advice, sent me to the school of life and of theatrical experience, rather than to one of those stuffy academies run by failed actresses who equate elocution with performance and starch the talent out of a good many promising youngsters. Then he let nature take its course."

"And . . . ?"

"And I became an actor the hard way, the only way: by acting, by leaving my blunders behind as stepping stones. I began by mimicking old toffs in the streets to the delight of my gang. Then some boys and I set up our own little theatre in an abandoned house in Cheapside and got up an audience for our terrible, funny little entertainments which we wrote ourselves. Sometimes we used threats to get other boys in to watch—oh, we stuck at nothing! When I got older I did readings and comic bits at workingmen's clubs. Then I used to pay a shilling for the privilege of playing small parts at the Percy Hall on the Tottenham Court Road. The shilling meant nothing to me—wasn't I getting to act on a real stage? Well, of course my ambition grew into wanting to be paid for my talents, which were meager and undeveloped then. I had met a boy at school with connections, stagestruck like me, who had got himself a job at the Elephant and Castle on the Surreyside as an extra gentleman—a 'super,' you know—the lowest thing imaginable, but it seemed to me that I had scaled the heights when he managed to bring me along. It was good-bye school and hello to the life of the stage!"

"How old were you then?"

"Fourteen, and I am now twenty-eight. It has been a long road, doctor. The Elephant and Castle was a dingy working-men's theatre that smelled of fish and chips, which the patrons brought along in bags under their shirts, and the most expensive seat cost a shilling. It was a stock company, and we changed the bill every week. I saw Mr. Holmes rarely at that time, but I often thought of what he had taught me about tricks and nerve in performing and about makeup and costume. I think he knew more about the theatre than any man I ever met treading the boards, but he never told me how he came to learn it. I am sure that doddering old Joe Cave, the manager, would have kicked me out of his company if I hadn't been able to show that I knew something, and that it came from Sherlock Holmes. At any rate I went from walk-ons and crowd scenes to small speaking parts, but after a time decided that my next move should be toward the provinces where I could play larger roles. So I answered an advertisement in *The Stage*, building myself up tremendously, of course, and I was off on the road."

Wiggins paused long enough to order two more pints. In the interim I found that my hand had strayed into my overcoat pocket and was absently fingering the octavo volume on theatres which I had rescued from Holmes' library.

When our drinks were before us, Wiggins continued: "I was in the provinces more years than I had expected, but they were my apprenticeship and filled me out as an actor without discouraging me too much. Well I remember the small seedy hotels in places where we changed the bill every night. I belonged to several touring companies in succession, some with managers who paid regularly and some run by scoundrels who absconded with everything portable when things got sticky. Then I was with the Empire music hall agents for a time as an acrobat and a clown. In those years I played all kinds of parts, men of all shapes and sizes, sometimes women; and when I was most hunched over, with a skullcap covering my hair, a beard stuck on my face with spirit gum, and lines of age marked on my cheeks in grease pencil, I would think of how Sherlock Holmes used to fool me, and I would enjoy my performance all the more."

I could tell that Wiggins was pleased to recall his history for me. He sat back.

"And there you have it, Dr. Watson—except for my decision to return to London and make it in the West End or die trying. I will spare you the weary round of agents which every out-of-work actor in London knows, and crawling up and down the Strand, hoping for a tip from friends. I am arrived and I intend to stay!"

"That is admirable. You seem to have been well seasoned for the stage."

"I have indeed. And, if I may say so, I hope that my season is a long one."

I had to laugh at this. "And I also."

"But enough of my history. What of your problem? Is it serious?"

"I think I may call it the deepest dilemma of my life."

"And it concerns Sherlock Holmes?"

"It does."

"Well, I promised help if ever you needed it, and I am at your service. Come, we will go to my rooms. They were once Sherlock Holmes' rooms—yours as well—and I can think of no better place for solving mysteries. Perhaps Holmes' magic has lingered and will inspire us. You know, doctor, I do not know your story, but already I am confident of good results!"

Energetically he pushed back his chair and stood. Once he had made a decision he acted with dispatch. He tossed some coins onto the table and led me out, more at a dash than a walk, onto the still-bustling Strand. He hailed a cab, and it was not long before we were rattling west along Oxford Street toward Baker Street.

This was a route I had traveled often, and in the same fashion, with Sherlock Holmes. Surprisingly Wiggins had grown silent. I glanced at him by my side; his look was placid and thoughtful. With his lean dramatic features he reminded me, in the glow of the passing streetlamps flickering across his face, of my old friend. I could almost imagine myself sitting next to Holmes once more, returning to our old digs.

11

WIGGINS LET US into the front door of 221B Baker Street. The sharp odor of burned wood struck my nostrils immediately; it would take some time for that to be aired out of the house. Wiggins led the way up the seventeen steps which I had climbed so often at Sherlock Holmes' call. It was like a pilgrimage for me, and I felt my anger and suspicion toward the detective begin to soften. How often had I come down these same seventeen steps with him, my service revolver in my overcoat pocket as it was now, to trail some miscreant along London's bleak and misty byways?

How I longed to see my old friend again!

Wiggins flung open the familiar door and stood aside to allow me to enter. I stepped across the threshold. I had not been in these rooms in over two months, not since I had packed away the last of Holmes' voluminous boxes of notes. By that lapse of mind which does not acknowledge change, I expected to see the sitting room as it had been before Mrs. Hudson and I had emptied it. For me it had the character of a shrine, though it had been cluttered and ordinary in spite of its eccentric touches. We had accumulated much, and in the periods when I had not lived with Holmes he had kept it all. (My first wife no more than my second had been interested in my bachelor hoard.) In addition to our two comfortable chairs by the fireplace there had been a wooden chair, a cane-backed chair, and an armchair for guests, as well as a sofa and a settee. Then there had been our breakfast table with its oil lamp, and in one corner the acid-stained old table littered with Holmes' chemical implements. As well, he and I had each kept a desk against one wall with, above, bookshelves bending under the weight of his reference books and boxes of cuttings. Added to this were the violin case, the tantalus and gasogene, and Holmes' rack of pipes; also the mantelpiece littered with the drying plugs and dottles left from his smokes of the day before, his unanswered correspondence fixed to the center of the mantel with a jackknife, the Persian slipper of shag tobacco, the coal scuttle full of cigars, the bullet pocks in the wall from his bouts of indoor target practice, our scientific charts and pictures, and the bearskin hearthrug. Too, my friend had saved all sorts of criminal relics which had a way of wandering into unlikely places, sometimes turning up in the butter dish. This bachelor confusion had been compounded by his untidiness in the matter of storing things in their proper places, if indeed they were ever assigned them, so that there had often been books and papers scattered about the room.

This singular scene of disorder was what I was prepared to meet, but what I saw instead was a room with the stamp of a totally different personality. Sherlock Holmes had been as careless in his housekeeping as he was careful in his attire; Wiggins, somewhat flamboyant in dress, was a model of simplicity and orderliness in the arrangement of his small home. If it could not be called elegant, it was at least orderly, and the smoke from the fire appeared to have done little or no damage. The familiar jumble of tables and chairs was gone, and in its place were many fewer pieces: three chairs, a divan against one wall, and a single small round table where I supposed Wiggins to take his breakfast by the bow window. The curtains were new beige draperies, and the wallpaper had been

changed to a lighter shade and a subtle pattern, so that the
patriotic *V.R.* in bullet pocks with which Holmes had adorned
one wall was hidden forever. The whole effect was light and
airy. I was surprised to find myself pleased at the change.

Wiggins saw me looking at the wallpaper. "Do you like it?"
he asked, dropping his cloak off his shoulders. "Very different,
I suppose. I picked it out myself. Mrs. Hudson and I agreed
that the room needed redoing after a quarter of a century of
Sherlock Holmes. I admire him greatly, but really, it was atro-
cious! I don't see how he could live like that. Faugh! Those
awful dottles from his pipe had stained the mantel terribly,
and the whole place stank of shag and nitric acid. And the
things that must have been ground into that rug! I tell you,
doctor, Mrs. Hudson was as glad to have the place redone as
I, and she gave me a free hand in picking things out. What do
you think?"

I gave my approval. It was all that Wiggins needed. Delighted as a child, he strolled about, pointing out this and that
—the newly painted woodwork, a light yellowish hue which
was echoed in the fresh golden tones of the new carpet, and
particularly his plants. There were green things everywhere
in pots and baskets of various sizes and descriptions. His ac-
cumulation of flora I found rather startling—no man of my
acquaintance had ever displayed the least joy in such things—
but Wiggins was effusive over palm and trailing vine alike. If
there were too much of anything in the room to my taste, it
was these. A great fern hung from a hook above the bow
window near his table, and a formidable potted palm reaching
nearly to the ceiling stood sentinel by his door. His single
bookcase, with bound plays of Pinero, Jones, Galsworthy, Bar-
rie, Wilde, and the outspoken Mr. Shaw, had as much leafy
stuff on its shelves as books.

I decided then and there that Wiggins and Sherlock Holmes
had something in common besides acting skill: they were both
singular characters who would leave their stamp upon life
wherever they paused in it.

As if to confirm my observation, I was introduced to another
of Wiggins' objects.

"You must meet the lady who lives with me, Dr. Watson," I heard him say.

Prepared to be both shocked and embarrassed, I turned from examining the spiky aurelia which he had just proudly shown me to find him whistling softly at a canary quivering on its perch in an ornate brass cage on a stand in one corner.

"This is Columbine," he explained, smiling across at me slyly. "I occupy my at-home hours only with her. I have named her for the lost love of my youth." He whistled again and the bird responded, twittering, hopping about its cage, keeping its little head cocked toward Wiggins all the while and ignoring me utterly. At last Wiggins took up a cloth cover and placed it over the cage. "Good night, Columbine. Our late hours shall not keep you from your dreams," he whispered.

He busied himself about the fire grate, chattering away about affairs of the stage until the coals were blazing, then he took my hat and coat and disappeared with them into the bedroom. I took a seat in one of two comfortable armchairs placed near the fire and looked about once more. There were no photographs or paintings on Wiggins' walls, but he had put up three or four theatrical posters of Bernhardt and Duse, unusual but appropriate decor. There was a magazine rack by the side of my chair. In it I found issues of *The Stage* as well as other theatrical publications, also some issues of *The Yellow Book* with rather unpleasant pen-and-ink drawings by Aubrey Beardsley on their covers.

Wiggins emerged from the bedroom. He had changed his clothes, and I stared at his new raiment. He was wearing a flowing floor-length garment with voluminous sleeves in which his arms were almost lost. It was made of some rough-spun material and was tied at the waist with a wide cerulean blue sash. Parallel stripes of the same vivid color decorated the cloth from foot to shoulder. It made him look quite barbarous.

"It is a caftan!" he announced, turning so that I could view the whole effect. "Isn't it wonderful? I picked it up for a song in a secondhand shop on the Edgware Road. No ordinary dressing gown for me! It is very comfortable. And now," he said, plopping himself down in the chair opposite mine, "let us get down to business."

He crossed his legs on the chair, emphasizing the oriental effect. I did not comment that in India I had seen such garments as he wore, but never on a white man in London—nor a white woman, for that matter. I was anxious to get on with my story and so deliberately disregarded Wiggins' dramatic effects.

I decided on the direct approach: "Moriarty is back."

I confess to being pleased to see my young friend start. His blue eyes became round with fascination and his mouth dropped open in a frozen expression.

"Not *the* Moriarty?" he asked at last.

"The only one." I spoke softly. Only the hiss of the coals accompanied my voice. Outside, London had grown still. "Wiggins, I shall tell you things entrusted to me in the strictest confidence by Sherlock Holmes, as well as new and highly disturbing facts which I have learned since his supposed retirement. I believe you care for him, that you owe him much, and that you can be trusted. Otherwise I would not confide in you."

Wiggins' look could not remain frozen for long. His eyes had lit up. "*Supposed* retirement—fascinating! I appreciate your trust, Dr. Watson. Please do go on."

He was now completely attentive. I saw before me the Wiggins of the night of the fire, alert and intelligent, aware that the game might be a deadly one and acting appropriately. I realized how much hope I had placed upon his help. As succinctly as possible I described the evening of Holmes' abrupt departure two months before and the reasons for it—that Moriarty had somehow survived Reichenbach and was dogging the detective's footsteps, seeking revenge. I did not yet reveal that I had seen Moriarty since then. Holmes had thought it best to disappear, I explained; his retirement to beekeeping on the Sussex Downs was a false trail.

"And you do not know where he has really gone?"

"I do not. Mrs. Hudson and I packed his things and sent

them by rail to Eastbourne Station. I have no doubt that they were met there by some agent of his, probably an unwitting one, and that in all likelihood even Moriarty has been unable to trace them."

"Just so. And how did Holmes seem to you when he left? Was he well?"

"He seemed in perfect command of himself. And yet . . ."

"Yes?"

"He spoke of Moriarty as he had never spoken of him before. There was a personal note—complete enmity, of course —and yet almost a sadness."

"That is certainly unlike Holmes. Of course if you have described Moriarty accurately in your chronicles—and that is the only way I have of knowing him—he is indeed singular, the most brilliant criminal mind the world has known. Perhaps Holmes was regretful at having finally to dispose of so challenging an opponent."

"Perhaps. He told me more, however. He said that he had known Moriarty in his youth."

Wiggins' eyes grew round again. "Indeed! That is new information. Did he explain the circumstances? No? Well, let us file it away. We will collect our facts as Mr. Holmes always did, then we will see what to make of them."

My young friend was now obviously greatly intrigued. His eyes danced and he leaned forward, his hands clasped tightly over his crossed legs.

"Before you tell me more, doctor, will you explain how you are involved in the affair and what exactly I may do for you?"

"Sherlock Holmes is missing; I am determined to find him. I want to warn him, to help him if need be. But there is another reason: I must have an explanation for the mystery which has arisen about him, indeed which has always existed, though I was too obtuse to see it or to question how little I knew about a man with whom I spent so many years. You named an aspect of the mystery when you wondered where he had acquired his astonishing stage lore. You said that he never told you."

"I admit that he did not, and it puzzled me greatly. Yes, he was always very close."

"Well, perhaps we can combine our questions and our knowledge to solve the mystery of his secretive nature together."

Wiggins remained in his Buddha-like position, the light from the fire flickering on his eager face, as I described the cryptic note Holmes had left in Mrs. Hudson's hands saying that I was not to do anything unless the detective himself instructed me. I told of my waiting, pondering, and worrying; of my visit from Gregson and Lestrade, who had hinted at an increase in crime which seemed to have the purpose of aggravating the international situation; and of the message at last in Holmes' hand, delivered to me on the previous evening by the page, Billy.

"Billy saw him, you mean?" Wiggins interrupted.

"Yes."

"Why, then Holmes is in London!" The young actor flung his arms dramatically wide at this obvious fact.

"Not necessarily," I cautioned.

I told the rest: of my decision to come to Mrs. Hudson in Baker Street, of my conversation with her and its astonishing revelation, of my descent at last into the secret laboratory and of what I had found there, finally of the arrival of Moriarty, with his perverse resemblance to Holmes. Wiggins had become immobile again, and said not a word. I reproduced my conversation with Moriarty in as much detail as possible and described his bewildering antics.

"A juggler like myself?" I heard Wiggins whisper in wonder.

I concluded by describing how Moriarty had deliberately set the fire.

"So it was Moriarty who drove off so furiously in the cab Athelney Jones was so anxious to trace! And I saw it!"

"It was."

"If I had only known. If I could have seen Moriarty's face—especially as you describe it! It is certain that Athelney Jones will never find that cabman."

"Quite certain, I am afraid."

"But, doctor, this is astonishing!"

"There is more."

Wiggins looked disbelieving, but now that I had begun I was determined that he would have it all. I told of my attempt to contact Mycroft Holmes, of my meeting with Simon Bliss in the Stranger's Room of the Diogenes Club, and of my subsequent discovery that, contrary to what Holmes had told me, his brother had belonged to that club for but a month.

"From the Diogenes Club I came to you at the Gaiety Theatre," I concluded, "and you have me now before your hearth. I do not know what to make of the strange facts I have described, but you can understand that, much as I have always respected and cared for Sherlock Holmes, they raise many questions about him. The one thing that seems clear is that he had deep secrets which he kept for many years from all of us who knew him; he deceived his friends. I cannot convey to you how wounded I feel by my discovery about Mycroft Holmes. It seems that Sherlock and his brother acted out that farce at the Diogenes Club for the specific purpose of misleading me. In any case I am determined to unravel this mystery, and the one sure way of doing it is for Holmes himself to explain it to me. Therefore I must find him and I would like your help in doing so."

There was a long silence during which Wiggins attempted to collect his thoughts. "I believe Sherlock Holmes is a good man," he said at last. "When I was an Irregular I was made aware in many ways of his affection for you, doctor. Therefore I believe that he must have had good reason for whatever he did."

I fervently wanted to believe this and confessed as much.

"I will help if I can," Wiggins went on. "I want to help because Mr. Holmes faces a formidable enemy, and I will do whatever is necessary to repay him for acting as a father to me, for protecting and guiding me when I was a wayward boy who might have gone bad. I shall always be his loyal ally, and it seems now that he may need all the allies he can muster."

"I understand. Thank you, Wiggins."

"Have you considered that these deceptions which you have uncovered may have at least as much to do with Moriarty as with Holmes?"

"What do you mean?"

Wiggins uncrossed his legs and stood up. He rubbed his hands together briskly and began striding up and down in front of the fire, his billowing blue-striped robe trailing after him and swirling as he turned.

"I don't yet know," he replied, "but it seems to me that the one outstanding fact, which if we could only explain it would explain all, is that Moriarty looks like Holmes."

I was pleased to see Wiggins already forming theories. His face did not frown in puzzlement, as did mine, but glowed with eagerness to set out on the solution to the problem I had set before him. His look of youthful fearlessness heartened me.

"And what do you make of that fact?" I asked.

"Well," he began, seating himself again and lowering his head into the folds of his caftan so that only his blond hair and gleaming eyes showed above his crossed arms, "you say that Moriarty claimed he was not Holmes' brother?"

"Yes."

He looked up. "But that they were close, very close."

"Yes."

"Holmes himself told you they were close; also he did not say that Moriarty was his brother. Therefore, as far as they go, the two men's stories are at least not contradictory. I would add to our considerations Moriarty's hint that Sherlock Holmes is not the detective's real name and that Moriarty is not his own. It is quite delicious! I do not see that anything more can be made of it now, but let us keep it all in mind. Now, the laboratory, doctor—that is another fascinating aspect. To have kept such a place for so many years! There was a hallway and four rooms, you told me. The washroom and the costume room do not seem important, though I would love to have gone through Holmes' repertoire of dress. But the library was singular. Holmes was an expert in many aspects of biology, yet there were no such books there—no physiology, anatomy, or botany?"

"Not one."

"Instead you found . . . ?"

"Books on mathematics and the physical sciences, mostly."

Wiggins frowned and ran his hand through his thick shock of hair. "The laboratory must have been for some purpose connected with those books. Can you recall any specific titles?"

"There were a great many volumes all told, hundreds I should say, but most were recent books, as well as the latest scientific journals. Holmes had his own peculiar filing system, so I couldn't discover any order, but I jotted down the names of the most recent books I could find—the ones most dogeared too—on the hunch that I might want to look them up later on." I fished a card from my billfold. "These are the names."

Wiggins took the card and began to read titles aloud: *"Notes on Recent Discoveries in Electricity and Magnetism, Elements of the Mathematical Theory of Electricity and Magnetism, Electricity and Matter* by J. J. Thompson, *Radioactive Substances and their Radiations* by James Rutherford." He looked at me blankly. "Doctor, you are the scientific man. I am but an actor. What do they signify?"

I shrugged. "I am only an ordinary practitioner of medicine. I have difficulty keeping up with my own field. I know nothing of magnetism and radioactive substances, little enough even of electricity. Those formidable titles are as mysterious to me as to you. My guess is that Holmes was experimenting at the forefront of some scientific development, inventing something in that basement which the world has never seen before."

"You are probably right: but what? And what did it have to do with Moriarty? You say that the laboratory seemed familiar to Moriarty, or at least that he claimed to have been in a part of it before?"

"Yes, the cage. I know nothing of machinery, but even a

child could have seen that all those wires and tubes and gauges
were connected to a thing in the center of the room, a sort of
cage made of heavy wire mesh, polished and silvery. Moriarty
jumped inside it, then went into a frenzy."

"Berserk?"

"He became a perfect madman. Said that Holmes should
never get him back into the thing again. Then he jumped out
and began to smash everything, finishing with the cage, on
which he did a most thorough job."

"'Not get him into it again.' His words are significant, I am
sure. So he knew something of what Holmes was doing? A cage
—how odd."

"Well, I only call it a cage, but it would not have held a
man."

"No?"

"Not confined a man, that is, though a man or two would
have fit into it. But it was certainly not for imprisonment."

"For what, then? What would the whole apparatus have
done to Moriarty while he was within the cage, if it had been
activated?" Wiggins unexpectedly began to laugh. "You know,
doctor, it sounds like an elaborate mousetrap to me, something one might see in a carnival of wonders. Well, it is another
subject we shall have to leave hanging."

He rose, stretched and bent to touch his toes several times.
Then he returned to the chair opposite me, folding himself
again into the Buddha position.

"You mentioned other books in Holmes' library—ghost stories, I believe?"

"Some of them could be called ghost stories; none of them
purported to be fiction. Frankly I believe all such matters to
be the result of overwrought imagination at best, but the people who produced the books and pamphlets which Holmes
had collected believed in their subject, or wrote about it as if
they did. I had time only to glance through the material, but
I found stories of demons and poltergeists, cases of levitation
and mysterious disappearances, people walking through walls;
all nonsense of course, but taken perfectly seriously by the
people who reported them."

Wiggins waggled a finger. "They are not nonsense if they bear upon our case. And consider: it was Sherlock Holmes who was studying what you call nonsense. No, it means something, make no mistake. Fascinating! It grows more convoluted. I would give it up for nothing! I thank you, doctor, for inviting me in. Yet we have nothing tangible. If only some object had been saved from that laboratory."

"But there was!" I cried suddenly. "It is in my coat!"

Wiggins yelped and sprang from his chair. He dashed into his bedroom and emerged an instant later with my overcoat, which he thrust into my hands. I pulled the small volume on London theatres from the left-hand pocket and placed it in his eager grasp. I explained the circumstances of my taking the book.

"And you have not examined it since?" He looked at me incredulously. "It may contain a significant clue!"

"It was barely twenty-four hours ago that I took it," I reminded him. "I have been very busy since then."

"Of course." His eyes gleamed. He turned the pages, examining the theatre designs closely. "Yes, I know many of these places. I have played in some of them. The Lyceum, the St. James, the Sans Souci, the Oxford, they are all here, of all types. A manual of stage design and stagecraft, a practical volume. Sherlock Holmes, a man who had very little to learn of the theatre, had it by his chair; it was perhaps the last book he studied before he left. And it was the only book of its type —that enhances its significance. We have highly scientific and technical books alongside some very questionable stuff on odd phenomena, and this. I don't suppose there is more?"

"There is, though it may mean nothing. Holmes left the book open to a particular page."

"But that is wonderful! It may mean everything. Which page, doctor?"

I had folded down its corner. I showed him the place. He examined the page silently for a long moment. I had time to notice that the fire had sunk low and rain was blowing against the window. Its blustery sound reminded me of similar nights before this selfsame hearth with my old friend, in which each

of us would be preoccupied with reading what we fancied—
I a Clark Russell sea story, Holmes some dusty old manuscript.

Wiggins rustled the page of the book. "It is the Pavilion at
Bermondsey," he said quietly. He was staring at me with a
smile, not his exuberant grin but a look of delighted puzzlement touched with incredulity.

"Yes," I confirmed. "The Pavilion."

"I was there today, doctor. This very afternoon."

It was my turn to look incredulous. "What?"

"You heard me correctly. If you will recall, I asked you to
accompany me. Not ten hours ago, at a matinee at the Pavilion
Theatre, the Great Escott baffled me with feats of magic."

12

"THE GREAT ESCOTT?" I said, alarmed. "Magic? I do not understand. Surely it is coincidence that you were at the Pavilion Theatre this afternoon."

I was not convinced by my own assertion. Sherlock Holmes had taught me never to trust coincidence.

Wiggins was slow in responding. "It seems that it must be coincidence," he agreed at last, "for no man influenced my visit to the Pavilion. I went only to see Escott, the magician my friends had told me would soon be the rage of London. They were right; the fellow is amazing. Yet . . ."

The smile stayed on his face, a smile of delicious inner excitement at this puzzle. Unable to contain himself, he jumped up and began to pace, swirling the caftan back and forth.

"It is wonderful, wonderful! It makes one reflect." He turned to me and clasped his hands tightly behind his back, rocking on his heels, staring toward the rain-spattered window beyond which stretched the labyrinth of London streets. Somewhere within it lay the key to our mystery. "It makes me understand the keen relish Holmes took in mystery."

"No doubt," I said impatiently, "but it is my mystery, and

I do not glory in it. I only want it solved. Does your keen relish give you any clue?"

"Not at present. Is there anything you have omitted?"

"I think not."

"Well, then, let us leave it for the night. You have seen a flurry of activity over the past twenty-four hours. I have just heard of your adventure. Let us sleep on it. In fact I invite you to spend the night here in your old room. That should stimulate your detective powers. Your wife is away, I believe; there should be no difficulty."

It was settled. I realized how tired I was in both mind and body and, not relishing a cab ride back through the wintry streets, accepted Wiggins' invitation at once. I found to my pleasure that though the sitting room had been changed, my former room, now rather bare, still contained my comfortable old bed which Billy, as Holmes' page, had used in my absence. I spent the night in dreamless—and nightmareless—sleep.

In the morning the rain had stopped and a gray light was seeping through the window as I opened my eyes. I was about to shut them again to roll over for forty winks more when I felt a gentle but insistent tugging at my shoulder. I looked up to see Wiggins bending over my bed, his eyes too bright for the hour I suspected it must be.

"Come, get up, lazy lie-abed!" he ordered. "We have work to do."

"What time is it?" I managed thickly.

"Eight o'clock."

I groaned, but Wiggins shook me again. I saw that contrary to all civilized expectations he was already fully dressed, impeccably too, in a handsome brown tweed coat and dark pants.

"Mrs. Hudson will be up with breakfast in twenty minutes. She is very glad to have you back. I have set a fire in the grate, and the room is warm as toast. No excuses, now! We must proceed with my plan of action."

He withdrew and, reluctant but tantalized by Wiggins' mention of a plan, I rose, made my ablutions, and greeted him at the table a prompt twenty minutes later. Mrs. Hudson had already set out our breakfast: eggs, rashers of bacon, toast, and coffee as in former days at Baker Street, and I found myself eating with a will. Wiggins smiled throughout breakfast, never speaking but humming a jaunty tune from *The Orchid* between mouthfuls of food, a feat I rated with his juggling ability. When we were through and had pushed back our chairs, I lit a cigarette to accompany my coffee.

With a wave of his hand Wiggins rejected my offer of a Woodbine. "No, I never smoke, doctor. It takes away my wind. You have not yet asked about my plan. Do you not wonder what it is?"

"I was about to ask you to explain it," I informed him. In fact I had only just been able to contain my curiosity until breakfast was through.

"To begin, let us discuss Mycroft Holmes," Wiggins said, leaning back, crossing his ankles and placing his hands behind his head, "for it is he who forms the first part of my plan. I have thought a great deal during the night about this singular brother of Sherlock Holmes. Naturally I reread your account of the Greek interpreter case as well. You actually saw Mycroft Holmes in the Diogenes Club on only one occasion?"

"I did, though I saw him later that same day in these very rooms. From here he accompanied Holmes and me on the chase to Brixton for the tragic and unsatisfactory end to that case."

"Inspector Gregson met him as well, I believe."

"Yes."

"You also said last evening that you had dealings with him in the course of one more adventure, an espionage case. Lestrade was involved in that, was he not?"

"You were listening very closely," I observed. "Yes, in '95 Mycroft Holmes called upon his brother for help in a very serious theft case, that of the Bruce Partington submarine plans. Mycroft showed up here at Baker Street to describe the problem, and Lestrade followed close after. I have committed its details to paper and hope one day to publish them. You are the first besides those involved in its solution to hear of it."

"You dropped some provocative hints last night about Mycroft's special position with the government. Can you enlarge
upon them?"

"I can tell you what Sherlock Holmes told me. Mycroft was
born with a faculty for figures. His early official career was as
the auditor of some Whitehall departments around the corner
from his club, but gradually his brilliance carved out a more
important niche for him. As well as his mathematical genius
he had an extraordinarily tidy brain with a great capacity for
storing facts. The conclusions of every department began to
be passed to him, and he became the great central exchange,
the clearing house of Whitehall, and therefore a man to whom
influential people looked for decisions. You can imagine how
important that made him. He drew but four hundred and fifty
pounds per year, was seen nowhere but in Whitehall, at his
club, and in his rooms, yet at times could be said, because of
his omniscient knowledge and keen analytical mind, to be the
government of England when weighty decisions were to be
made."

I realized that Wiggins was staring at me fixedly. Then he
began to laugh. I flushed with chagrin.

"I am sorry, doctor," the young actor said at last when he
had contained his mirth. "You recited that very well. It is a
wonderful example of lesson-learning. But do you believe it?
The government of England indeed! And at four hundred and
fifty pounds per annum? You have described Sherlock Holmes
to me as fantastic and incomprehensible, as indeed he may
seem to us for the moment, but this brother of his is surely a
fairy tale!"

"What does his brother do, then?"

Wiggins looked disappointed. "You miss my point entirely.
Frankly I doubt that Mycroft Holmes exists."

"But I have met him!" I exclaimed in protest at this ridiculous suggestion.

"And you have met me, but you have only my word, and the
hardly conclusive evidence of a playbill, that I am Frederick
Wigmore, just as you have only Moriarty's word that he is

Moriarty, and, for that matter, Sherlock Holmes' that he is Holmes."

This thoroughly disconcerted me, but I saw the point of it immediately.

Wiggins grinned slyly, leaned forward, and reached across the table to tug at my sleeve. "And you have only the evidence of your mirror that you are Dr. John Watson."

"Really, Wiggins," I exclaimed, withdrawing my arm. "You needn't joke. This is serious. Who is Mycroft Holmes, then, and what is the meaning of his game?"

"I don't know, doctor. Mycroft Holmes may yet prove to be himself. But I took the liberty of speaking to both Gregson and Lestrade on the telephone before you awoke. They were terribly disgruntled at the hour on a winter Sunday when they had every right to lie abed. My excuse was the fire; I said that I wanted to inform them that no further disasters had occurred. Then I drew them out. I wanted to find out if they could verify anything you had told me about Mycroft, particularly his important connection with Whitehall. I did it subtly, never fear; they were not suspicious in the least. Can you guess the result of my prying? They both confirmed that Mycroft plays a mysterious but significant part in governmental affairs. How did they know? Why, because Sherlock Holmes had told them so! That was their only evidence and, like you, they had never thought to question it. What do you think of that?"

My head was reeling. "I think Holmes is very persuasive."

"Indeed, but that is not the issue. The question is, has he persuaded them, and you, of a lie? And if so, why?"

"But what has all this to do with your plan?"

"Mycroft seems a key to your mystery. Inadvertently you have stumbled upon something which has been going on for some time, at least fifteen years. Holmes told you he had known Moriarty in his youth. I would not be surprised if in fact this game or deception began that long ago. However, we cannot be certain of it now. What we can do is find Mycroft Holmes—or the man who calls himself by that name."

"But how?"

"We shall begin at the Diogenes Club," Wiggins announced, "and we shall go there at once!"

With that he jumped up from his chair, disappeared into his bedroom, and emerged a moment later wearing a deerstalker hat matching the tweed of his jacket. He slipped into his own overcoat, handed me mine, and, taking up his malacca stick, ushered me out the door. We hailed a cab and pulled away toward Oxford Street before I had the opportunity of asking what he planned to do on Pall Mall that I myself had not accomplished on the previous night.

"We are not going exactly to the Diogenes Club," he explained as our hansom rattled along. He had snatched up his vivid yellow scarf and now finished wrapping it around his throat. Above this his lips were fixed in a smile of pleasure. His nostrils flared in the brisk air, and his bright eyes stared keenly ahead, the whole effect reminding me of Holmes' look of anticipation when he was on the trail. "I am only acting on a hunch. Sunday morning is not the time to explore Whitehall nor even a gentleman's club, no matter how eccentric it may be. But Mycroft's suspiciously circumspect life led him habitually to one other place, according to Sherlock Holmes: to his own rooms. And those were across the road from his club."

"They were supposed to be across from it. Surely you do not expect to find them actually there?"

"I do not expect anything, doctor. Admittedly it is only a straw. But we must grasp at what clues we have. For some reason a deception was perpetrated which caused a man named Mycroft Holmes to join the Diogenes Club for one month in 1888. This Mycroft was supposed to reside across Pall Mall from his club. Sherlock Holmes was thorough in everything. Assuming him to be the originator of the deception, it is likely that he would have engaged the rooms which he described to you, if only for a month, just to make sure that all ends were neatly wrapped up. I certainly doubt that we shall find Mycroft Holmes in them now, but the trail which leads from the Diogenes Club may be picked up there."

"So we are heading for the hotel opposite the club?"

"Exactly."

Shortly afterward our cab turned from St. James's Street onto Pall Mall. Wiggins raised the trap and called out to the driver to stop. We alighted just in front of the Diogenes Club and looked across Pall Mall. I had not bothered to notice it before, but there was indeed a small, respectable-looking hotel of four stories exactly opposite the doors where we stood. We crossed Pall Mall and passed into the lobby of the Trafalgar Hotel.

I knew that the Trafalgar, because of its location, would not be a traveler's hotel but a place where gentlemen, many of whom held important positions in nearby Whitehall, would keep permanent rooms. The atmosphere into which we entered was thus restrained, masculine, and distinctly clublike. There was but one desk clerk on duty, a thin, middle-aged man with a well-trimmed gray moustache, who regarded us with stuffy curiosity. Wiggins approached and with perfect aplomb inquired after Mycroft Holmes. To my surprise, the clerk replied, "You mean Mr. Sherlock Holmes' brother?"

To Wiggins' credit, he did not bat an eye. "Of course," said he matter-of-factly. "May we go up?"

The clerk smiled with distant and official regret, first at Wiggins, then me. "You have not kept up with your friend. He has not lived here these fifteen years. In fact he stayed with us but a month."

Wiggins looked significantly at me. To the clerk he commented, "You have a remarkable memory."

"I am a great follower of Sherlock Holmes' exploits. He has done the Empire much service. It was an honor to have his brother with us at the Trafalgar, and I have not forgotten that time."

"Did he leave an address?"

"He did," the clerk replied, "but it was only for the forwarding of messages—though there have never been any. Nevertheless I am afraid I cannot give it out to strangers."

Wiggins hesitated but an instant, then grandly stretched out his arm in my direction. "Allow me to introduce my companion. This is Dr. John Watson, Mr. Sherlock Holmes' biographer. It is he who requires the address."

The next five minutes were for me the endurance of, first, sputtered disbelief from the clerk and then, when irrefutable proof of my identity came forth, an effusion of praise for my descriptions of Holmes' adventures, followed by a plea for an unpublished anecdote which the clerk might make his own, and, last, when it was clear that we were on an urgent errand involving the great detective, complete capitulation regarding the forwarding address of Mycroft Holmes. Wiggins stood by with an amused expression during my uncomfortable moments, but he took care toward the end to ascertain the description of the man who had registered as Mycroft Holmes. It was a description of the man I had met.

"I have kept his address in my own book," said the clerk, reaching into his breast pocket and drawing out a small dog-eared volume. "Ah yes, here it is: Mycroft Holmes, 288 Kennington Road."

I saw Wiggins stare hard at the clerk. "Kennington Road, you say?"

"Yes."

Wiggins was suddenly brisk. "Thank you. Come, doctor, we must be off."

He took my arm and, more abruptly than I thought necessary even under the strained circumstances, rushed me out the door. Outside, I noted a glow to his cheek that could not be accounted for by the crisp air, and he wore again the smile of delighted puzzlement which I had seen the night before. He went directly to look for a cab.

"You are onto something?" I asked, by his side.

"Kennington Road," he replied in a voice full of rich conjecture. "Kennington Road. Does it mean nothing to you, doctor?"

"I cannot say that it does. Just over Westminster Bridge, the direct way to Brighton. It is not a road which I have been on often, though I did visit Morse Hudson's gallery there with Sherlock Holmes in connection with the Affair of the Six Napoleons some years ago."

Wiggins ignored my reference to Holmes. "Brighton," he repeated with a faraway look. "I have performed more than once in Brighton. It is a playland and a high spot of any music hall performer's round. People are ready to laugh and applaud in Brighton."

"It is December," I reminded him, wondering at this irrelevancy. "In this season Brighton is as bleak as any spot on the south coast."

"But the Kennington Road leads there, and so we shall go to the Kennington Road." He glanced at me. "You know, I once lived on the Kennington Road."

By now I was prepared for any revelation. "I suppose at Mycroft Holmes' address," I suggested with some sarcasm.

Wiggins was unruffled. "That would be a coincidence, would it not? No. But I know the neighborhood well. Because it is the way to Brighton, Kennington Road is the home of many a successful—and not-so-successful—music hall artist. An intriguing fact, is it not? On Sunday morning one can see smart ponies and carts outside the better houses, ready to take resting variety players on day trips to Norwood or Merton."

"Perhaps we shall run across the Great Escott, then," I said impatiently, not certain where Wiggins' train of thought was leading. "He can perform magic tricks for us."

Wiggins stared at me and then laughed. "Perhaps we shall at that, doctor. Juggling tricks—would that suit you? But here is a cab at last. It should be no more than half an hour's drive to our destination."

Wiggins' estimate proved accurate, showing that he was indeed familiar with the route. He explained, as we passed the solemn Houses of Parliament to cross Westminster Bridge, that he had traveled this way often during the six months he had shared rooms on the Kennington Road with fellow performers. Many of the houses along that thoroughfare had once been fine, fronted with iron-grille balconies, but most had deteriorated into rooming houses and apartments. It was in front of one such place, number 288, that our cab pulled up.

A few children played and sang on the pavement nearby,

and a barrel-organ man ground "After the Ball" from his machine. A blowsy red-faced woman regarded us suspiciously from the steps of the apartment before us. "What might you want?" she demanded, planting her beefy fists on her hips and confronting us as we approached. The children stopped playing to watch the encounter.

"We are neither bill collectors nor hawkers, I assure you, ma'am," Wiggins said at once. He doffed his cap and nudged me to do the same. He favored the woman with the same smile which had so captivated the girls at the stage exit of the Gaiety Theatre and began to chat about people he had known when he had lived nearby. I thought nothing could eradicate the stout woman's terrible look, as I thought it fixed upon her countenance by an unfortunate accident of birth, but Wiggins managed to bring a crooked grin to her gap-toothed mouth after a moment, and she ended by gazing fondly upon him and chattering away as if to a long-lost friend. I noted with amazement the result of Wiggins' formidable charm.

"Mycroft Holmes?" the woman, whose name was Mrs. Grimsby, repeated in her gravelly voice when Wiggins told her whom we sought. "No such chap 'ere." She was quite certain.

Wiggins shot me a glance. "He may have lived here many years ago," he said to Mrs. Grimsby.

"I have owned this house twenty year," she responded. "Was he 'ere longer ago than that?"

"I think not," Wiggins admitted.

"Might you 'ave the wrong house?" she suggested.

"No."

Wiggins made the mistake of allowing disappointment to show on his face.

"You do look sad. It breaks my 'eart!" With an impulsive lunge Mrs. Grimsby embraced him in her meaty arms and shook him. Wiggins' eyes rolled, but he withstood her grasp admirably. "Come, now, tell me what the man looks like," Mrs. Grimsby said, releasing him. "I have a sharp eye and know every soul on the Kennington Road by sight."

With a relieved look, Wiggins indicated me. I gave the description: "He is rather fat—absolutely immense in fact—with light gray eyes which are clear, thoughtful-looking, and sharp, and he has broad hands, rather like the flippers of a seal." I recited this without much hope.

"Do he take snuff?" Mrs. Grimsby asked after a pause.

"Why, yes."

"Out of a tortoiseshell box?"

"I have seen him do so."

"Why, then, he do live here! It is Mr. Fish!"

"Fish?" Wiggins interjected.

"Yes. Mr. Alfred Fish. He is a music hall man—or is when he chooses, though now he does more singing at the Hare and Hounds, when he's in 'is cups, than on any stage. He has stayed with us fifteen year if it be a day."

I was both elated and astonished, but Wiggins' face burned with excitement. I had not seen his eyes so bright.

"Tell me one thing more, Mrs. Grimsby," he said feverishly, daring to grasp both her arms at once. "Is Alfred Fish here now?"

She guffawed at the foolishness of the question, and her belly wobbled. "Oh, no sir! The local stays open till two on Sunday, and Mr. Fish and 'is cronies puts in full time. You will find 'im up the road, drinking and gossiping."

"Thank you, thank you, Mrs. Grimsby," Wiggins said, and I thought he would hug her, but he stopped short of this expression of gratitude. With a tug at my arm to follow, he started off down the pavement at something just short of a trot. I kept pace as best I could, wondering if Mycroft Holmes and Alfred Fish, the music hall man, would indeed turn out to be one and the same.

The Hare and Hounds was just on the corner, a typical suburban pub. In its vestibule two street musicians, one blind on harmonium, the other on clarinet, played "The Honeysuckle and the Bee" with more vigor than virtuosity. Wiggins pushed through the door of the lounge and I followed on his heels, the music trailing after us. Inside was a scene of conviviality. We stood and surveyed the illustrious gentlemen lined up at the bar, "the elite of the music halls," Wiggins described them, dressed in checkered suits and gray bowlers, flashing their diamond rings and tiepins. They lifted their glasses of stout and declaimed and gestured floridly.

"They are engaged in the second profession of the variety artist," Wiggins whispered to me. "They are expected by the circuit to drink with the patrons after the show, and they naturally develop an independent taste for it. I myself can remember some terrible mornings after."

Suddenly he was no longer at my side.

"Alfie!" he exclaimed from across the room, and I saw him throw his arms round a huge man who had just turned from the bar.

"Wiggins!" the man exclaimed. There was a look of astonished delight on his face, but as he returned Wiggins' embrace his eyes met mine over the young actor's shoulder. His expression became frozen in horror as if I were an apparition, for the man I saw was Mycroft Holmes, and there was an accounting due.

13

THE NOISY banter, the clinking of glasses, the pathetic
music from the vestibule went on, but I ceased to hear it. All
my attention was focused thirty feet across the room upon the
two embracing men. Wiggins I knew; the other I only recognized. Mycroft Holmes or Alfred Fish or some third party
impersonating both—which was he?

Wiggins must have felt the man grow rigid, for he released
him and stepped back. I could see the man fully now. Though
I had not seen him for eight years, he was unmistakably Mycroft Holmes—or the man I had known by that name. He was
older, of course. The top of his head was a great bald dome,
but he had longish hair streaked with gray at his temples,
curling over the collar of his coat at the back of a massive neck.
He was tall, over six feet, and appeared to have grown even
stouter than when I had last seen him (I placed him at nearly
twenty stone!). His small feet were tucked into impeccably
polished black shoes. His height, combined with his balloon-
like stomach, projecting from triple chin to groin and bound
in a great checkered waistcoat, gave the impression of a public
monument balanced on too small a pedestal. He remained

frozen on that pedestal just long enough for me to take in a full impression. Then, with a grunted "Farewell" to Wiggins, his tiny feet began to carry him with remarkable speed around the crowded bar toward a side entrance.

Wiggins halted his escape easily, gripping him firmly by the sleeve. So discreet was my young friend that not a patron noticed the brief struggle. The fat man outweighed him by nearly double, but Wiggins applied a pressure which caused a look of extreme discomfort, then resignation, to pass across the fat man's face. He ceased struggling, cast a rueful smile at his captor, shrugged, and pulled from his coat pocket a huge white handkerchief with which he mopped his perspiring face. He drew up his massive shoulders into an imitation of dignity and waved one of his flipperlike hands toward a corner table.

"Shall we, Wiggins, old chum?" he said in the voice, if not the manner, of Mycroft Holmes.

"I think we must." Wiggins did not loose his grip upon the man's arm. "That was very rude of you, Alfie, after so many years."

"Nothing personal, of course, old chum." Again the rueful smile.

At the table Wiggins motioned to me to join them. "Allow me to introduce an old friend from former days," he announced triumphantly as I stepped near. "This is Alfred Fish. You have met Dr. Watson before, have you not, Alfie?"

Alfred Fish's face grew red, and his attempt at a bluff smile was not successful. "I have indeed. Hello, Dr. Watson." He thrust one of the huge hands at me.

It was with hesitation and misgivings that I took it. I found it guiltily moist, not cool and dry as it had been when it impersonated the hand of Mycroft Holmes.

"What have you been about, Mr. Fish!" I exclaimed indignantly.

We seated ourselves, scraping our chairs, and Wiggins called for drinks. I continued to glare across the table, but Alfred Fish avoided my accusing look and made no answer to my demand.

With a sigh he pulled a cigar from his breast pocket and lit it in deliberate fashion, making popping sounds with his lips and cheeks as he puffed it into a glow. On one fat finger he wore an ostentatious ring with a huge blue stone. Gradually his flush of chagrin faded and he became cool and matter-of-fact. He leaned back as far as his bulk would allow and placed his fingertips on the edge of the table. He began to tap them rapidly. His light gray eyes fixed themselves upon me at last, but they were obviously a little affected by drink and had lost the keen edge I remembered.

"So you see me as I am at last," he said. "You are displeased with me. He is displeased, is he not, old chum?"—this to Wiggins—then to me again: "I understand your feelings, Dr. Watson, but I was only doing a job, acting in a professional capacity, you might say, for acting is my profession as young Wiggins here can confirm. And I was doing it for our mutual friend, Sherlock Holmes, so there seemed no harm. The job was to fool you, it's true, and I did not understand why. Holmes refused to answer my questions and swore me to secrecy, but to be frank the wages were very generous. Too, he and I go back a long way, and I trusted him just like you did. So you must forgive me." He laughed. "I'll be damned, I do not know why I am raving on, for Holmes himself must have sent you. Surely there is no other way you could have found me. How is my old chum? Retired, so I read in the papers. Is he settling old affairs, sending you here—admitting to the trick at last? You must know there never was a Mycroft Holmes but me and that I played him to Holmes' script. I'll be damned if for fifteen years, ever since my month at the Diogenes Club, I have not wondered why." He sucked vigorously at his cigar and, straining, reached over his belly to tug confidentially at my sleeve. "Be a chum, Dr. Watson, and put a fellow out of his misery. What was Holmes' game?"

I jerked my arm away. "Do you mean that you cannot tell us?"

Fish stopped puffing on his cigar. Slowly he pulled it from between his lips. His watery eyes had grown round. "Sherlock

Holmes is the only man who can explain it to anyone. Has he
sent you here and not told you why?"

"He did not send us here, and we have no explanations. We
count on you for them and mean to have them! Now, my good
fellow . . ."

"Not sent?" Fish interrupted. His jowls shook. "I'll be
damned, then how did you find me?"

At this moment the harried-looking barmaid arrived with
our drinks. She stared at us curiously with her hard eyes. I
glanced down the bar and noted more than one look turned
with grim interest toward us. I realized that our voices had
grown loud.

"Friends of yours, Alf?" one burly fellow called. He looked
as if he might be a circus weightlifter. I had no doubt that his
suspicious expression could easily turn belligerent if his crony
were threatened, so I was relieved when Fish reassured them
all with a cheery wave that was as fine a piece of spontaneous
acting, considering his agitation, as I had seen.

"Perhaps," interjected Wiggins softly with a smile that was
an equal piece of showmanship, and leaning close, "we had
best act in a quiet and gentlemanlike way. It seems that we are
all in the dark and want enlightening. Let us help one another."

The barmaid set three tankards before us and hurried off.

"Do you believe this fellow?" I exclaimed, forcing my voice
to remain low and turning my back to the room.

"Alfie and I were both booked by the Empire Variety and
played many a bill on the same stage, so I know all his tricks,
as he knows mine. I do not believe he is pretending now."

"Thank you, old chum." Alfred Fish displayed a broad smile
of satisfaction. Evidently a man of many and simultaneous
vices, he set his cigar on the table edge and produced the
tortoiseshell box which I remembered from long ago. He in-
haled snuff from it and fastidiously brushed the wandering
grains from his paunch. His eyes puckered. "I remember those
old days with joy. You were a baby then, but you learned fast.
He was a quick study, Dr. Watson."

"Thank you, Alfie." Wiggins smiled. "When I heard your name from Mrs. Grimsby, I rushed to see if it could really be my music hall friend."

"Grimsby!" Fish's laugh was a detonation of wheezes. "Then it was the old battle-ax sent you here?"

"In a roundabout way."

Wiggins described our progression from the Diogenes Club, including a summary of my interview with Simon Bliss. He added that our reason for coming was that Sherlock Holmes might be in danger. Scrupulously he avoided any mention of Moriarty.

With a cautious expression Fish tucked away the tortoise-shell snuff box in a recess of his voluminous coat. "I understand. It is serious business, then." He picked up his cigar and stared at it as if to bring it into focus. "I'll be damned if I don't want to help in every way. But you see, I am not sure that I can."

"Why not?" I demanded impatiently. "Surely the charade is at an end."

"Well, I am on a retainer from Sherlock still, in case he should need me again at some time as Mycroft Holmes—the cheques from Lloyd's arrive regular—and the stipulations of our unwritten contract are that I play no other roles in London and that I tell no one of our secret. It is only accident that you know as much as you do. I'm not sure that I am free to tell you more, though I know little enough."

"You must, Alfie," Wiggins insisted. "It is to help Sherlock Holmes—and as a favor to an old chum."

"An old chum, is it!" Fish exclaimed. His eyes puckered again and he chewed at the end of his cigar. "For an old chum, I would do anything. It was like this.

"I hadn't seen Sherlock Holmes in many years when he came to me early in '88. It was quite a surprise. He explained that he had a part for me and would I be interested in trying out for it. I was down on my luck then, as he seemed to know, and I would have grasped at anything, so it seemed a godsend. 'It is an unusual part,' he warned me. 'It must be played under highly unusual circumstances, and you shall receive no applause or recognition for it save my own approval. But it is well-paying and if you are good at it it may prove to be a long run.' Well, applause is never low on an actor's list of requirements, but I'll be damned if a full stomach and a roof over my head were not then foremost on mine, so I jumped at the chance. I had some qualms when my old chum said it was to impersonate his own brother and when it became obvious that it would deceive you, doctor, but it seemed harmless enough, and so I did it. By the way, the other characters in the thing were real enough—Melas, the Greek, and the other poor unfortunates in that case which, as you know, was not one of Sherlock's successes. We waited some time for an opportunity to present itself, a place where I might reasonably be brought into a case. I settled myself into the Diogenes Club, getting used to my role of eccentric brother, and when I met Melas in the lobby of the Trafalgar Hotel and heard his peculiar tale I knew that that was our chance. So I got hold of Sherlock right away, and he brought you along."

"It was rather a spontaneous meeting," I recalled.

Fish's huge stomach rocked the table with his sudden laugh. "If weeks of planning make a thing spontaneous, then that was spontaneous!"

"And the Bruce Partington affair?"

"Sherlock set that up completely as well. Through his own methods he already knew of the theft of the submarine plans and of the mysterious death of Cadogan West on the Underground. I was only an actor in the drama, following my chum's script again."

"And you have no clue to why?"

Fish finished a long gulp of ale. "I'm damned if I do," he vowed with beery sincerity, banging his pint down upon the table.

Wiggins had sat quietly through this exchange, sipping slowly at his drink. "The thing was arranged for your benefit, doctor," he observed. "That seems obvious. Now you are the central figure in the drama, with the spotlight full upon you.

Now, tell us"—he smiled slowly—"what is your part in it?""
"My part?"

He and Alfred Fish gazed intently at me, making me feel as
if a spotlight had suddenly shone on me and that I must perform. But I did not know how to respond.

"Do not joke, Wiggins. I have no part. I am in the open. You
know I am only the transcriber of Holmes' adventures; I have
no importance outside of that."

"Oh, you misrepresent yourself," Wiggins insisted. "You
have helped the detective in many ways; but yes, your major
significance in his life has been in presenting him to the
world."

"And a loyal chum you have been in that!" Fish added.

"I agree," Wiggins said. "The doctor's reputation as a de-
pendable and discreet reporter is unquestioned. I have always
believed every word he wrote."

"Of course!" Fish said. "Dr. Watson is a truthful man. He
tells no lies."

"And yet what he wrote about you was untrue."

Fish sucked earnestly at his cigar. "I'll be damned, Wiggins,
that is different. He did not know at the time that I was a fraud.
There was no deception there."

"No?"

"Well, it was not Dr. Watson's deception."

"Yet people were deceived, a vast number of them."

"The reading public, you mean. Was there any harm in
that?"

I interrupted. "What are you getting at, Wiggins? Have you
some explanation?"

"I do not, but I believe that your position as Holmes' biographer, his mirror as it were, is the lead we must follow in finding
the reason for his rather elaborate game. I still believe he
meant no harm to you by it. But he engineered the affair, and
so it must have been necessary to him for some reason. I too
ask your question: why? I am only thinking aloud." He tossed
off the last of his ale. In an offhand way he said, "By the way,
Alfie, will you show Dr. Watson 'the cloth and the coin'?"

A great smile suffused Alfred Fish's face at this mysterious request. "Delighted!" he exclaimed. "This is for the barmaid." He tossed a sovereign upon the spotted tablecloth. "But perhaps that is too generous," he added at once, looking at me innocently.

I thought it was generous to the point of foolishness and said so without qualm.

"Well then," he responded, placing one hand under the table beneath the coin. He rapped the sovereign with the knuckles of his visible hand and the coin vanished with a thump, reemerging between the thumb and forefinger of the hand which he had placed beneath the table and now withdrew with a flourish.

"Why, it is only a trick!" I said.

Wiggins and Alfred Fish burst into uproarious laughter.

Wiggins was the first to recover. "There are a great many tricks being played," he said. "Let us not mislead the doctor further. You have described yourself as an actor, Alfie, and it is true that you are as versatile—if not as subtle—as any man I have seen on the stage. But you have not explained your speciality nor given your *nom de guerre.*"

"Why, that is no secret among chums, and I hope that Dr. Watson has forgiven me enough so I may call him my chum. I am none other than 'Alfred the Great, Master of the Mystical Secrets of the East'!"

"He means that he does card tricks," Wiggins wryly interpreted when I responded to this announcement with a blank look.

"Wiggins!" Fish appeared deeply hurt. He beckoned to the barmaid for another round of drinks. "You represent an old chum very ill indeed, Wiggins. I am more than a card man," he explained to me. "I am a master of sleight of hand, of the rings and the cane, of appearances and disappearances and all sorts of illusions."

My look was skeptical. "And do you juggle?" I asked.

"Never!" He sat back and his several chins shook. "It is beneath me." He nodded at Wiggins. *"He* is the juggler!"

Wiggins laughed, and Fish joined him.

"Touché, Alfie. Yes, I have done some juggling in my day. I will admit that your sleight of hand is beyond me, though I never tried very hard to learn it, but . . ."

"Wait!" I interrupted. A thought had just struck me; I wondered that the idea had taken so long to arrive. I spoke to Alfred Fish: "You told us that you and Holmes 'went back a long way.' What did you mean by that?"

Fish accepted his pint from the barmaid. "Only that I had known Sherlock many years before he asked me to pose as his brother." Unconcernedly he sipped his ale, the fact seeming to mean very little to him.

It electrified me. "How many years?" I asked breathlessly.

I glanced at Wiggins. He was scrutinizing the portly magician as closely as I. He must have read my thought: here was a man who might have known Holmes before even young Stamford. The night before, I had expressed to Wiggins my deep curiosity about the years prior to 1881. Had Fish known Holmes during those years? Was he privy to the facts of Holmes' origin, his family, his birthplace, his education and travels? If he was, there might be a clue somewhere, something he had overlooked, to explain the Mycroft masquerade, or more, a clue to Holmes' strangely reticent manner.

Fish returned his pint to the table and dabbed the corners of his mouth with his handkerchief. He reflected for a moment. "I first met Sherlock in—let me see—'78. Yes, it was just ten years before he approached me about the Mycroft Holmes engagement."

The answer was somewhat disappointing. The difference was only three years. I had hoped that Alfred Fish had known Holmes as a very young man, perhaps when he and Moriarty were associated. To have had that explained!

If Wiggins was disappointed in Fish's answer, he did not show it. "And how did you meet him?" he asked eagerly.

Fish hesitated. "That is another of those things of which I was not to speak."

"For an old chum!" Wiggins prodded.

"All right—I met him on the stage."

"On the stage?" I cried.

"Come, doctor, you cannot be surprised. So Holmes was an actor?"

"Yes, a struggling young one like myself, though I'm damned if everyone in our touring company—we were with Sheffield's Repertory at the time, doing the Fens—could not see that young Sherlock Holmes wouldn't struggle for long. He was magnificent! I could not believe that he was as inexperienced as he claimed. He knew things about the theatre—about holding an audience, milking lines, gesturing, moving—that even our crusty veteran of a manager had not mastered. And yet he belittled his skills, said they were nothing or that they just came to him. But I didn't believe it, for he knew makeup as well, and how to raise and strike a set, and things that seemed miracles about lighting and music. I was closest to him, though he would let none of us too near. I used to walk the streets of each new town with him. He had a passion to explore. He wanted to see everything, and he asked questions about it all, peculiar questions, as if it were new to him and he must learn it. He was secretive, and I did not pry, but I had my own explanation for his ignorance: he was not English, or at least he was not raised here."

"Why, he is as English as any of us," I protested. "Surely that cannot be denied. His ancestors were country squires."

"Yes, but which country?" Wiggins responded. "You believe they were squires only because Holmes said that they were. How much do you trust his claims now? Go on, Alfie, I am fascinated."

Fish bit off the end of a new cigar. "I have good reason for thinking Sherlock was not English. You see, he talked in a strange way. Oh, he spoke our tongue all right, and nearly perfect, but he had an accent, ever so faint—an actor hears those things. And he used phrases, turns of speech, I had not heard before in any part of England, and I had been in every corner of it even then. It wasn't American lingo, but what it was I couldn't tell. I thought he might have come from the

Continent, and I wondered about it aloud to him once, but he didn't say anything, so I left it alone. In those days acting was not nearly so respectable as it is getting to be now, and all kinds of shady fellows whitewashed themselves with makeup and made themselves new men in the footlights. It was possible that Holmes was one of these. And, then, so skillful was he at mimicry that he soon erased the accent. Two months after I met him you would not have known he wasn't English born, and four months after that he was gone."

"Gone?"

Fish lit his cigar. "Yes, he left Sheffield's Repertory. I knew he was planning to go, though I'm sure I was the only one. I exclaimed to him once about the great West End career in store for him when he reached London. 'My goal is London,' he told me, 'but I am giving up the stage.' 'Why?' I asked in astonishment. 'Because I have a job to do,' he answered. 'This country is as good as any to do it in, and London is its heart, so I will go there to begin, but it cannot be done from behind a proscenium.' I didn't expect more from him, for he was very secretive, as I've told you, but he added, 'There is reason for me to loathe the stage, Alfred, and to stay off it forever—for my own good and the good of the world. I have only endured it these past months in order to set aside a little money and to learn a few necessary things. It will take remarkable circumstances to get me onto it again!' "

Fish sipped his ale and looked from Wiggins to me. "It was hard, you can imagine, not to ask more about that, but I knew my young chum had given me that much because I did not pry. Our conversation happened on a Sunday evening in May. We were strolling under the stars, near Lincoln, I think it was. The smell of spring was in the air. 'Thank you, Alfred,' Sherlock said, and shook my hand. I never felt so close to him. A week later he was gone, stolen off in the night, and I didn't see him again until he appeared ten years later, when I was down on my luck, to propose the Mycroft Holmes impersonation. Because of his retainer I have kept comfortable since then. After he left our troupe I had to scramble to keep my career going, so I forgot about him and never connected him, in spite of the unusual name, with the Sherlock Holmes you wrote about, doctor. And that is all I know."

Alfred Fish tilted his massive head back and blew cigar smoke at the ceiling. Loud guffaws and chatter still emanated from the jostling music hall artists at the bar. Neither Wiggins nor I spoke for a moment.

"His family?" I suggested at last, hopefully.

Fish shrugged. "So far as I know, Mycroft Holmes *was* his family. If there is more to it besides the nonexistent brother, he never told me about it."

"And how did he happen to join your company?" Wiggins wanted to know.

"He replaced a young chap who was to come up from London but who canceled at the last moment. We were playing Camford at the time and advertised in desperation with placards outside the rented theatre. Holmes was the first to respond—walked in off the street. At first we took him to be a student down on his luck, for he was ill-dressed, but I don't think he was a student. At any rate, he was so good, even with his odd accent and stiff ways offstage, that Barker, the manager, hired him at once."

"You lost track of him for ten years, but after he chose you to play his brother you saw Holmes often, I suppose," Wiggins pursued.

"No. He asked me never to contact or to mention him. His cheques come from a sort of trust fund in my name at Lloyd's. I didn't see him at all while you and I were with the Empire Agency, Wiggins. In fact I acted as his brother very few times, the last being in the Bruce Partington affair. 'Watson is asking questions again,' he said at the time. 'I shall need you, Alfred.'" Fish looked at me. "I'll be damned if I knew what to make of that."

"Questions?" I was dumbfounded. "I believe that I was as discreet with Holmes as you were, Mr. Fish. I only wondered occasionally why Holmes was so damnably close, as you did."

Wiggins was alert. "You wondered about it in print, however, did you not?"

"Perhaps some question or other crept into my writings now and then, but I found it hard to write about a person without origins. Holmes was vivid enough to me, but readers must have more; they want to know a person's background. I told them mine, fully; it was only fair to explain that I did not know Holmes' and that I wondered about it as much as they."

Wiggins placed a hand on my arm. "You needn't defend your actions. In your place I would have done the same. But we must not disregard the fact that you questioned his past history." He turned to Fish. "However, I am most interested in Holmes' comments to you on that spring evening in Lincoln. There was reason for him to hate the stage, he said. That is strange. I wonder about the cause of his feeling, considering his talents. But the really remarkable statement came next, that he intended to leave off acting for his own sake and 'for the good of the world.' If he were a terrible performer, his words would make perfect, if exaggerated, sense, but we all know that he was a consummate actor. So, what, gentlemen," Wiggins glanced from one to the other of us with his look of happy bewilderment, "are we to make of it?"

There was silence.

"I am at a loss," I confessed at last.

Fish released an odd sigh.

This seemed a prelude to something, and Wiggins looked at him sharply. "Yes?"

I stared at the now faraway look in Fish's watery eyes.

"Well, I can see young Sherlock on the stage." The old performer smiled, peering down the years. "He was a wonderful comedian. The audience was his always, and with a word or a wiggle he could have them roaring in an instant. But he was nonpareil in melodrama. I watched him from the house once. You get a different perspective then, when you yourself are not groaning on the boards. I felt his full force. It went right through us all. It was hypnotic. I could not take my eyes off him. He tugged my heart a dozen different ways, he did, and though I knew what he was doing I could not stop him. I wanted it to go on. Afterwards I thought about it. It was amazing, but I'm damned if I entirely liked it. The audience applauded terrifically, but my hands never moved. My palms were sweating. What a power he had! He wove a real spell. Napoleon must have had such a power." With these words, Fish's voice trailed away. "That was the way he was, but I don't know what it means."

"It is deep, very deep," Wiggins said, and for once his usually bright look was changed to a frown.

None of us spoke for a time. The exuberant clamor at the bar formed a background in contrast to our thoughts. Mine were in a muddle. Holmes had always insisted upon gathering facts before guessing at meanings. I had plenty of facts now, it seemed, but I could make neither heads nor tails of them. They crowded about in my brain like the anonymous faces of a mob, resisting all order. I knew that they must make sense somehow, felt even that there was a connection I was not grasping, was avoiding perhaps. But it slipped out of my reach, and I was left profoundly depressed and helpless.

Wiggins' expression was still thoughtful, but his eyes had regained some of their glow, and I was about to ask him what he made of things, when the call, "Time, gentlemen!" came from the ruddy-faced barman. We rose, tossed coins upon the tablecloth, and joined the other patrons streaming noisily out onto the Kennington Road. Dark and lowering clouds rolled overhead, and a sharp wind whipped at the gaunt branches of the trees in the park across the way. We turned and, holding our hats, walked in the direction of Mrs. Grimsby's lodging house.

"Ah, here is a carriage," Wiggins said. He hailed the driver, and a four-wheeler drew up alongside us. Crumpled papers and leaves blew against our ankles. Alfred Fish protested that our visit had been too short, but Wiggins insisted we must go, promising that he and Fish would get together soon to talk over old times.

"By the way, Alfie," Wiggins said as he slipped into the carriage beside me, "did I ever tell you who taught me to juggle?"

Fish seemed as surprised at this question as I. "You never

did," he admitted, squinting against the wind. "Who was it, then?"

"Sherlock Holmes."

"Then our chum was a talented man indeed," Fish responded, "for it was he who got me into magic. He knew some amazing feats."

I started at these words, not immediately certain why.

"I suspected as much," Wiggins said breezily. "Good-bye, Alfie!"

Our carriage rattled away, back toward central London. Wiggins turned to favor me with a smug smile as the rain, which had threatened, began to patter down upon the leather roof.

"But what does it mean?" I exclaimed.

Wiggins wrapped his yellow scarf about his throat. "It means that we must pay a visit to the Pavilion Theatre of Varieties at the earliest possible opportunity."

14

THE RAIN CONTINUED, gaining in force until it swept the streets in great waves, battering our unfortunate cabman and the poor horse which doggedly plunged ahead. Wiggins and I were silent for a time, my young friend sitting to my right with an amused expression, reminding me, in his deerstalker cap, even more of Holmes than he had on the previous night. Though bursting with questions, I remained quiet because I wanted to sort things out for myself rather than have Wiggins explain to me what he saw. Yet by the time we reached Westminster Bridge and were rumbling over the roiling Thames, I had concluded very little to my satisfaction and was about to speak, when Wiggins turned to me with a surprised look to exclaim, "Doctor, we have not eaten—that is dreadful! It is three P.M., and I am famished. What do you say to lunch?"

That Wiggins could think of his stomach at a time when my thoughts were in such a turmoil piqued me, but I said, "I am not hungry, but I will accompany you. I should be glad of a chance to talk."

"Splendid! Marcini's?"

I knew Marcini's well. Holmes and I had occasionally dined there in our days of rooming together. I acquiesced, and Wiggins called directions to the driver. Past the Houses of Parliament we turned into Whitehall in the direction of Trafalgar Square; within fifteen minutes we were at the restaurant on Jermyn Street.

Marcini's was a pleasant place, reasonably priced, elegant without being pretentious. My young friend and I strolled through the foyer into the dining hall. Imitation marble columns supported a frescoed ceiling; a colored tile floor stretched under the tables arranged around the great central sideboard, with its burden of glasses and decanters and two huge wine coolers. A waiter whom Wiggins addressed familiarly as Alexander led us along a red-curtained brass rail to a table spread with white cloth and silver. A palm in a tub nearby set us apart in relative seclusion.

When we were seated with the menus before us, I could suppress my question no longer: "Then the Great Escott is Holmes, you believe?"

Maddeningly, Wiggins raised his eyebrows only over the menu. "What do you think of turtle soup?" he asked with a bland smile.

"I do not give a damn for turtle soup," I replied, forcing my voice to remain low. "Is Escott Holmes?"

"Well, either he is or he is not, that is how I see it. That is a splendid pheasant the waiter is carrying by. However it is a perfectly awful afternoon, and as a consequence I am feeling particularly English. It will be roast beef and Yorkshire pudding for me. That was invented for typical English days such as this!" He beckoned to Alexander and gave this order with gusto. Sullenly I asked only for tea. When Alexander had gone, Wiggins rubbed his hands together briskly and leaned forward. "Now, doctor, as to Escott's being Holmes, what I meant by 'he is or he isn't' was that Escott"—his voice dropped—"may be Moriarty."

I was aghast. "But the evidence points to his being Holmes—the book and the magic!"

"Just my thinking. I only wish to point out that things have not turned out to be what they were presumed to be in this case of yours, so we must be prepared for the unexpected."

"But you have seen Escott yourself. Is he or is he not the detective?"

"You must remember that I was not looking for our old friend when I went to see the Great Escott. Frankly, he did not look like Holmes, but Holmes in disguise has never looked like himself and has fooled both you and me, who know him well, many times. In any case, because of Moriarty's remarkable resemblance to him, I could hardly distinguish between them even if I were sure that under Escott's features lay those of our missing friend."

"That is true," I conceded. "It is damnable to have to wait until tomorrow afternoon to know for sure!"

"Presuming that we will know even then. Escott may surprise us by being Escott. We must face the fact that Sunday is the performer's day of rest. Let us get some pleasure out of it as well. Ah!" Wiggins beamed. "Here is my roast beef!"

He consumed with dispatch a meal that would have done credit to King Edward on a weekend at Sandringham. I managed a few biscuits with my tea. Afterwards he invited me to his rooms for a glass of brandy, and I accepted. On the way back to Baker Street I asked him about Alfred Fish. "You roomed together in vaudeville days?"

"No, but we knew one another well enough. Music hall people are a jovial and outgoing crowd. One makes friends easily."

"And Fish was a magician?"

"He was when I knew him. He seems now to be letting Holmes' monthly retainer take the place of a stage career. He was not the equal of Maskelyne and came nowhere near the Great Escott, but I remember he was very sly, with a good patter. He always went over well, even on bad nights, which is more than I can say for myself."

"And his story about young Holmes, do you believe it?"

"I think he told us the truth, so far as he knew it."

."It is still hard to believe that Holmes is not English by birth. Do you trust Fish's judgment?"

"Yes. He is no fool. Unfortunately his suggestion complicates our problem, as every new turn in this affair seems to do. Now we must wonder where Holmes did come from, and why."

"And do not forget that 'job' of his which he was so anxious to carry out in London. What can it have been?"

"Perhaps we already have the answer," Wiggins surprised me by saying. "I see no reason to think it was not the job he actually took, that of consulting detective."

"But why should that make him leave the stage? According to Alfred Fish, Holmes felt the new job as a kind of calling."

Wiggins shrugged. "Why is any man called? After all, to be a guardian of justice is not so ignoble a goal. For over two decades has not Sherlock Holmes been the foremost such guardian in England, perhaps in the world?"

"That is true," I agreed. "But the laboratory—he came to London and built that as well, and kept it a secret for twenty-two years. Where does that fit into his plan?"

Wiggins' look had been puzzled but amused; now he appeared totally bewildered. "I have not the least idea, doctor. I believe that only Holmes, and perhaps Moriarty, can give us the answer. I myself cannot get out of my mind the image of Holmes spellbinding his audience like Henry Irving, yet causing Alfie's palms to sweat, as if there were something dangerous in his performance. Alfred Fish is a strong man; he does not shudder easily." Wiggins turned to me, and all the usual lightness was gone from his expression. "I am much mistaken if it is not a very strange phenomenon we are investigating, doctor, and we must prepare ourselves for surprises which may shake many of our assumptions."

These words showed me that Wiggins knew little more than I, and that he felt the oddness of the case as well—but they also jogged my memory. A phrase which Holmes had used on the very night of his departure two months before drifted back into my consciousness. It had seemed a mere turn of speech at the time, and I had ignored it, but now it took on special, if puzzling, significance. I was about to repeat it for Wiggins when we pulled up at 221B Baker Street and, with his usual alacrity, my young friend leaped out of the cab, umbrella raised against the wind and rain, to toss some coins to the driver. He ran up onto the porch to unlock the front door. I followed. Just before entering the familiar haven, I paused to glance over the area railing before the house. Boards had been rudely nailed across the broken windows; the dim streetlamp illuminated nothing inside. I shuddered at the memory of my confrontation there with Moriarty, and the unsolved mystery of the laboratory flooded over me again.

For the present, Holmes' phrase was swept from my thoughts.

We were passing through the entranceway before climbing the stairs to Wiggins' rooms when the door to Mrs. Hudson's parlor opened and she bustled out to greet us.

"To have you back on such a day!" she exclaimed, obviously much relieved. "After what happened Friday night I am suspicious even of the weather. I hope," she spoke to me in lowered tones, "things are well with you, Dr. Watson, and with Sherlock Holmes."

I had no reassurances to give her, but was spared from telling her that by the interruption of a familiar and altogether unwelcome voice: "Mr. Wigmore and Dr. Watson together. And at Baker Street! I am surprised. I did not know you knew one another. Can you not keep away from your old rooms, doctor, or are you writing about the theatre now, and giving up crime?"

I smelled the scent of lavender upon the air. At that moment a bulky form insinuated itself into view from behind Mrs. Hudson. It was Inspector Athelney Jones.

He brushed biscuit crumbs from his sleeve and dabbed at his pudgy lips with his handkerchief. "Mrs. Hudson and I were having tea. She kindly offered it while I waited. Thank you, Mrs. Hudson. I will talk to Wigmore now." He turned to Wiggins. "I only paused a moment on this dreadful afternoon on the chance that you might return. Gregson and Lestrade told me of your calls to them this morning. I must say, it is most thoughtful of you, and thorough. But why, I asked myself, did you bother? Has something new crossed your mind, something you neglected to mention during our previous interview?"

This was more enterprising than I had ever seen Athelney Jones. There must be great urgency to draw him away from his fireside into the storm on a Sunday afternoon. I wondered how Wiggins would parry Jones' question. I looked at my young friend and saw an expression on his face such as I had not seen before: one of utter and complete vacuousness. He pursed his lips several times in succession, sucked at his cheeks, brushed madly at his hair.

"Oh, inspector, it is so good of you," he said with a kind of idiotic relief in his tone, "so good. I have been terrified, simply terrified. I only want to know that Scotland Yard is near to protect me." He stepped backward, stretched out a trembling arm as if to support himself and nearly toppled Mrs. Hudson's aspidistra from its bamboo stand. He grappled with the thing and managed to save it only barely, then stood peering, wild-eyed, through its foliage.

Mrs. Hudson stared at this performance with wide eyes. "I shall leave you gentlemen to your business," she said curtly, and withdrew into her apartment, closing the door and leaving Jones, myself, and the suddenly transformed Wiggins to play out our scene.

I looked at Athelney Jones. His eyes, rolling between their puffy pouches, spoke eloquently of his attitude toward this foolish young actor—"theatrical person" must have crossed his mind—but he forged ahead as cheerily as possible, unable to keep the disappointment from his voice: "So you have thought of nothing new to help us?"

Wiggins emerged from behind the plant to raise shocked eyebrows. "Indeed not, inspector. It is I who need help and protection. Why, I may be forced to change my rooms! Do you still think the fire has something to do with Sherlock Holmes?"

Athelney Jones brushed this aside. "We do not know. But

speaking of Holmes, we have discovered an interesting fact about you, Mr. Wigmore. You knew Holmes some years ago; you once were part of a band of urchins whom he employed to run errands for him and to act in a not altogether legal fashion. Don't deny it!" Jones looked stern. "Why didn't you tell me of this before?"

Wiggins did not bat an eye. He looked very contrite and his voice began to quaver. "I am so ashamed of those years, inspector, but I was a poor boy who knew no better. And Mr. Holmes did help me. Oh, I hope you have not told this to Mrs. Hudson, for she was not fond of me then, and rightly so; I was an ill-mannered guttersnipe. It was another piece of Mr. Holmes' kindness to suggest that I apply for these rooms when he knew that he was to retire, but of course I did not wish to tell Mrs. Hudson who I was. She would never have let them to me then. I have been two-faced, Inspector Jones, but now you see me as I really am. Can you forgive me?"

Such was the audacity of the young fellow that moisture gleamed in his eyes, threatening to gush down his cheeks. He lowered his lashes, sniffed, and shuffled his feet in great chagrin. I had never witnessed such a shameless performance in my life, but Wiggins knew his audience. Athelney Jones was embarrassed and revolted at once, and he responded by waving both fat arms in the air.

"Well, well, I shall trouble you no more, Mr. Wigmore. You are in no danger, I am sure. Do not call upon Scotland Yard again unless it is absolutely necessary. I must go now. Are you leaving, doctor? Perhaps we may share a cab?"

I was not anxious to spend time with Athelney Jones, but on the other hand I did not want to appear to wish to spend it with Wiggins. I did not want Jones to wonder why we were together.

"I met Mr. Wigmore on the night of the fire," I said. "When I learned that he had been one of the Baker Street Irregulars, naturally I wished to speak to him further. We have just had lunch at Marcini's to reminisce about old times. However it is the hour for me to return to Queen Anne Street. I shall be happy to share your cab."

I glanced at Wiggins. He seemed to understand completely. He simpered. "So pleasant, doctor. A superb lunch. We must get together again *very soon.*" His emphasis on the last words was an unmistakable reference to our agreement to meet tomorrow at the matinee at the Pavilion Theatre.

I shook Wiggins' hand and departed with Athelney Jones.

It was now about five o'clock and growing dark. Already the streetlamps were lit, spreading their sentinel glow down the thoroughfares. The wind had ceased and the rain fell straight down, hissing on the pavement and on the roof of our hansom. I was surprised that I did not have to endure Jones' effusiveness on the journey as I had feared. In fact he was rather morose, and when the lamps of a passing carriage illuminated his face I saw that he was deep in thought, with his lips pressed grimly together.

As our cab turned at last onto my street, I questioned him about his mood.

"These are dangerous times, Dr. Watson, dangerous times," he muttered in response, mopping at his face with his handkerchief. Moisture gleamed on his upper lip and he seemed almost to be talking to himself. "The international situation is very grave; the balance of power is upset. We can keep things in line for a time, but what will future years bring?"

"Why, the world seems well in order," I observed, more to draw him out than anything. I had wanted to dismiss Gregson's and Lestrade's similar comments as hyperbole, but confirmed a second time by Athelney Jones, who was closer to the seat of power, they gave me pause.

"It seems in order, does it not?" he said, "But you do not know. Whitehall is in an uproar. They have sent me on the trail of Holmes. We need him badly now."

The cab pulled up before my house.

"I am sorry to be unable to help you," I said.

"Yes?" he replied abstractedly and went on thinking aloud: "It is as if some power were manipulating things, foiling all our best efforts. Well, doctor, you will say nothing of this, I trust."

I had stepped down from the hansom and stood on the wet

pavement, shielded by my umbrella. "Of course not. Good-bye, Inspector Jones."

"Good-bye." He sank back into his seat, and the last I saw of him before the cab disappeared was his handkerchief mopping his perspiring face.

It was very cold to be perspiring.

I entered my house. It was chill and dark, having been unoccupied for a day and a night. Immediately I switched on the ceiling light, but in the instant before the entranceway brightened, I shuddered. The familiar appearance of the objects around me was reassuring, and as I placed my dripping umbrella in the hall stand and hung up my coat, I laughed at myself, albeit nervously. I knew the source of that shudder: Moriarty. In my search for Sherlock Holmes, which had led me far in so short a time, I had not had time to worry that the most dangerous criminal mastermind in Europe had very nearly snuffed out my life not two days ago, and that in all probability he was not far away. By a forged note he had attempted to trick me into leading him to Holmes; he had employed at least two disguises for that purpose. Obviously then he had been unsuccessful at tracing Holmes and hoped that I might show the way. Was there any reason to suppose he had given up on me? None. He would be nearby, or one of his agents would be. I reviewed all the faces I had seen in the course of the last two days. I was not aware of being followed; nevertheless, any one of them might have been observing me, tracing my steps, listening discreetly, reporting. Moriarty's web was far-flung, was it not?

And what was I to do now that I felt close to finding Holmes, seemed on the brink of a great discovery? I hung fire over that decision for a moment, but the answer came soon: Press on, do not hang back now.

I would keep my appointment with Wiggins at the Pavilion Theatre.

My wife was due back on Thursday. Because of the exertions and dangers of the past two days I felt an urge to write to tell her that I was well. This I did, not mentioning anything of my adventures, of course. I said too that I hoped she was enjoying her holiday in Kent and that I looked forward to having her back. Then, after a few hours in which I attempted unsuccessfully to read, I retired early.

I dreamed. My dreams were not so vivid nor so elusively suggestive as the nightmare in which Holmes and Moriarty had exchanged faces. Instead, fragments of the puzzle and images from my pursuit tumbled through my brain as if an explosion had scattered them. There was the note Billy had brought, ingeniously forged; there were the six glittering test tubes Moriarty had juggled and the six stones with which Wiggins had done the same; there was Mrs. Hudson's distraught face and Wiggins' jaunty smile, his yellow scarf, caftan, and little yellow bird fluttering about; there was Athelney Jones wheezing into his large handkerchief. The whole cast of *The Orchid* appeared and sang their songs and danced, bowed, and were swept away to be replaced by Alfred Fish, who tossed hundreds of gleaming sovereigns upon a cloth, then made them and his own bulbous presence vanish with a snap of his fingers. Simon Bliss of the Diogenes Club doddered toward me, waved his long pipe stem under my nose, and chuckled knowingly. Sherlock Holmes' features appeared, waxen and unreal: "Come at once, come at once!" they repeated like a mechanical doll before they too broke apart and whirled away.

The last image before I awoke abruptly to a gray dawn, the dawn of the day in which I hoped to see my old friend again, was that of the strange silver cage in the laboratory, the cage which had been at the center of the whole fantastical apparatus and which, I believed, without being able quite to say why, was the very heart of the mystery.

15

I HAD PATIENTS to attend to on Monday. I kept my morning appointments but canceled my afternoon ones. By noon I was ready to return home to change my clothes before meeting Wiggins at the Pavilion Theatre.

I had an unexpected visitor just before I left my Gloucester Road office: young Billy, who burst into my presence nearly as out of breath as he had been when he had last come through my doors. The boy's cheeks glowed and his eyes sparkled as he explained his rush. He was carrying a package for his employer —he was a delivery boy for one of the new Oxford Street mercantile houses—and had detoured to ask what had come of the note. "I could tell you were worried, doctor, though you kindly tried not to show it. Is Mr. Holmes all right?"

His concern moved me, and I felt he deserved the fairest answer I could give. He had worked for Holmes; I must trust the lad's discretion. "I do not know, Billy. He may be in some danger, but I am pursuing the matter as best I can. At least there is no evidence of his having been harmed."

Billy took this well. "Do not worry, Dr. Watson," he said, patting my arm. "Just think how smart Mr. Holmes is. If there is danger he will take care of himself, I know he will. Well, I must dash or Mr. Selfridge will think I have made off with his goods. Good-bye. Let me know how things turn out."

And he was gone, leaving me with more reassurance than I had been able to give him.

I returned to my house, changed into a suit and top hat, slipped on my overcoat, and went out to hail a cab. The Pavilion Theatre was in Bermondsey, south of the Thames. I gave the cabman instructions. He turned out to be a Bermondsey man himself and said he knew the Pavilion well, so I felt assured of getting there in plenty of time for the beginning of the show at two P.M.

Soon we had crossed Waterloo Bridge and were on Long Lane, heading east. The roadway was still slick from the rain, but the clouds were scudding away, allowing a thin sunlight to trickle down on the show of life and movement that thronged the noisy street. This was a working-class district and formed a contrast to the fashionable Strand. The buildings were of yellow brick turned dingy by soot. Many of them, once private dwellings, had become shop-fronted, and many of these were pubs—the Nag's Head, the Turf, the Wellington. Here was the cry of costers competing with the singsong of knife grinders wheeling their rigs along the sidewalks. Top hats were a rarity. The men moving purposefully along or lounging in groups on corners wore caps and plain tweed suits; the women shopping and gossiping were also simply dressed. Here children were in evidence as they were not in Westminster; they ran and played everywhere, often dangerously near the wheels of passing cabs and lorries. Many of their parents had not been born in London but came to it from the country in search of a new life; there were not jobs for everyone, and so crime was bred in these streets.

I thought of this as I watched the children at their rough, aimless play, away from grass and trees, and I wondered if the evil Moriarty had once been such a child and had played thus, had perhaps been perverted to crime by grim necessity.

I felt in my pocket and pulled out the small octavo volume

which had been my silent companion, along with my service
revolver, since the fire in the laboratory. As Wiggins had
noted, it was a kind of manual for scenic designers and showed
the stage equipment of various theatres—the mechanisms for
raising and lowering curtains and flats, tracks for locomotion
across the stage, revolving stages, and traps, called "vam-
pires," by which scenery and props and even actors could be
raised and lowered through the stage floor. Because of new
playwrights like Ibsen and Shaw, theatrical effects and settings
were becoming simpler, Wiggins had informed me; the elaborate spectacles were dying. Even so, the book was a necessary
guide. I opened it to the pages on the Pavilion, wondering if
they might give me a clue as to what to expect or to why
Holmes had been interested in this particular theatre. All I
discovered was that though many music halls were converted
public ballrooms, schools, or even chapels, the Pavilion was
newly built and had all the most up-to-date equipment.

My cabman was about to let me out directly in front of the
Pavilion's wide Jamaica Road entrance when I spotted Wiggins on the opposite curb and called out to the driver to halt
there. He did so, and I stepped down.

Wiggins had dressed for his part. He wore a dun-colored
overcoat and cap, but he had not bothered to disguise his
personality, and his habitation in these nondescript working-
man's garments gave them an almost dapper look, as if they
were the height of fashion. Still, he made me feel conspicuous
in my dark coat and silk hat, which I had always worn whenever Holmes and I had attended a concert. I had put them on
automatically.

"Good afternoon, doctor," Wiggins greeted me cheerily. He
stood, hands in pockets, rocking on his heels, in a fine imitation
of the loafer's raffish pavement air. "There she is. What do you
think?"

I looked across at the Pavilion. Its surprising and, I thought,
rather vulgar façade rose two stories above the buildings beside it. It was not so large nor so magnificent as the Alhambra
in Leicester Square, but it affected that same peculiar Moorish

style of decoration which was then so popular, with twisting gold colonnades supporting its pinkish minarets and great blue onion dome. "Pavilion Palace of Varieties" proclaimed exotic letters in an arc above the entrance, through which the Bermondsey crowd was already eagerly passing.

"It is certainly colorful," I responded.

"We are twenty minutes early; let us go in now to make sure of our seats," Wiggins urged. "I was in the 'gods' on Saturday afternoon, but I insist upon the best seats for this performance!"

I followed his quick steps across the street. We entered the lobby, also decorated in lurid Moorish style, and purchased two stalls in the fifth row. Wiggins wished to take his place at once, and I followed him, but just before passing into the auditorium I paused to examine one of the large playbills plastered in an ornate frame. It proclaimed a bill of varied acts. The headliner was Gus Elen, followed by Harry Champion. I had never seen either man, being in no way a devotee of the halls, but I knew their reputations as beloved Cockney comics. There followed at least twenty mysterious names and acts, among them, "THE COCHRANE FAMILY, Five in Number, comprising Sarah, Nellie, Maggie, Butch, and Bill, in their *American Songs and Dances*," "ROBB WILTON, who will open his *New Budget of Comicalities*, including his *Impersonation of the Midland Railway Guard*," "THE FLYING PONGO, Daredevil Aerialist," "YOUNG & DEAN, the Eminent Negro Entertainers," "The World-Renowned BOSQUET TROUPE in *The Wild West*," "BELLA BIJOU & LILY GRAY, Sensational Duetists," and so on. I was surprised to find "THE GREAT ESCOTT, Mystifying Magician" as far down the bill as sixteenth. As we walked down the aisle to our seats I commented on this to Wiggins: "You described Escott to me as the sensation of London, yet I find him near the bottom of the bill."

"The *future* sensation of London," Wiggins reminded me, turning to make his way into the fifth row. "Once even Marie Lloyd was unknown and played bottom of the bill, as did I.

One way or another," Wiggins winked broadly at me over his shoulder, "Escott will become the sensation of London. When you have seen him, tell me if you do not agree."

For the time being I had to be satisfied with this.

We settled ourselves in our places. My young friend's face remained bright with pleasure as he looked about eagerly, turning this way and that, once or twice rising in his seat and twisting full round to stare up into the crowded balcony. The joy of being in this beloved place seemed to have made him forget his worried pronouncements of the previous day, but I was wary. I searched faces, as I had in the lobby and outside the theatre, looking for a telltale oscillation of the head or an evil gray-eyed glance that might signal the presence of Moriarty. But I discovered no such hints in any of the ruddy faces about us. At last I sat back. Wiggins continued to wave and mouth greetings, mostly to pretty young wenches who smiled back at him saucily but whose escorts frowned and expostulated with their ladies.

At last these preliminaries were concluded, and Wiggins leaned back with a sigh of deep satisfaction. "Ah, doctor, this is the place! I believe the best of England is here: her life and sense of fun, without all her awful pretensions. Here a man can laugh and experience wonder!"

Above us rose tiers of gilded oriental splendor set off by red velvet draperies. This ripe setting was filling rapidly with an incongruous crowd of raucous Londoners. It was not at all the crowd with which Holmes and I had listened politely to Madame Neruda at St. James's Hall nor the crowd which had nodded in time to the melodies of *The Orchid,* and I felt uncomfortably out of place, the more so because of my anxiety over the impending appearance of the Great Escott. Admixed to the roar of color and sound was the odor of fish, which patrons blithely munched from paper wrappers, and the smell of spirits as well, no doubt from nips into the public houses along the way.

"I am out of my element," I said nervously in the face of this.

"I feel the same way, sometimes, at a fine dinner," Wiggins

replied. "I think I would rather be here!" He nudged my arm and grinned. "Unbutton your coat, doctor. Do you know where these theatres of variety come from? No? From a fine English impulse: our love of singing while tippling, or tippling while singing. Do you want grand origins? There have been musical clubs for two hundred years. Not your Pall Mall variety, where stuffy veterans of Empire sit in stuffy rooms in overstuffed chairs and mumble over the bloody heathen, but places of wit and merriment, and of bawdy. And poets and princes and actors and rakes alike made them up, come together to make merry. At the Neapolitan on St. James, the Duke of York and the Prince of Wales rubbed elbows with Beau Brummel and Sheridan, and later Byron and Thackeray and Edmund Kean could be found at the Coal Hole, Strand. That's egalitarianism for you! Thank God for Edward!"

I had not expected this patriotic conclusion and wished to get us back to the subject at hand. "Well, the Pavilion seems to me not the place for a king," I said, "nor a poet. The question is: why is Holmes here?"

"If he is here, doctor. That we shall see."

There were ten minutes to go before the orchestra was to strike up the overture. Wiggins filled the time with theatrical reminiscences: "I have heard stories of the days fifty years ago when the clubs began to charge admission and amateurs who had been content to sing for taproom applause became aware that their ability to amuse might be worth a weekly wage in the new music halls. One Johnny Golightly—I never knew his real name—told me what it was like auditioning in those days. You would trudge twenty miles with your carpetbag and line up in wind and rain. Then, with little warning, you'd find yourself pushed onto a tiny platform in front of a crowd roused to blood lust. The real music halls were drinking establishments, so you might easily be stunned by a bottle while trying to recover from stage fright. At the very least, boos, old boots, and a dead cat would come your way. The wisest thing to do was to break into a clog dance, partly to soothe the savage breasts, but mostly to make yourself a moving target. Thousands retired, heartbroken if not maimed, from the ordeal. But for the ones who survived it was worth it. I did not have that awful experience of the early audition—things were tamer when I broke into the circuit as an acrobatic clown—but I suffered terrors enough. It was a wonderful life!"

I could not understand Wiggins' joy in what sounded more like a perilous obstacle course than a profession, but I asked him no questions. A moment of truth was approaching, and I was absorbed in my own reflections. An idea had been hovering at the edge of my consciousness for some time. I had refused to examine it, but now it forced itself upon me.

Wiggins had said the key fact of our mystery was Moriarty's resemblance to Sherlock Holmes. I knew that it was more than a resemblance; it was an uncanny likeness, distorted by evil personality but otherwise exact in every detail. There was an inner likeness, too, a similarity in their powers to plot and dissemble.

Could it be, I hardly dared ask myself, that Holmes and Moriarty were the same man?

Having expressed the thought at last, I shuddered. Protests against it flooded my mind. Yet two related facts would not let me relinquish the idea: to my knowledge no one had seen Moriarty save Holmes and myself, and I had never seen them together. I had to admit that the unexplained resemblance between the two could be explained by some strange warping of personality which caused good to alternate with evil in a single mind. It was fantastic, but possible.

The conductor, a swarthy little man with a moustache waxed to fine points, darted out of the wings and onto his box before the orchestra. The audience cheered, then quieted. With a flash of the fierce smile of the petty tyrant, Maestro Franco tapped his baton in staccato fashion. He raised the stick. The house lights dimmed, and on the downbeat the *Zampa* overture engulfed the house.

In spite of the show's having started, I was so full of my new idea that I had to express it to Wiggins immediately. I leaned over and whispered excitedly into his ear: "I have just thought of something: Moriarty and Holmes may be the same man!"

Wiggins turned his head toward me with a smile. He did not cease tapping his index finger in time to the music. "I have thought of that myself," he whispered back. "It is a remote but very real possibility. However I have been toying with another idea which seems to me to have far more merit. Perhaps there is no Moriarty."

"Why, what do you mean?"

"I mean that Moriarty may be a creation of Sherlock Holmes' fertile imagination, just as Mycroft Holmes was. Holmes may have hired another actor friend from old days, one who looked something like himself, to play the archfiend. Makeup can work wonders."

I was thunderstruck. This possibility had not crossed my mind at all. I drew back to stare at my young friend and was disconcerted to find that he was chuckling loudly enough for me to hear him over the spirited blare of the orchestra.

He drew close again to whisper, "There is still mystery and danger, doctor; do not mistake my mirth. But I have regained my sense of humor. To know so much and so little, and to have infinite possibilities for speculation open to one I think is very funny, do you not?" And he burst into laughter again.

I wanted to tell him in no uncertain terms how little humor I saw in the situation, but at that moment the overture raced to its end, and the enthusiastic applause of the audience drowned out the beginnings of my response. The curtain, flanked by two grotesque caryatids, sprang apart to reveal Bertram Stiles, in garish checks, the chairman of the program, whose drolleries were lost upon me. Shortly, the leering Mr. Stiles introduced Nell Simpson, "The Chelsea Thrush," and I had to suffer her trills in silence.

I sat anxiously through turn after turn, unable to like or dislike anything, but only occupying my seat, waiting for the Great Escott to appear. There came singers singly, in pairs, and in troupes; they ranged from operatic to sentimental to saucy, at which last the audience cheered loudest. There were comics like Gus Elen, who affected the broad Cockney of

Cheapside, and comics who played drunken toffs and one who
played a woman no better than she should have been. And
there were acrobats in spangled tights and dancers and
clowns. I connected none of these with the names I had read
on the bill, though Mr. Stiles introduced each act clearly. I sat
stiff as a board and perspired in the overheated atmosphere of
the auditorium, while Wiggins laughed and cheered beside
me, or leaned over to malign the skills of the acrobats or to
praise a pretty ankle.

But at last, inevitably, the moment I had waited for arrived.
My heart beat fast.

"And now, that marvel of the mystic arts, that peer of pres-
tidigitation, the one, the only . . . Great Escott!" exclaimed
Bertie Stiles, and bounded off the stage.

I sat on the edge of my seat. The lights dimmed, the wood-
winds began a low, mysterious air, and the red velvet curtains
opened to reveal a dimly lit scrim covered with hundreds of
silvery question marks upon a dark field. Gradually a bluish
glow spread up from the floor behind the scrim, producing
that strange stage effect of suddenly being able to see through
a wall. Standing alone, absolutely upright and still, silhouetted
by the rising blue glow behind him, was the tall cloaked figure
of a man. He remained immobile as the tempo of the music
accelerated and the drum made odd tapping sounds like the
rattling of bones. At last the whole back of the stage was
blue-lit, and the scrim rose foot by foot. The Great Escott
stepped forward, a clear spotlight flooded his figure, and in
rich, full tones he said slowly, "Good evening, ladies and gentlemen."

It was not the voice of Sherlock Holmes; it was languid and
sonorous, and there was already evident in those few words a
faint accent which I was unable to identify. I thought at once
of the accent which Alfred Fish had described the young
Holmes as using, and I wondered if I could be hearing it now.
Neither did the Great Escott look like my old friend. He was
taller by several inches, and stout; not obese, but as he whirled
off his black velvet cloak, his paunch showed, though he car-

ried it with the well-bred dignity of middle age. He was dressed in impeccable evening clothes: tailored trousers, white tie, and black swallowtail coat, and the front of his gleaming white vest was fastened with ruby studs. He had draped his cape over one arm and wordlessly, meticulously, while the music droned on, removed his fawn gray gloves one finger at a time. These he placed on the cloak. The hands which emerged were narrow and white. They could have been the hands of Sherlock Holmes, but the head was not my friend's. The hair was black, shiny with pomade, combed severely back, long and curling around the collar. The features were pinched, the mouth carefully pursed, and the generous cheeks and narrow nose were rosy with the unmistakable inflammation of the habitual drinker. This man had obviously succumbed to the offstage malady which Wiggins had described.

The Great Escott's arrival had been impressive: the gradual lighting, the seductive beat of the music, and the grave air of the magician himself had done their work on the audience, which had grown absolutely silent. But I was disappointed. With his stout figure dressed in black and white, Escott looked like a great pompous penguin to me. Surely he could not be Sherlock Holmes.

He said nothing, barely smiling as he pulled playing cards from the air, rapidly one by one, until he held a full pack, then fanned them, spread them up his arm, folded them back neatly, and tossed them into the air, whence they vanished as mysteriously as they had appeared. I heard my young friend gasp at my side. I too was amazed. Wiggins leaned close to me.

"I told you he was skillful, doctor. I have tried that one. It is difficult; he does it better than any man I have ever seen."

The Great Escott might be a drinker, as his red cheeks and swollen nose proclaimed, but his habits in no way affected his performance. His further feats demonstrated that. He produced metal rings which he tossed and joined and separated miraculously. He picked up the cloak which he had placed on the small stand by his side, swirled it about, and a half dozen pigeons flapped up from its folds to hover about his head. He whirled the cloak around them and they vanished, to be re-placed by a shower of flower petals upon his person. Coolly he brushed the petals from his lapels, then smiled his faint smile at the audience and accepted their applause. A pretty wasp-waisted soubrette carried onstage a gaily painted box into which other boxes had been cunningly fit. Escott began sepa-rating these, all with open tops, until five of them were ranged in ascending order along the stage. He produced a slender wand from the air and tapped the smallest box; a spray of flowers grew from its interior. He tapped the next; three pi-geons flew up from it to perch on his shoulders. From the next a small dog leaped, yapping, to run about the stage and stop, still barking wildly, in front of the fourth box. A black cat emerged from that. The dog began to chase the cat back and forth until both jumped and vanished into the fifth and last box, leaving utter silence. Escott strolled over, tapped the fifth box with his wand, and its sides fell open upon the stage, revealing thin air. The magician looked up quizzically. Pres-ently, from backstage, barking and yowling were heard. Es-cott glanced in a bored manner to the left. From the side of the stage loped the black cat, chased by the yapping terrier. The animals streaked from one wing of the stage to the other behind the magician. Escott faced the audience once more and gave a meager shrug. He proceeded to collect the boxes, placing each inside the other until all were fit together; only the flowers from the first and the pigeons cooing on his shoul-ders remained of the remarkable illusion. He placed the reas-sembled collection of boxes on the stand, lifted the pigeons from his shoulders, and nestled them gently among the flow-ers. Slowly the flowers sank back into the boxes until they and the pigeons were gone from view. Escott peered down into the set of boxes, looked up, blinked, stepped back, struck the large outer box suddenly with a crack of his wand. Its sides fell and clattered upon the stage to reveal—nothing. The flowers, the birds, and the four smaller boxes had vanished!

The audience applauded wildly.

Throughout all of this a feeling had grown upon me, the

feeling of being spellbound. Whatever his shape and appearance, Escott was a gripping performer. The effect was due in part to how he had set the scene, but mostly it was Escott. He moved deliberately yet lightly, and with complete confidence. He knew that nothing could go wrong. His face might be flushed with drink, but its masklike control and the unreadable basilisk eyes held me. I had seen that face—or its like—before, in India. It was the face of Buddha, whose disturbing, impenetrable smile I had avoided while at the same time being drawn to it during my two years in the East. Here it was again, hypnotizing me and the rest of the audience as well. And the hands, with their long white fingers, which flowed and wove together like dancers in unison, beckoning, entrancing me.

I tore my gaze away to look at Wiggins. He was staring up at the magician with a placid half smile of complete absorption. I looked about. All the other faces within my view were staring likewise. During the previous acts there had been noise and movement from the audience, good-natured banter, catcalls, the singing of well-loved songs with the performers, the crunching of fish and chips. Now there was silence, without so much as a cough. I began to feel uncomfortable and looked again at Escott. The ruby studs glittered as he moved, his hands undulated, his large body swayed on its dexterous feet, his face remained a mask, mysterious, commanding. I found myself perspiring. I wanted not to stay, wanted to rise, to flee up the aisle. I realized why: this was the same feeling I had had with Moriarty in the laboratory, the sense of being manipulated by a compelling but heartless and tyrannical power.

And then I was reminded again of Moriarty and of the depth of the mystery in which I had become embroiled, and complete confusion reigned in my mind: out upon the stage was wheeled, by two young women in tights, the silver cage from the laboratory.

16

W IGGINS WAS SHAKING my arm. "The cage!" he hissed into my ear. "It is the cage from Holmes' laboratory which you described to me!"

"Yes," I answered, hardly aware that I was speaking, "but it cannot be, for I saw the apparatus destroyed. Yet it is just like it."

"My God!" Wiggins exclaimed softly, his baffled tone expressing my feeling. "What can it mean?"

That was the question in my own mind. It was my question about all which had occurred during the past three days. But I had no time to think about it now, for my attention was held by the events onstage.

Except for his words of greeting, Escott had performed silently until now, but he spoke at last, stepping close to the footlights so that his face was illuminated from below in a ghostly fashion. "Dear friends," he began in deep penetrating tones that reached to the balcony, the hint of an unidentifiable accent still in his voice, "you are about to see the most wondrous feat of this and future ages. It is not an illusion but a fact. In moments I shall vanish from this stage. I shall not disappear into a box or behind a cloth and then, when the box is opened or the cloth removed, be gone. No, I shall vanish before your very eyes. I shall return"—he smiled his little flicker of a smile —"just in time for the evening performance. I learned this amazing ability in a distant country which only one man other than myself has ever visited; of the two of us only I am the master of the feat. Not Maskelyne, not any magician on earth, can reproduce it, for it is not a trick to be copied. You shall witness a true disappearance."

Escott said this with such quiet force that I, and I am sure everyone in the audience, believed it.

"Wiggins, have you seen this before and failed to tell me of it?" I whispered.

"I have not. I know I would have recognized that cage as the one in your story at once. I would not miss the next few moments for the world. It means something that he is doing it now, doctor, with you here at last. It is Escott's show, Escott's game. Let us see how he plays it." And he gazed raptly toward the stage.

The music had faded while Escott spoke, but now it rose again, this time in an undulating rhythm of gradually increasing tempo. The blue backlights died to be replaced by a single brilliant spotlight illuminating only the cage and Escott, leaving the rest of the auditorium in contrasting blackness. The cage was exactly as I remembered it, a simple cube made of meshed and shining metal strands, with a single door in its front. It must be a duplicate of the one I had discovered in Holmes' laboratory.

The two young women who had wheeled it out had walked off, leaving Escott alone with the apparatus. He lifted his black cloak from the little stand nearby and clasped it round his neck again, then turned to face the cage. There was a drum roll, the music reached a climax and ceased. In the silence that followed, Escott reached out and swung open the front side of the cage. I could hear the faint shiver of metal as he did. He stepped into the apparatus, turned to face the audience, and shut the cage upon himself. It was barely tall enough to accom-

modate his height, with an inch or so of space remaining above
his head. His expression was somber and, if anything, more
fixed than before. He breathed deeply several times, then his
gray eyes began to roll upward in their sockets as if he were
going into a trance. Slowly he reached out with both hands to
grasp the outer edges of his cloak, drawing it about him until
all but his head was cocooned in it; he looked like a corpse
standing in a black shroud. He remained this way for a full
moment, during which I am not sure that I took even one
breath.

And then, incredibly, he began to revolve.

I thought at first that he had stepped slightly to the right, but
a quick glance at the tips of his boots protruding from beneath
the hem of his cloak showed that his feet were tightly together. Yet his body turned until he was sideways, then he was
backward, then frontward once more. His body proceeded on
this circuit about its own vertical axis again, and again and
again, turning ever faster. My gasp of breath was simultaneous
with that of the rest of the audience, Wiggins included. We
made one startled sigh of astonishment, then we stared,
transfixed, at the dervish whose face became a pinkish blur
and whose figure was transformed into a bullet-shaped column
vibrating softly at the center of the cage.

Suddenly a kind of blackness engulfed the whole interior of
the cage, a sparkling blackness, as if a piece of starry night had
been drawn into it. Yet we could still see Escott clearly, or
rather the blurred outline which his spinning figure made. At
last that began to dissolve into bright motes. I seemed to see
each particle of his being separate from the whole, flash once,
and die like a burned cinder. Finally there was nothing but the
strange glinting cloud of darkness within the cage. Abruptly
the stage lights flooded on, and the cloud was gone, leaving
only the shining wire apparatus on the bare stage. After a
stunned silence the audience roared with applause and cries
of "Escott! Escott!"

The spell was broken.

Excited conversation began. Bertie Stiles bounded back onstage as the two women wheeled the silver cage away to announce crisply that Escott would return for the evening performance. And then the Bosquet Troupe, in "The Wild West," was on.

Awed, I whispered to Wiggins, "He is the sensation of London indeed!"

"He is more than that," Wiggins responded. "Those first tricks were masterful, but I can explain them all, if not perform them. But that last was a wonder. I do not understand it" —he rose suddenly and stepped past me—"but I intend to find out about it now. Stay here, doctor. I shall be back." And he was gone down the row before I could protest. I saw him hesitate in the aisle, then walk forward and disappear through a side door near the stage.

My impulse was to jump up and follow him, but I trusted Wiggins. He knew his way about backstage far better than I, and he was shrewd and resourceful. So I acted as he had instructed, though it was hard indeed in my agitated state to sit through the final thirty minutes of acts until the bill reached its end.

The cage, the cage! It was indeed at the heart of the mystery, as I had guessed. But how? And who was the Great Escott?

Bertie Stiles announced the concluding act. Wiggins had not returned. I twisted round to look in agitation up and down both aisles and glanced repeatedly toward the door through which my young ally had slipped out of sight. At last I saw him emerge from the door; shortly he was at my side, his face flushed and his eyes showing all their old sparkle. At that moment a roar of laughter greeted Harry Champion's last Cockney wisecrack, Maestro Franco's orchestra sent the comedian off with a jaunty air, and the red velvet curtains swept together, followed by the flare of the house lights. At once the Bermondsey crowd was on its feet, gathering coats and caps and dropped articles and making its way out.

"What did you discover? Did you speak to Escott?" I demanded as soon as the last musical note had died. I took up my coat and top hat and started to rise, but with a hand on my wrist Wiggins pulled me back into my seat.

"A moment, doctor. My job is done; I have helped as much as I can for now and am pleased to have been able to do so. I must rush, for I am on in *The Orchid* in less than two hours, but you are to remain here; those are your instructions. Escott has agreed to speak to you, but don't look for him. He will find you, and you are now in his hands. As for us, Dr. Watson, I hope that you will not forget me and will visit me at Baker Street when this is over to tell me the end of it, if you may. It is still a great mystery to me, but it may be that the fewer men who know the secret, the better off the world will be. At any rate, for now, good-bye."

He rose and put out his hand. He had replaced his cap at a raffish angle and stood grinning at me in his engaging way. I grasped his hand, intending to say many things, to ask questions, to assure him that I would not forget him, to thank him. But he released my hand after a firm squeeze and was down the row before I could speak. He turned in the aisle for one last wave and then was lost in the departing crowd.

Soon the crowd was gone, and I was left alone in the Pavilion's opulent auditorium.

Four charwomen entered and roved up and down the rows with cloth satchels over their shoulders into which they swept all the detritus of the matinee. The stooped and wrinkled old woman who passed nearest me squinted at me curiously but said not a word; I smelled her beery breath as she went on her way. Within ten minutes the women had completed their sweep and were gone out a side door. The house lights dimmed until the auditorium was lit by only a ghostly gray glow, and I remained seated, feeling increasingly foolish. Had Wiggins meant that I should wait in the lobby, or outside the theatre perhaps?

But he had not, for shortly there came an unmistakable signal: the heavy velvet curtains parted slowly, to reveal the stage, mysteriously blue-lit again. The silver cage was in its former place.

I was inured to surprise; I hardly reacted to this. Surprise had become the rule in this case. I felt close to an answer at last, to a tying together of all the scattered fragments into a comprehensible whole, and I only longed for that to happen. Without fear, without forethought, I rose from my seat, walked to the stage, climbed the short flight of stairs beside the orchestra pit, and stepped upon the boards.

I turned to look back. The empty auditorium brooded before me. Suddenly I felt what it must mean to have to perform. I sensed that the great hall waited, full of impending wrath or derision, should my performance displease. Uneasily I turned my back on the house. I began to feel nervous, and chilly prickles crawled at the nape of my neck as I approached the cage. I reached out my hand to run my fingers along its fine wire mesh, as I had done with the cage in Holmes' laboratory, but my touch gave no clue to the secret of the apparatus, to what its deeper meaning might be or how it had helped the Great Escott to disappear.

I stepped back and surveyed this thespian landscape, so unfamiliar to me. I could see now the bank of blue electric lights recessed below the back of the stage floor. Directly above were hanging lights, invisible to the audience, as well as the bottoms of various curtains, scrims, and flats, ready to be lowered for their scenes and effects. Yet it was familiar because I had seen it in the book on London theatres which was still in my left-hand coat pocket.

I was reminded that my pistol was in my other pocket, and I reached in to grasp it for reassurance.

I looked down. There was something else familiar from the theatre book: the floor of the stage was not solid but was riddled with traps, hinged openings through which props and performers could be raised and lowered. I understood at once that these were probably the devices whereby Escott's box trick had been effected, though they could hardly explain the miraculous illusion of the cage. I thought about that incredible disappearance again, and about Escott's magnetic power, which had frightened me. Alfred Fish had had the same uneasy response to the stage presence of the young Holmes.

I returned to the cage and put my hand upon it again. My eyes began to trace one of its strands of silvery wire; they followed it as it wove in and out among other strands. The thing was a remarkable piece of workmanship, simple yet elegant; in fact it seemed, as my eyes continued to trace the wire, that the whole thing was made up of one continuous length which twisted back and forth and interlocked upon itself. I wondered what kind of metal it was and if Holmes himself had fashioned it. Or had Escott made this cage?

Suddenly the phrase which I had thought to communicate to Wiggins, the words Holmes had spoken to me on the evening of his departure, came to my mind again. The detective had admitted aspects of his conflict with Moriarty which he chose not to reveal. "My old friend," he had said somberly, "I shield you from a truth too strange for you or any man of this century." Staring at the metal cube, unlike anything I had ever seen, I pondered that intriguing phrase.

Would I ever see Holmes again, and if so would he reveal to me the "truth" he had spoken of?

I grew impatient. Someone had turned on the bluish lights, had replaced the cage, had raised the curtain. I assumed it was Escott, and I was anxious to speak with him, but I was annoyed at the delay. Were melodramatic settings a requisite for his real-life encounters as well? I looked into the wings to either side of the stage; they were gloomily dark, and I was not anxious to explore past the margin of stage light. Could the magician be there, observing me?

I called his name, first timidly, then more loudly: "Escott! Escott!" Only a faint echo of my own voice came back to me from the vast deserted auditorium.

I was about to venture into the offstage darkness when I heard the sound of footsteps along one of the aisles. I turned and saw a man approaching. He wore a cap pulled low over his face and, as he drew nearer the stage, I saw that his boots were scuffed and that his mismatched coat and pants were none of the best. He looked like many of the idlers I had seen on the street near the Pavilion, and he walked, hands in pockets, with a shambling dejected air. I wondered at his presence, but he appeared so common, like a down-at-heels laborer, that I experienced no trepidation. Perhaps he brings a message, I thought.

He came up the stairs, stepped upon the stage, and walked toward me, his cap still casting a shadow across his features. At last, when he was barely six feet away, he halted, removed one hand from his pants pocket, and poked up the brim of the cap with a dirty finger.

"Good evening, doctor," came the soft, precise words of James Moriarty.

Without hesitation, in spite of the great jolt which that unmistakable voice gave me, I jerked my revolver from my coat pocket and had it leveled at his breast in an instant.

"You do not find me unprepared this time," I said.

He reached up and pulled off the cap to toss it away across the stage, revealing that amazing head which looked so much like that of my friend, yet which expressed only evil intent. He laughed his contemptuous laugh.

"You are always unprepared, doctor. In your hands that revolver is a foolish toy. You do not frighten me with it, nor will it prevent me from acting just as I please. But I shall suffer you to hold it for the time being if it makes you feel better. Admit it, you did not expect to see me in the person of this Bermondsey loafer."

"I did not," I confessed.

"Honesty, honesty! I can count on you for that, doctor, except in one thing. On our previous meeting you convinced me that you did not know where Holmes was, and yet you have led me to him at last. Your deception, then, is one point of cleverness, a major point at that, which I must concede to you."

"Holmes? Is he here, then?"

"Oh, do not fumble when you have been found out. Admit defeat graciously. Escott is Holmes—he must be! I know it as well as you do."

"That is ridiculous! Escott looks nothing like Holmes."

"And you do not look like a fool, but you are one! Mend your ways, doctor! The cage is here and Holmes is here. Come now, lead me to him!"

Moriarty's body had hunched over as before, and his head had begun its peculiar oscillation. His eyes glittered with a feverish urgency, and I knew that he might be devilishly clever, even brilliant, but that he was also thoroughly mad with some incomprehensible mania about my old friend. Was he right? Was Escott Holmes? I did not know, but in any case I must protect myself. I raised my revolver higher and pointed it in no uncertain way. Moriarty scowled and took a step toward me.

"Stand back," I warned. "I should be glad to put a bullet through your breast!"

Moriarty halted. He smiled. "Would you shoot your old friend Sherlock Holmes?"

His body came out of its crouch, pulled itself erect, became the upright, lithe, and dignified figure of my old companion. The palsied head ceased twitching, calmed; the chin rose; the eyes took on the clear look of kind and reasoning intelligence; the thin lips spoke: "My dear doctor, give me the gun."

It was the voice of Sherlock Holmes; before me was the very image of Holmes. The man held out his steady hand, beckoning with the slim, sensitive fingers of my friend.

"The gun, doctor."

He took a step forward.

I held the gun tighter and stepped back, filled with confusion. What was this before me? I thought of my surmise that Holmes and Moriarty were the same man. If I killed Moriarty, would I also kill Holmes? This scene was worse than the nightmare I had had, for there was no waking from it. I must make a decision, and it seemed that the crucial point, the moment toward which all my efforts had led, was unexpectedly upon me now. Moriarty had been right: I was unprepared, yet I must act. My arm trembled. I reached up my other hand to steady it.

"Stand back!" I warned.

The Holmes-Moriarty figure continued to advance.

"I must have the pistol, Dr. Watson."

I heard a sound at my feet, a click. I saw a startled expression suffuse the Holmes face, a face which was suddenly rising into the air!

But it was not the face which was rising; it was I who was falling. I gasped at the unexpected sickening sensation. There was empty space beneath my body.

One of the traps in the stage floor had sprung open under me, and I was plummeting into darkness.

17

I MADE NOT a cry, but I heard a distinct yowl of disappointment from above me, in Moriarty's voice, not Holmes'. I dropped perhaps ten feet but landed on something soft which gave beneath me and broke my fall. I found myself unharmed but sprawled upon my stomach in a pile of sand. Before I could blink twice I heard a bang from over my head, and the faint bluish light from the stage winked out. The trap above my head had swung shut, leaving me in darkness.

I groaned and scrambled about on the sand, attempting to find my footing. A hand gripped my sleeve to help me up and a rasping female voice said, " 'Ere now, doctor, we must be up before we can run, and run we must!"

"Who is that?" I gasped and jerked back my arm.

I became aware that I was not in total darkness but that here and there light was seeping down through the cracks around the edges of the traps. About me was a large space peopled with the ghostly forms of props—tables and chairs, papier-mâché trees, stuffed animals, and the like. Before me was the blurred shape of the person who had gripped my arm.

"I am Alice!" the form asserted bluntly in its wheezing old

woman's voice. I smelled an incongruous mixture of soap and sweat from her person, and overlaying both of these the strong odor of beer.

"Alice?" I repeated blankly. I took a step back. She might be old, and she might be a woman, but I was glad to feel my revolver still in my hand. I gripped it tighter and raised it halfway.

"You must trust me, doctor. We 'aven't much time. This will 'elp." She struck a match and put it to an oil lamp which she held in one hand. Its glow spread up over the face of the snaggle-toothed charwoman who had passed me wordlessly in the auditorium. "You see, it *is* Alice!" she exclaimed triumphantly while she grinned broadly up at me.

Now I could see her all too clearly. She was short and plump and wore a sort of shapeless smock of indeterminate color. Her cheeks were, if anything, redder than Escott's, her hair gray and stringy. On her sharp chin sprouted hairs like pig's bristles, and one of her eyes wandered aimlessly while the other fixed itself in a bright and not altogether welcome gaze upon my countenance.

"But I do not know you!" I insisted, pleased only to be certain of that.

Alice was unaffected by my rebuff. She thrust her face into mine. "But I knows you, Dr. Watson. Mr. Escott sent me. Now, no nonsense! That fellow above, whoe'er he may be, is a nasty one, I've 'eard, and no fool besides. He'll be down 'ere in a flash."

Alice was right. I could hear rapid footsteps from above, moving in the direction of the wings. Moriarty was in search of the way below, and he would find it soon.

I made my decision: "All right, I'll follow."

Alice beamed out of her one fixed eye while the other somersaulted in pleasure. "Good! This way, now."

She reached out to grip my hand and, shielding the lamp so that it gave off only a muted glow, led me between racks of costumes of various sorts, around artificial palms and false boulders, through bits of architecture from every age, so that

I felt like an explorer of some strange landscape in which time had gone mad. At last we passed through a small door, up a flight of musty stairs, and out a heavier door into an alleyway whose high brick walls oozed moisture.

"Be quick, now," she hissed, still tugging at my arm. We scuttled over the cobblestones until we reached a narrow street which I guessed was in back of the theatre. It was dark now, and few lamps lit this deserted byway. A shabby-looking carriage waited in the rising mist where we emerged from the alley and, without speaking to its heavily muffled driver, Alice —mad Alice I began to think her—jumped into its interior with surprising agility and beckoned me to follow. I clambered aboard and swung the door shut behind me. Before I had settled myself, the driver had snapped his whip and we were off at a brisk trot, proceeding along even more narrow and obscure ways than the one where we had started our journey. Obviously we were not traveling into a reputable part of London, and I grew alarmed.

"Where are you taking me?" I demanded.

Alice sat opposite me. For answer she reached down complacently to smooth her voluminous garment over her knees; then, with a quick and altogether unexpected flick of one hand, had snatched my gun from my grasp before I could tighten my grip upon it. She placed it on the seat by her side. Inwardly I cursed my carelessness.

"I am sorry, my dear Watson, but we would not want you accidentally to shoot poor Alice," came the voice of Sherlock Holmes. "She is a good soul and has served me faithfully."

I sat bolt upright and blinked. I looked about the carriage compartment for Holmes, but it was all too plain that Alice and I were its only occupants. The old woman held up the lantern before her face with one hand; with the other she stripped the unsightly whiskers from her chin and plucked out the glass eye whose pupil had bobbled so outrageously. She spat out the cotton wadding which had bloated her cheeks and lifted off the wiry wig which had hidden a skull of noble proportions. Her squat shapeless body stretched within the smock to become a fine lean figure. The man smoothed back his hair and gazed at me keenly. From the folds of the smock he produced a familiar cherrywood pipe and proceeded to light it. The hint of a smile strayed across his thin lips as he gazed at my stupefied expression.

"I must congratulate you, Watson," he said. "You have found me at last."

There was no question in my mind. About the figure on the stage of the Pavilion Theatre who had advanced upon me looking exactly like Holmes, demanding my gun in Holmes' voice, I had felt a horrible ambiguity. Is it he or is it not? I had asked myself countless times in a mere dozen seconds. But about the identity of the man before me now I had no doubt: it was truly my old friend.

Yet my dilemma was not at an end, for I had discovered that Sherlock Holmes was not what he seemed. He had deliberately deceived me for years. Remembrance of my anger and of the dangers I had faced over the past few days flooded over me. And here, in the person of this absurd Alice, the detective had toyed with me again, and sat across from me now with his smug smile, sucking on his pipe placidly as if we had just met over tea in front of the fire at Baker Street. Yet inside of me too were the loyalty I had wordlessly pledged and my longtime trust in him, feelings not easily displaced. How was I to react?

I leaned across the carriage and, to my astonishment as well as his, flung my arms around him in a hearty embrace.

"Holmes!" I exclaimed.

And tears of relief formed in my eyes.

"My dear fellow, you astonish me," Holmes said when I had seated myself once more. "I am surprised that you are glad to see me after what Wiggins related of your adventures of the past few days. I never expected that you would be so resourceful—nor so meddlesome. You really put yourself in a position of great and needless danger."

"Meddlesome!" I exclaimed. "Holmes, I did it for you."

"Well, I believe you, and I am grateful, but your appearance

tonight at the Pavilion has been a serious setback to my plans.
I have had to postpone the capture and the disposal of that
viper, Moriarty. Don't think that that little display with the
cage was for your benefit. It was for his alone, and I would have
had him but for you. Still, I am glad to see you and may be able
to use you. In fact, already a new plan is forming in my mind
in which you figure prominently. After all, it is fitting that we
who have accomplished so much together in the past should
accomplish this last task together. Oh, here is your revolver.
I am sorry to have taken it from you so rudely, but when I
revealed myself I did not want you to confuse me with Moriarty and shoot me by mistake. That would have been most
unfortunate."

A deluge of questions rushed into my mind. I hardly knew
what to ask first. "So you were Escott?" I said at last.

"Of course. My dear fellow, do you mean to say that I fooled
even you? That is flattering. But I did not fool Moriarty. Oh,
no. I counted on his seeing through Escott, who was merely
a matter of elevated heels, a pillow paunch, an altered voice,
and a little makeup. Escott—and the cage, of course—were
my lures."

I let that tantalizing hint alone for the moment. "And Wiggins found you backstage?"

"I allowed him to find me, for of course I saw you and him
in the fifth row at once. Moriarty was but three rows behind
you. It was hard to remain the calm and impassive Escott after
that jolt, but I believe I sustained the character admirably.
Wiggins has turned out well, don't you agree? Of course his
tastes in everything are not mine, but then we must allow for
a little individuality. He is a fine actor of the light sort, highly
amusing. I have seen his performance in *The Orchid* twice,
both times in a different disguise. I do not go about as myself
these days."

I repressed my desire to ask who that self might really be.
"And Wiggins explained to you how we came to the Pavilion?"

"Yes. He was pretty near to certain that I was Escott after
your interview with Alfred Fish—a fine chap, if a little too

given to drink—and after seeing the theatre book, of course. Most careless of me to have left it where I did, but I never expected that anyone would find his way into my little hide-away, much less that it would be you. Or that you would lead Moriarty there—most distressing!—and that you would then follow my trail with such skill and persistence. My dear chap, in my absence I would recommend you to Scotland Yard above Gregson or Lestrade or the pompous Athelney Jones any day."

I ignored this questionable flattery to bury a hidden suspicion: "Then Wiggins really knew no more than I?"

"Well, he may have suspected more. And I am sure that his bright mind is ringing the changes on the evidence even now. But if you mean was he in on any secret of mine, he was not. My actions were, had to be, all on my own. When he met me in Escott's dressing room this afternoon it was the first time he had seen me since I suggested he take our old rooms at Baker Street."

The carriage rattled along streets which seemed to grow narrower and darker. Holmes continued to sit easily, puffing at his pipe. The strong smell of shag tobacco almost covered the odor of mad Alice which drifted to my nostrils from the unsightly smock the detective still wore.

"And Alice," said I, "why the old charwoman?"

"I have kept her in readiness for many years. In fact she has appeared before. In the case of the marble cupids, one of my solitary ventures during the reign of your first wife, she was instrumental in discovering the secret panel in the wainscoting of Marlinspike House. Incidentally, Moriarty's dark shadow was over that case as it has been over so many of my investigations. I needed to survey the Pavilion's auditorium after it emptied this afternoon. Your presence was obvious, but I was certain that Moriarty would be there too, lurking about. What better way to discover him, yet remain undetected myself, than to appear under Alice's frightful wig. And there my old enemy was, his scuffed boot tips protruding clumsily from behind one of those dreadful Persian columns below the balcony. I have not been so near to him since we struggled at Reichenbach, and the very thought of it now makes me shudder with the desire to rid this world of him. It is my one and only purpose!"

A flash of understanding came over me. "It was that which brought you to London! That was the 'job' which you told Alfred Fish that you must accomplish!"

Holmes was no longer at ease. His look was grim, and he ceased puffing at his pipe. "In part, it was," he admitted.

"I heartily hope you accomplish it!" I exclaimed with a rush of feeling. "The man is a devil!"

"He is that," Holmes agreed.

A new thought came upon me. "The cage—that extraordinary trick. How did you manage it?"

A smile of pride effaced the dour look at once. "It is one of my greatest feats. In spite of Escott's denial, it was an illusion you saw, the most important of my career. It involved carefully placed mirrors and lighting and some projections of that marvelous new invention which will revolutionize the world, the cinematograph. I was not certain that it would come off, but with the aid of my limes man and some accomplices backstage, who of course had no idea of my real purpose, it seems to have done its job. It will have set Moriarty afire, and he will become careless; I know him well. Of course I must abandon my apparatus; he will surely destroy it too, and I dare not return to the Pavilion. But there is a third cage, which will contain more than an illusion. When Escott appears again it will be the trap with which he will ensnare and finish Moriarty —and Holmes as well, I am afraid."

"And you as well! But why?"

"My enemy and I must depart together, Watson. It is no mere death which will rid the world of us. No, no, I cannot answer your questions now, for I must leave you presently."

He reached down and stripped off Alice's foul-smelling garment. Beneath it he wore the crisply pressed trousers, tunic, and coat of an army lieutenant. He produced as well a military cap which he placed upon his head. A tiny moustache from his breast pocket completed the transformation.

"Be patient," he adjured. "You shall know the story soon; in fact before the sun sets tomorrow you shall be in full possession of it. I doubt if you will believe it. You may in fact call me mad, for there is madness in this, though it is all on the side of Moriarty." He peered out the window. "Ah, I see that we are approaching my destination. There is not much time. Listen carefully. After I am gone you will be driven to an hotel. Give the cabby two shillings and go in immediately. At the desk you will find a dark slender young man, an Indian—his name is Edalji, but that is no matter. Give the name of Dr. Venables, and in return he will give you a key to room 327. It is a comfortable room suited for travelers; retire to it at once. Supper will be sent up. Do not on any account go out. Sleep well; I shall see you there promptly at eight o'clock tomorrow morning. I assure you that these precautions are necessary. You are now in this thing more deeply than ever before. Moriarty surely suspects you of being one of my agents, as in fact you are. We do not want him to discover you before the dramatically opportune moment."

The carriage slowed to a halt at a dark intersection where decrepit half-timbered buildings leaned precariously toward one another over the narrow way. Holmes opened the door and stepped down upon the mist-shrouded pavement.

"I shall see you in the morning, Watson." He stiffened, clicked his heels, gave a military salute, turned, and was gone.

The carriage moved off again, the rattling of its wheels echoing hollowly against the dank walls.

Presently these narrow lanes opened into streets and then onto a major thoroughfare which I recognized as the Waterloo Road, and shortly after that the carriage drew up in front of the York Hotel not far from Waterloo Railway Station. As Holmes had bade me, I paid the cabman his two shillings and walked directly into the hotel. It was a modest, clean establishment. The young Indian was at the desk.

"I am Dr. Venables," I told him as instructed, and wordlessly, without a flicker of his dark eyes, he dropped a key marked 327 into my palm.

I took the lift to the third floor and let myself into this room;

it contained but one personal article: a man's nightshirt laid out upon the bed. Supper arrived, and I ate it. I left the tray outside the door and locked myself into the room. Before retiring, I sat by the window for at least an hour, staring down at the traffic that bustled to and from the nearby railway terminus and organizing my thoughts, arranging the questions which Sherlock Holmes must answer for me in the morning.

Precisely at eight o'clock there was a knock at my door. I had dressed and was waiting patiently.

"Who is there," I called.

"Holmes," came the answer, softly.

I unlocked the door and opened it, expecting to see my old friend, but was dismayed to find before me a man who, from his bulging carpetbag and awful houndstooth jacket, must be a commercial traveler of the most persistent sort. He grinned at me broadly with every tooth in his head and cocked back his brown bowler with his free hand, which he then thrust almost into my face.

"Jenkins!" he announced with a blare of good fellowship. His roguish black handlebar moustache twitched. "Jenkins, of Escott's Appliances."

"Escott's Appliances!" I exclaimed, and looked closely.

It was Holmes.

"Hurry, Watson," he snapped without losing one tooth of his grin. "Do not keep Mr. Jenkins out in the hall. He may have something valuable for you in his carpetbag, something you cannot do without." And he brushed past me into the room.

"I suppose these disguises are necessary," I said, shutting the door after him, "but I wish that you would warn me."

"When first one practices to deceive, one must go on deceiving, particularly if a man who is as apt at disguise as oneself is one's enemy. I am sorry to have startled you, but it is your turn to play the game at last, and about time, I should think. How is your Italian?"

"My Italian? I do not speak it at all."

"Never mind. I shall be your interpreter, as you once were mine. What do you think of this?"

He had opened his carpetbag upon the bed and withdrew a costume I recognized. It was the black cassock and broad-brimmed hat of the old Italian priest whose identity Holmes had assumed when we had fled from Moriarty twelve years before, a flight which had terminated at Reichenbach.

"You do not mean that I should wear that?" I asked, dismayed.

"Precisely," Holmes affirmed with a smile, "and you must get into it at once, for we are scheduled to catch the 9:05 from Waterloo to Eastbourne."

A quarter of an hour later I did not recognize myself. I stared into the half-length mirror above the dressing table at an aged Italian cleric with side whiskers along his jowls and a hat which effectively covered the hair of John Watson, M.D., beneath. Holmes stood by my side, having just applied the last subtle touches of makeup to give my face a liverish complexion, and smiled with satisfaction upon his handiwork. He placed the ecclesiastic's beads in one of my hands and a well-worn breviary in the other.

"You look rather uncomfortable in your role, my dear Watson, but let us assume that this priest is dyspeptic. You will do nicely, I think. Now listen carefully again. I shall leave you now. In five minutes' time, take the black satchel which I have removed from my carpetbag and placed by your door, leave your key at the desk, and walk out upon the Waterloo Road. Do not take a hansom, for the station is but two blocks away. When you reach it, go directly to platform three, from which the Eastbourne train leaves in forty minutes. Here is your ticket; it is for a reserved carriage and the number upon its side will tell you which one. You will have but one traveling companion, the unpleasantly effusive Mr. Jenkins of Escott's Appliances, and he will join you shortly. My dear fellow, you do look splendid, and soon, as is proper, I shall confess all to you. Now I must go."

He grabbed up a pillow from the bed, thrust it into his depleted bag to puff it up again, and marched out the door.

Again I followed his instructions; again there was not a hitch.

Upon the thoroughfare I found the air cold and crisp, but the mists of the night before were gone and a feeble but heartening sunlight played upon the activity of the street. I passed numerous restaurants and private hotels on my two-block journey. Once in the terminus, with its green and buff distempered wood walls and vast arched roof held up by cast-iron supports, I made my way through the throngs, passed the station bars and bookstalls and waiting rooms which never closed, and arrived at platform three. By this time I had become, if not pious, at least used to my ecclesiastical costume.

The train was waiting on its track. A porter in black serge trousers and bottle-green waistcoat tipped his cap to me and asked if he might be of assistance. I did not know how to react. I decided, if I were Italian and presumably unfamiliar with the English tongue, that I must not speak it at all. I waved my ticket at him and uttered some gibberish; he led me to the proper carriage and helped me aboard. Shortly, Jenkins of Escott's Appliances joined me with a wink, and soon after that the engineer opened a valve to clear the boiler, and every sound in the station was blotted out in a rush of escaping steam. Then there was a tiny jolt of movement, and at exactly 9:05 the train pulled away.

Five minutes later we were rolling swiftly south, out of the environs of London.

"Now," said I to Holmes, taking off the cleric's hat and placing it on the seat beside me, "about Mycroft Holmes: there never was such a person?"

"You are to the point this morning, Watson. Well, I do not blame you. Perhaps you ought first to know that I am fairly certain none of Moriarty's agents, who are watching every railway line, detected you beneath your cassock nor me behind Jenkins' toothy smile." He too removed his hat, Jenkins' awful brown bowler. He produced his pipe from the carpetbag and proceeded to fill it with tobacco. "No, there never was a Mycroft Holmes."

"And you hired Alfred Fish to impersonate this wholly fictitious person of your invention?"

"I did."

"Why?"

"To protect my secret, to give myself the origins which you so obviously wondered about to the extent of putting your idle questions into print. My public knew me through you, and they believed what the honest Dr. John Watson wrote. If you told them that I had a brother, that you had even met him, then they were bound to believe you."

"Wiggins suggested that that was your reason. So it was just a screen?"

"A necessary one, I felt."

"But what a chance you took. Couldn't you have invented a nondescript brother instead of that fantastic creature Mycroft Holmes? You even told me that he was at times the pivotal figure in British government!"

Holmes lit a match and puffed his pipe into a glow. "Bold strokes! Bold strokes! The finest deception is the most outrageous. I wanted Mycroft to be powerfully believable, so I made him larger than life, and eccentric. An Englishman is always convinced by eccentricity, for it is a way of life with so many of his fellow countrymen. Of course I made sure that my brother was so lazy and retiring, however brilliant, and his job so specialized, that it would seem perfectly logical for you, indeed anyone, never to have seen or heard of him before. The Diogenes Club was ready-made for him, and my old stage acquaintance, Alfred Fish, was ready-made for Mycroft's embodiment. Together we worked up a background, complete with forged papers and references which I had no trouble obtaining, and he was admitted to the club by September of '88 in time for the curtain to go up on our little show. I fancy it was a most daring and meticulously devised red herring."

Holmes did not repress his satisfaction at this.

"Did this secret you were hiding have anything to do with the job you had set for yourself, the destruction of Moriarty?"

"Moriarty is inseparable from my secret; in a way he is the cause of it. It is the secret of that so-called foreign land from which Alfred Fish surmised I had come to England, the secret of my origins, which you shall hear soon enough. In fact it is Moriarty's secret as well. I set myself the task of finishing him because it became clear to me soon after he and I had parted that he would be a curse upon this earth, that he must be stopped at all costs, and that I was the only man to do it, the only man equal to his machinations. So evil is he, Watson, and so mad, that his goal is none other than the subjugation of every human soul and, failing that, the destruction of civilization, beginning with the Western governments, including the United States. Mark my words, there will be a great war involving both hemispheres, a worldwide war, in fact, if Moriarty is not stopped. He is even now sowing mistrust and ill will among the nations of Europe and hopes within a decade to bring his foul scheme to bloody fruition."

I could not believe it. I could not believe that one man, however powerful and ill-intentioned, was capable of toppling a single nation, much less the glorious edifice of Western civilization with mighty England at its head. It was true that Edward and the Kaiser, though uncle and nephew, were not on the best of terms, but Lord Lansdowne and Mr. Chamberlain would smooth those troubled waters. Despite the hints, first from Gregson and Lestrade, then Athelney Jones, that the international balance of power was precarious, and despite my usual trust in Holmes' judgment, I objected. After all, he was not speaking of a backstreet stabbing, nor the theft of a crowned head's private correspondence. These were complex matters of state.

"It is nonsense, Holmes," said I. "How could anyone know such things? How could anyone know that there was going to be a great war among the European nations, and America too? Why, she is three thousand miles away! It is ridiculous. You have gone too far if you wish to convince me that you have deduced the inevitability of such an event by your methods."

"I have not deduced it, Watson; I know, if I fail, that it will occur. Make no mistake, there's an east wind coming, such a wind as never blew on England. It will be cold and bitter, and a good many of us may wither before its blast. Yet I hope it is not inevitable; that is what I count upon. The raising of such a gale is Moriarty's aim, but it may not be too late to blunt the edge of the storm."

I did not wish to argue this question further. I wished only to get to the heart of the matter. "Your secret: you have promised me that, and I think you owe it to me at once. I have trusted you in the past and will believe what you tell me."

"You do not believe that there will be a great war."

"Well, but that is different. How can one know such a thing positively, and that it will occur ten years from now?"

"I can know it because I am who I am. I am sorry, my old friend, if I doubt that you will believe me, but it will require a great leap of the imagination to follow where I am about to lead. There is only one man I know who has made such a leap, and his excursion is accepted by the world only because it is considered fantastical entertainment, not to be taken seriously."

"Why, who is that?" I asked.

Holmes regarded me steadily. "Mr. H. G. Wells, in *The Time Machine,*" he said.

18

OUR ENGINE HOOTED as we rounded a gentle curve. We were now approaching the South Downs; a stop at East Grinstead was just ahead. I was silent as our train pulled into the station. I did not know what in the world to make of Holmes' last statement, but I began to have premonitions that he was correct when he said that I would find it hard to believe him. What was he about to tell me? I had followed Mr. Wells' story when it had been serialized with some notoriety in *The New Review* in 1895, but had not found it to my taste. Besides being based on an absurd and unscientific premise, it was unedifying and depressing.

"I wonder if you would mind," Holmes said as the train started up once more, "my being silent for a while. It may be the last time I shall see this countryside which I have come to love, this land of farms and cottages and rolling hills, and I should like to contemplate it quietly."

In our few moments together before the train had pulled out of Waterloo Station I had asked him our destination. He had explained, "We shall be safest outside of London. I insist that you spend the day with me at my little farm on the Sussex

Downs, the farm to which I truly planned to retire before it became absolutely clear that my old enemy had returned. We shall walk along the coast, gaze out upon the Channel; perhaps on this fine day France will be visible. We can talk at leisure. I will show you my beehives." Therefore I was certain of plenty of time in which to question him, and I readily assented to his request, particularly as I sensed a new and different note in his voice, one of nostalgia for what was slipping away, and something else as well: a hint of tiredness, as if the exhaustion of his duel with Moriarty, perhaps the exhaustion of his life-long battle against wrongdoing, was catching up with him at last.

And so I watched his face for a time as our train rolled toward the south coast. It was a pale, thoughtful face, drawn and a little sad, and my heart went out to him. In those moments I forgot all my anger at his deceptions. Wiggins surely had been right; he had had good reason for all of them and had meant no harm to his friends.

Our train halted at Polegate. At this stop Holmes emerged from his pensive mood to become again the alert man of action. "And now, out of your prelate's robes," he urged. "Be quick about it! We shall disembark soon at Willingdon."

I struggled the cassock off over my head; my own clothing, somewhat rumpled, was underneath. Holmes handed me a handsome beaver hat from his carpetbag and stuffed the rolled-up priest's garment into the bag in its place. He exchanged his own loud coat for a muted tweed from the same miraculous haberdashery. Without Jenkins' obtrusive grin he looked most respectable.

"You are not exactly dressed for the country in your evening finery," he observed, "but you will simply be mistaken for a local squire. It is not a bad thing to be taken for. By the way, in case of questions I am Mr. Worthing and you shall be my friend, Squire Sacker—what do you say to that?"

I said nothing, for at that moment the whistle sounded for Willingdon. The train pulled into the rural station, and we got out. Holmes led the way to a nearby livery stable, in back of which a small but comfortable trap was billeted. After a wave and a hearty "Hallo!" to the smith, Holmes jumped up into the trap, and I followed him.

"Morning, Mr. Worthing. Off to Birling Farm?" asked the smith, who was leading a cart horse across the muddy yard to be shoed.

"I am, thank you, Mr. Franklin," Holmes replied. "Splendid day!"

With a cry of "Away, Victoria," to his mare, he flicked the reins, and we were off down a narrow dirt road.

"It is but half an hour to my country home," Holmes told me.

We were heading west in the direction of the Seven Sisters cliffs; directly south was Beachy Head. I was content to sit quietly and take in the countryside, as was Holmes. This was the heart of the rolling chalk downs upon whose springy turf it was a joy to stroll. The undulating hills, green and damp, were about us. Along one side of the road meandered a hedge-row of hawthorn and wild rose, on the other was a low stone fence. Here and there the little red and gray roofs of farm-steadings appeared and disappeared from view in a leisurely manner, and smoke trailed up from their chimneys. The sky remained clear; it was crisply cold, but the winter sunlight warmed my cheeks while my breath was a faint white cloud. The sharp smell of laurel was in the air.

Soon we came to a fork in the road. The main branch, ac-cording to a wooden marker, led to Fulworth, farther west. Holmes took the south turning.

"Fulworth is an old-fashioned hamlet in a hollow of the bay toward which we are now traveling," he explained. "It is the nearest town to my villa and is pleasantly rustic. It is rather isolated and keeps to itself, quite what is wanted."

At last, through a cutting between two hills, I glimpsed the sea perhaps a mile distant, and the tang of salt air reached my nostrils. At this point, Holmes turned the trap right, onto a narrow lane, a signpost at the entrance to which announced Birling Farm. We proceeded about five hundred yards down a gentle slope into a sheltered dell and drew up before a large, inauspicious-looking house with a gravel walk and wide bay windows set on either side of its heavy wooden door. It was two-storied, with what appeared to be a garrett in the sloping slate roof above. It was whitewashed, but the weather had begun to send streaks of brownish color down its walls from the eaves.

"Welcome to Mr. Worthing's estate, Watson," Holmes said, jumping down from the trap. He stood with his hands on his hips, surveying the house with the proud but critical eye of the proprietor. "It wants work which, alas, I shall not have the pleasure of putting into it. It was my dream to retire here. There on that slope, sheltered from the sea breezes, are the hives. In the spring the hills are lush with white clover. England is a beautiful country; she makes one feel at home."

He unlocked the solid front door, and we went inside. It was not cheerful. The parlor was low-ceilinged, and there was little furniture—a couple of rickety chairs and an old table with a spotted oilcloth upon it. The dank smell of disuse hung in the air, and it was chilly and dark.

"You see, Watson, I had not even begun to move in, but there is a little food in the larder which we can eat later." He arranged some kindling and logs in the wood-burning stove and struck a match on the grate. "There is not much to see— the other rooms are bare—and it will be unpleasantly cold until the fire heats the parlor. I am ready for conversation now. Let us walk upon the cliffs."

We took a path toward the sea. A heavy layer of leaves prevented the way from being too muddy. The bare branches of beech and chestnut trees raised themselves over our heads; on the hills oaks and hawthorn bushes grew together in slate-green clusters. This vegetation gave way to a broad sweep of gorse which stretched off toward the chalk cliffs and the sea.

The path reached a point at which I and my friend could walk side by side. Holmes did not wait for me to reopen the subject. "My origins, Watson: where did I come from, who were my people? That is what you wish to know. Well, I wish to tell you so that one person on this earth beside Moriarty will know. That person ought by every right to be you, and so it shall. There was no Mycroft Holmes, no grandmother related to Vernet; there were no country squires in my background, and young Dr. Verner who bought your practice in 1894 was not my distant relation; there is no Alice nor Jenkins nor Escott nor Mr. Worthing. In fact, there is no Sherlock Holmes, and never has been. He does not exist. My life has been a series of disguises, the most visible and meticulously fashioned of which has been the great and amazing detective, the man who was and still is your friend, and will be while he breathes the air of England. I hope you understand that every subterfuge was necessary to me and had no purpose of harming any soul."

"I do believe that," I affirmed.

"Well, then, I come from far away, not distant in space, for I was born an Englishman, but distant in time. I come from a world fantastically changed from this one, not altogether for the better. In fact, my dear Watson, I shall not be born for three hundred years."

We walked in silence for what must have been several moments. A brisk wind blew up from the cliff edge, which we had neared, moving the grass in great waves. The Channel to our left was a rippling blue gray sheet beneath the clear winter sky. The cry of sea birds pierced the silence at intervals. I became aware that something was wrong, that a force was pressing on either temple, causing my head to ring, and that my breath was short. "Holmes, I must sit down," I said weakly.

"My dear fellow!"

He took my elbow. There was a thorn stump nearby, and I settled myself on that. I realized that I was perspiring heavily. Holmes loosened my collar. I looked into his face; I searched his eyes. I could find no denial of what he had said; I saw that he meant it and believed it. And in that instant I half believed it too. It was that, the shock of this extraordinary knowledge, that had overloaded my poor brain. A flood of evidence was pouring into it, battering against my unwillingness even to consider the idea of travel through time, with which I was perfectly familiar from the H. G. Wells story. I was forced to admit that all the evidence fit, all the scattered fragments which I had been unable to reconcile fell together: the mysterious youth, the lack of connections, the deliberate isolation, the reticence concerning all things personal, the willingness always to give credit to the police for crimes which he alone had solved, so that he would not be harassed with questions, and most of all his fantastic skills and his extraordinary knowledge which he had brought with him—I hardly dared think it —from the future! That he had come from there was a secret which could indeed cause a man to invent a brother, in fact to invent himself.

Holmes stood before me, a look of deep concern for my well-being upon his features. At his back was the sea. I struggled to gather my thoughts, to remember all the questions which I had intended to ask him. The sea breeze blew in my eyes; my vision which had been red and blurred suddenly became preternaturally sharp. I stared beyond Holmes out toward the horizon where, faintly, the shape of the continental coastline could be discerned. Upon the broad expanse of water, figured with a wash of small whitecaps raised by the wind, a sailing dinghy with the name *Seamew* on its bow crossed my vision. A boy in a white public school sweater was at the tiller, staring intently at the horizon. I saw, or imagined I saw, an abstracted half smile upon his lips, the smile of the young dreamer. I thought of the youthful Holmes who had joined Alfred Fish's theatrical troupe in Camford, seemingly by chance.

"Then who are you?" I managed at last. My voice was hoarse.

"I will tell you, but I shall not do it by means of a name, for it is too late for that. My given name does not matter; in this world I am Sherlock Holmes and shall remain so until I leave it soon. Do you feel well enough to walk on? I am certain it has been a great shock to you."

"It has indeed. I want to trust you, Holmes." I rose with his help, and we proceeded along the cliff edge. I began to feel myself again. "Is it really so, then?"

"It is really so."

I came to a conclusion. "I believe you, then. But you said Moriarty also shared your secret. Is not that dangerous?"

"He has always known it, for it is his secret as well. He too is from the future."

At these words, the night in the laboratory flooded back into my memory. In a flash I saw Moriarty's leering face, and behind him the silvery cage. I saw his incredulity and frenzy at finding it there, heard him say that he had seen it before, boast that Holmes would never get him into it again.

"The cage!" I exclaimed. I halted and faced Holmes, gripped his sleeve. "It is the time machine!"

He nodded. "My deductive methods have not been lost upon you, Watson. You are quite correct."

"And it brought Moriarty here as well?"

"It did."

"And your laboratory was for the purpose of rebuilding or recharging the machine!"

"Excellent!"

Holmes laughed, and I was glad to hear his laughter. The tension within me snapped. For the first time I realized that the mystery was solved, however fantastic its solution, and that if I did not have all of the answers yet, I had found the man I had searched for, and he would give them to me in good time. We were together again, Holmes and I; that was the greatest relief.

I laughed as well, the sound rising in my throat to become a joyful cry.

Holmes was somewhat taken aback. "I expected anything but this of you, Watson, though I am glad to hear it. It proves that the great Sherlock Holmes is not infallible. You have occasionally surprised me in the past, and I am happy to find that you are still capable of doing so. The surprises, then, will not be all on one side."

We walked along farther. We passed a slippery path descending to a shingle beach below the chalk cliffs. Here and there were curves and hollows which must have made splendid swimming places in the summer months. This admirable beach extended for some miles in either direction, save where the little cove and village of Fulworth broke the line ahead.

"I will tell you my story now," Holmes said. "It will explain my arrival in your time, an event planned deliberately by Moriarty. It will explain why it was necessary to rebuild the apparatus which brought my enemy and me here together. It will explain my aptness at disguise, a skill shared equally by him. And it will also explain why I am the only man capable of dealing with him and why I have decided to do so by carrying him away with me in one of the rebuilt machines, the third cage which I mentioned to you—an event I arranged after I left you last night and which will take place tomorrow evening, with your help."

"You return to your own time tomorrow?"

"Yes, my old friend, I must. The trap is set, the last contingency eliminated. I have not much more than twenty-four hours left in your world. I am content only in this: that I can spend them with you."

He was silent for a moment and then began his story.

"It is not easy for me to describe the world from which I came, for two reasons. One reason is that it is vastly different from yours and to make it comprehensible would take more time than we have; it would take years and volumes of words, and even then that distant world might seem incredible. The other reason is that I have been gone from it for a quarter of a century. This is now my world, this England, this green and fertile land which still is not spoiled—though she is beginning to be ruined by the ignorance and greed which make men blind to why she is worth taking care of." He looked with passionate regret upon the vista before us. "There is not such a coastline as this, nor such a sky, nor such a meadow in my world!

"And yet there are wonders. For men of imagination, mine is a fascinating time. Can you imagine, Watson, that I have walked upon the moon?"

I stopped and stared at him in disbelief, but he took my arm and led me on. The gorse bushes crackled against our legs.

"You must be warned, old friend, that there are even more fantastic assertions to come. I said that you might call me mad; I would understand if you did so at any moment. It must be hard for a man reared under Victoria's scepter to conceive of what I describe, and yet, Watson, I believe you will come to it, for it is logical; elementary, I might say. Think of the past century of progress; think of the wonders it has seen: the transatlantic telegraph, the telephone, moving pictures, the electrification of London, the railway lines which cross the world, the motorcar which frightens the horses on our country lanes but which they will be forced to watch pass them by from their pastures. Do you think mankind will stop at these feats? No. Soon men will fly in powered aircraft, faster and ever faster, and, not content with that, will invent rocket ships and fly to the moon. They have already imagined it; it is prefigured in Jules Verne's *From the Earth to the Moon.* What man can imagine, man can do, Watson. He will fly even to the planets; he will find a way to reach the stars.

"I see that you still doubt, but here is something that you will understand: empire! You served the British Empire in India and Afghanistan. Imagine an empire whose mother country is the whole planet Earth and whose colonies are the planets of this solar system and their moons, and then the planets of the nearer stars. In those terms, is it so inconceivable?"

"I can imagine it, Holmes," I said after a silence. "It is believing it which is difficult."

Holmes laughed again. "Good, Watson!" He patted my back. "You are halfway there."

He went on: "Alas, I cannot paint a picture of continuous progress. Man will conquer space and time; he will conquer diseases and many forms of misery which plague him now. But if he can do these things he can also invent new weapons and new torments—and he shall, for he will never conquer his own nature, that paradoxical duality which gives him the capacity for producing both good and evil. I have a special insight into this duality, Watson, for I have been witness over the years to a strange form of it. It is that about which I shall tell you now.

"In that future world I was—can you guess it?—an actor, a man who becomes in a sense other men. You and Alfred Fish and Wiggins, and others I am sure, wondered where my performing skills and my knowledge, outstripping that of even your seasoned veterans, came from. Now you have the answer; but not completely, for you must understand what being an actor meant in those future days. It was not a profession one fell into by chance, as did Wiggins. Early in life a child's predilections were carefully charted and the proper course for his life set out for him—that is, the course on which it was decided his natural abilities and interests would make him most successful and happy. I know it is a strange concept for a man of this age, and there is much about it that I question after being here for so many years, but it is nevertheless the way things were done in my world. And so, before the age of five, I was destined to become an actor.

"Now let me tell you what that meant. I was entered at a tender age upon a course of study intended to turn me body and soul into a performer. It was a highly specialized course of study; in the future, specialization is a form of survival. Before I tell you what I learned, however, let us look more deeply into the future. Today you have the opera in Covent Garden; you may choose from Madame Neruda at St. James's Hall or Marie Lloyd and Little Tich at the Oxford; you can watch Beerbohm Tree thunder at Her Majesty's or Wiggins prance at the Gaiety. But in not twenty years these live entertainments will begin to atrophy because of the cinematograph, and then they will fade still more because of Mr. Edison's gramophone, which will bring the sounds of an orchestra into your sitting room whenever you desire them. More inventions will follow. People will become bored by the old entertainments; the jaded audience will ceaselessly demand new experiences, new sensations. They will need performers who are more and more extraordinarily gifted and highly trained to rouse them. The situation will fluctuate over the next three centuries; at times people will be pleased to revive the old styles. In any case, actors will have to be remarkably versatile to make good. I was remarkable, Watson; in fact, I was one of the great performers of my era, for reasons which I will make clear. I think you would call me a genius in my craft—but so was Moriarty.

"From the age of five, I studied all the modes, old and new. I learned to rhythm the iambic pentameters of Shakespeare and the elegant alexandrines of Racine; I learned the trage-dian's art and the clown's; I studied the deliberate and sym-bolic art of the Noh; I manipulated the puppets of Bunraku; I wore the golden mask of Oedipus; I mastered the telling of fables for children and the spinning of intrigues for older minds. I became a spellbinder. Too, I learned to dance and to tumble and to play, among other instruments, the violin. You have written that in my moods I scraped my bow at random across the strings of my Stradivarius; that was the music of the future you were privileged to hear, old friend, the few notes of my time I allowed deliberately to sound in your age. I learned the disciplines of the body: the martial arts of Japan, the meditative arts of India, and other skills which three hun-dred years had developed. I studied the playwright's art as well. In short, I became, as I had to become, the complete performer. I could tame a lion or play Hamlet equally well; I could walk on fire, charm a snake, duel with the devil as Mr. Shaw's superman, execute an exquisite entrechat, wrestle a bully to the ground, raise a laugh from twenty thousand throats.

"So, too, could Moriarty. Even then he was my enemy!"

19

H O L M E S and I stood on a high bluff; the village of
Fulworth lay below, a straggling and picturesque collection of
houses about a main street leading to a wharf where fishing
boats bobbed on the rising tide. Upon the horizon a mist had
formed, obscuring our view of the continent. The Channel's
whitecaps had altered into long swells rolling in toward the
coast.

We turned back in the direction of Birling Farm.

"You are now at the heart of the matter," I said to my friend,
"Moriarty. Much as the cage puzzled me, Moriarty's resemblance to you baffled me more. You said that you had known
him from your youth. I supposed that you must be related, that
you were brothers, identical twins even. I asked Moriarty
about that, but he denied it. I remember his words clearly:
'Closer than any two beings,' he said. What did he mean?"

A pained expression crossed Holmes' face.

"You had a father, did you not?" he asked after twenty paces
of suspenseful silence.

I did not understand this change of subject. "Of course."

"And a mother?"

"A dear woman. Alas, my parents both died before I went to India, though they lived long enough to see to my education. I have neither kith nor kin in England, save my wife, Violet—but you know all that. What have my parents to do with the matter?"

"Your mother was a dear woman, you say? I believe you, Watson. Neither you nor I are given to reminiscence. I am sorry to have heard so little of her over the years. I wish that I had the tenderness of such a woman in my past to soften my memory and strengthen my heart."

"You are an orphan, then! I wondered that you never spoke of relations."

"I am an orphan of the human race, as is Moriarty. We are, alike, orphans."

"What do you mean?"

"I mean that I never had a mother, that I never had parents at all, nor did Moriarty."

I grew annoyed. Was Holmes toying with me again? Yet his look, staring away over the surging Channel waters, remained deeply serious. "But that is impossible! You were born, of course. I am certain that your mother must have loved you, and there were people who cared for you in her stead."

"I grew, but I was not born in the sense that you mean. The same is true of Moriarty and others like us." Holmes stopped me with a hand upon my arm. "You are amazed, old friend, that he and I look so much alike. I tell you, it goes deeper than appearance. We have the same bones, the same organs, the same tissues . . ."

"You are the same man!" I exclaimed, thinking that the theory of a divided personality, which I had expressed to Wiggins, was confirmed. I stepped away from Holmes in confusion. At any moment would he begin to hunch over, to leer and hiss and threaten?

Holmes smiled reassuringly, and I felt my panic ebb. "Moriarty and I are not the same man, Watson; we have separate bodies. I only mean that physically, at least, they are alike." He strolled on, and I kept by his side. "I have attempted to suggest the wonders which the future will bring. I do not lie when I tell you that I have walked upon the moon and upon the surfaces of planets other than our Earth. It is not a lie that I arrived in your England from three centuries in the future. I ask you to believe these things, and more; I ask you to believe that Professor James Moriarty is my exact duplicate. We were not born, Watson; we were, to borrow a term from a book not yet written, *decanted.*"

I experienced a great rush of anger. "Holmes, I am a medical man; you cannot fool me! I will believe your time-travel story; that is logical. But that you were not born of man and woman—it is too much to ask! Decanted? Poured from a flask? Will you tell me next that you were conceived in a watch glass and weaned in a beaker?"

Holmes began to laugh. "Watson, you are a wonder! Excuse me, but the aptness of your expression is better than you know."

I ignored his mirth. "And Moriarty is your exact physical duplicate? You cannot make me believe it."

To our left was a ridge of low hills. Beyond them, sheltered from the coastal winds by their rise, were the meadows with the beehives which Holmes had indicated when we had arrived at Birling Farm. He pointed in their direction. "I did not become an apiarist for no reason." he said.

That he could bring up his hobby at a time like this! "Your bees! Your bees! I do not wish to discuss your bees, Holmes. You must settle this preposterous assertion about yourself and Moriarty at once! You owe me that, and you shall not escape it."

"The bees are apropos, Watson; they illustrate the truth. Did you know that there are only three kinds of bees within a hive? A single queen, a few hundred drones, and many thousands of workers. The drones are all alike, indistinguishable; so too are the workers. Each drone and worker is a duplicate of the fellows in its class."

"Yes, but those are bees. We are speaking of human beings."

"I am speaking of life, and all life forms have something in common: they are made up of cells, and within each cell of each being is the genetic pattern of the whole being, be it animal or plant—or Sherlock Holmes."

"Genetic pattern?"

"The science of genetics is only beginning to be invented, but you know of the work of Mendel and others on inherited characteristics and of animal breeding according to desired traits. Imagine Mendel's investigations refined; imagine instruments which can examine and chart the mysteries of life's reproduction."

My anger had fled; I felt only a deep apprehension. "It frightens me, Holmes. What would men do with such knowledge?"

My friend halted again and turned to gaze at me. He spread his arms. "I am the answer to that," he said simply.

The wind from the sea caught his coat and flapped it about his lean body. I frowned, I stared. His face told me that it was true. "You are some form of man-made life, then?" I asked. I felt the same ringing in my ears, the same appalled but half-believing wonder which had followed Holmes' assertion that he had traveled backward through time, but the intensity of my feeling did not defeat me now. I was determined to stand up to anything.

"There is no such thing as man-made life, even in my world," Holmes said. "But the future is capable of duplicating from identical cells human beings with certain desirable characteristics. I am sure that as a medical man you would be fascinated with the process, however you might question its uses, but there is no time to explain it now. Suffice it to say that the first experiments with the growing of animal life forms from cells, without benefit of sexual reproduction, will begin in less than half a century. Human sexual reproduction exists in my world, but alongside it there are beings such as Moriarty and myself, drawn from a carefully bred selection of cells, beings with certain potentialities. I told you that I was destined from a young age to become a performer; in fact that was my destiny before I was 'born.'"

I was appalled. "But the breeding of human beings, Holmes!"

"Do not you English speak of 'breeding' in your upper classes?"

I did not respond for a moment. I saw the aptness of his point. "You claim that you and Moriarty are physiologically alike, that you have the same mental capabilities because you somehow grew, or were grown, from identical cells?"

"I claim it; it is true," he said with a clear-ringing certitude that shattered my disbelief.

An idea struck me. "Then you were not necessarily the only two duplicates. In the future, there are others like you?"

"My physical duplicates exist, yes."

The thought of multiple Sherlock Holmeses staggered me. The thought that there might be more creatures like Moriarty was even more staggering. I asked Holmes about this at once.

"There is only one Moriarty," he assured me.

As we walked on, I tried to take it all in. At last my thoughts grew well ordered enough to frame two questions: "If you grew from identical cells, why is Moriarty's personality so different from yours, and why are you here in Edward's England?"

"We are here because Moriarty wanted a world to conquer, a primitive world—you will forgive the designation, Watson—yet one civilized enough to afford the luxuries on which he thrives. The difference in our personalities is harder to explain. It seems to go deeper than mere upbringing, for we were raised alike. I believe that Moriarty must have been damaged in some way in his growth, not so as to affect his mental capacities—he is brilliant—but in a way that perverted all his finer tendencies. He is a fiendishly clever monomaniac who can conceive of nothing worthier than the satisfaction of his basest needs. You will recall my ruminations on good and evil during our last evening together at Baker Street. I said that I believed there was no such thing as a completely evil personality, but Moriarty comes as close to one as I can imagine. In my weak moments I pity him, Watson; but he must be stopped. I alone am responsible for doing that."

"But why?"

"I cannot help it, for he is me. Within him are my potentialities, as his are in me. He is my mirror image; I cannot escape it. In him I see my dark side; that must be obliterated. And then, as I told you, I knew him in my youth."

"You were raised together?"

"We were."

Holmes' expression altered. No longer did he gaze out upon the Channel. His eyes were directed ahead, along the meandering path skirting the cliff edge, but I could see that he took in not a single tussock or gorse bush. Instead he looked three hundred years into the future, paradoxically into his past.

"Moriarty and I and others like us were brought up together in an England vastly changed from this one, in a white, clean place which was intended to create happy children who would be satisfied with the futures which were planned for them. We were experiments of a sort and, as you have surmised, there were many like us. As well as superior perception and intelligence, we had from the start a cleverness at mimicry and a desire to show off—a histrionic sense, I might call it. There were other groups as well, with different physical and intellectual potentialities, gifted in science or mathematics or teaching. There were submissive groups, too, whose members hated decision and were inclined only to obey."

These last reminded me of the worker bees, and I objected. "But it is appalling, Holmes!"

"So I see it now, but I did not judge then. The groups intermingled and played together while young. Though members of the same group looked alike, subtle personality differences naturally appeared and, being perceptive, we distinguished among ourselves. It was my earliest training in closely observing human differences, and it has stood me in good stead in my detective career. These small differences, which later diverged considerably, showed up in our ways of holding ourselves, of gesturing, of speaking. Personality changes appearance as well as behavior; Moriarty is vivid proof of that.

"From the beginning, the predilections of the groups were obvious. My kind mimicked the others, was flamboyant, seized the spotlight whenever possible, was highly competitive and jealous of attention. I am certain that we were the most obnoxious children who ever lived! I remember Moriarty clearly. Even as a boy he stood out from the rest of my group. He was as skilled a pupil as any of us, but his need for attention seemed stronger, his desire to be center-stage greater, his jealousies more numerous and deeply felt, and his need to control more intense."

"He was a little tyrant, you mean."

"Yes, Watson, he was that, though the traits showed only gradually. He was a person of great self-control and hid his disappointments behind that soft insinuating manner which you have observed, but under this sly exterior his brain seethed with hatred. I believe his self-centered perversity hampered his growth as an actor. Whereas I learned with relative ease, taking joy in my accomplishments, Moriarty had constantly to struggle with his burden of ill will. He kept up with me, but what a price he must have paid! It was that which made him hate me."

"Now I understand why the creature has pledged to destroy you," I said. "I know where your acting skills came from and why you and Moriarty look alike, yet are so different. You said he traveled to this time in search of a world to conquer. But why are you here? Did you come to this age to save it from him?"

"If I could claim that, I would be proud indeed. No, it was Moriarty who brought me to your time."

"But you are the one man who can thwart his schemes!"

"His mind works in strange ways, Watson. He brought me here to challenge and prove his powers. A brief digression will make his warped reasoning clear to you. I have told you that my studies made me a master performer. By the time I was twenty-five I was a phenomenon. My name was known on more worlds than this earth. As I have suggested, there were many forms of electronic entertainment of spectacular, sometimes peculiar, kinds which it would take too much time to describe, but the art of the live performer had kept pace with new techniques and had developed its own kind of spectacle. Actors remained as fascinating to the public as people of the theatre have always been, and throngs flocked to great arenas to see their favorites. I was young and flushed with success. Night after night I stepped before those vast roaring audiences and took them in my hand, tamed them, moved them, made them laugh, cry, gasp in astonishment, call my name. I was a wonder, and the public loved me.

"Moriarty too was a wonder, but it was by a kind of force of will. He glittered, he was spectacular, but he was not loved, and he was not at ease. He saw me as his rival, but he had in mind a different sort of arena for our conflict. He knew that his power was limited in our time but that in a past age he, with his skills at deception and his knowledge of future science and organization, might make himself a king and thus satisfy his overweening need to be the best performer, indeed the determiner of the world's destiny. Too, I believe he had in mind a kind of revenge against his era for whatever slights his mad brain had conceived it had given him; by going into the past he hoped to change the future in some dire way. It was all part of his scheme.

"But there was a hitch: if he disappeared, he would leave me free; me, who symbolized all that he hated, a kind of careless skill and ease which he could not subjugate. His ego would not allow that. And so he laid a plot to entrap me and, by force, to bring me with him into your era, which had been carefully chosen by him. He tricked me into submission, bound me, haughtily laid his plan before me. Then, by means of an illegally obtained time mechanism, very like the cages which I have managed to reproduce, he transported us here. Our beings were disintegrated into their essential particles, shot through the twisted fabric of time, and reassembled on a lush green hill on a summer day in 1878, not five miles from Camford."

Holmes ceased speaking for a moment. He looked again out

toward the rolling swells of the Channel. We had stopped on
the rise of the bluff before turning down to Birling Farm. The
wind whistled about us, blowing our coats. In the distance a
horse whinnied. A jackdaw upon the stone fence cawed rau-
cously, then flapped off toward the east. The small dinghy was
no longer in sight; I hoped that the boy's boat bobbed against
the Fulworth pier and that he was safely before his home fire.
It was nearly three o'clock, and the sky was rampant with
lowering black clouds, boding rain. The air was thick with the
impending storm.

"And my age, this England, was where you were to play out
your drama?" I asked.

"Exactly, Watson." Holmes took my arm and led me back
toward the farmhouse. "Moriarty is really quite mad. 'And
now we shall see who is top dog, who will rule the world!' he
snarled, as if that mattered to me. Yet it is the only thing he
can see and, by bringing me here, he has forced me to make
it my business out of necessity, because I have had to stand up
to him. I am the only man aware of who he really is and what
damage he can wreak. His madness has the touch of genius."

"And so he tests himself against you?"

"If he can finish me, he will have proved to himself his
superiority. After that, the attainment of his final goal is inevitable, for your world cannot hold out against him. Now you see
the full seriousness of the matter, Watson, and you know why
I have dedicated myself to combating crime and advancing
methods of detection whenever and wherever I could, also
why I have not confined my efforts to England's shores.

"I cannot forget that first golden afternoon upon your English meadows. The numbing shock of the time transmission
wore off; Moriarty released me from the bonds with which he
had held me. We stood, stared at blue sky, smelled a warm,
scent-laden breeze, heard the twitter of birds we had never
seen before upon such a beautiful hill. I was spellbound by the
glory of my surroundings; Moriarty saw them otherwise, as a
world to be exploited. 'A different England, pristine and ripe!'
he crowed triumphantly. 'We shall see what to make of it. I

will go my way for now, and you yours. Time enough for our
meeting later; it is inevitable. We cannot divide this world;
one of us must have it all!' He turned and walked away from
me. The last I saw of him until years later, when he had formed
his diabolical organization and his shadow began to fall across
my investigations, was his body—my body!—horribly distorted by hatred and egoism, lurching away down a country
road, disfiguring the landscape by its passage."

I knew the rest. Holmes had joined Alfred Fish's repertoire
company in Camford only days after arriving in this time
because it afforded the kind of work he knew best.

"I watched and learned from the actors," Holmes explained,
"changed my accent and manners, became a young Victorian
gentleman. When I had learned my part, I made for London,
but not specifically to get in Moriarty's way. I did not know
then what had become of him, though I feared what he might
do. No, when I told Alfred Fish I had a job to perform, I meant
only that I had decided to dedicate myself to combating deviltry wherever it might arise, as a kind of preparation for what
Moriarty would do. Too, I did not wish to continue acting on
the stage. I realized that within me was the capacity to become another Moriarty, and I had experienced quite enough
of the egotistic exhilaration which my ability to sway an audience gave me. So I decided to use my acting skills as a criminal
investigator, the first quality of which is to be able to see
through a disguise. I was well trained for that. In addition I
brought to my new profession my zeal, my intelligence, and
of course my layman's understanding of scientific police procedure from the future, which I adapted to your age.

"I must confess to some further deceptions, for which you
will forgive me, I hope. I was never a university student, and
those early cases I described to you—the Musgrave Ritual, for
example—were manufactured from whole cloth. The most
fortuitous occurrence since my arrival here was my meeting
with you, old friend, twenty-two years ago, while I was estab-
lishing my reputation. You have been invaluable in helping
me to enlarge the world's respect for decent investigative

methods and for that, as well as many other services, I shall always be grateful."

I felt a glow of pride. "Thank you, Holmes. In London, then, you set up your laboratory in Mrs. Hudson's basement?"

"Yes."

"I see why that too had to be secret. It was another of your 'bold strokes' that you located it so near to your lodgings. It is a stupendous achievement, I am sure, that you were able to reproduce the time mechanism with our primitive materials and means. The scientific books by Rutherford and his like helped you by showing you our latest developments, I suppose. But the books on supernatural affairs?"

Holmes smiled. "An interesting study, Watson. If only I had time to investigate it further. My age, the future which had invented time travel, was only beginning, with extreme and perfectly understandable caution, to explore what the new discovery might mean. To raise only a few questions, what if by traveling backward in time one altered the future? What would happen when one returned to one's own age? Indeed, could one even do so? I will be a pioneer in that study. I collected all those records of mysterious disappearances and ghostly sightings in hopes that some of them might really be instances of time visitors—from my own time perhaps. I was searching for any clue to how to return to that age. My investigations proved inconclusive, however, and I was forced to reconstruct the time-travel mechanism single-handedly. When I believed I had finished Moriarty at Reichenbach, I ended my researches for a while, determined to remain in your England and to devote myself to her. But when I realized that Moriarty had survived, I knew I must rededicate my efforts to the time cage, which would remove us from your age. That method of disposing of Moriarty seems just and proper; I am fixed on it. Alive or dead, he shall go back with me!"

We had reached Holmes' farmhouse. We entered. The metal stove had warmed the parlor somewhat, and we drew up two rickety chairs before the blaze. We had both forgotten our appetites. I knew that this was probably the last time we would sit thus before a fire. That thought, and the passionate feeling behind the story my old friend had just related, put me into a somber mood. I sensed the end of a long but necessary struggle and wanted only to be of service, as always.

Holmes had said that his altered plans included me. I asked him what part I should play in the climactic act.

He had regained his spirits. He rubbed his hands briskly in front of the blaze, then took out his pipe, lighting it with a coal from the fire. He sat leaning forward, elbows on his knees, fingertips pressed together before him, while billows of smoke escaped from between his thin lips. The flickering glow from the stove illuminated his determined expression, as eager as it had ever been when the conclusion to an adventure drew near.

"There has been much playacting in the thing, Watson, and so it is fitting that it climax onstage, don't you agree? Tomorrow evening, Wednesday, the Great Escott gives his final performance at the Oxford Theatre of Varieties near Soho Square. His appearance is unannounced, a spur-of-the-moment arrangement I made last evening with an old client who owed me a favor. Your part in it is simply to arrive home tonight. Moriarty will be watching for you; you are his only sure link with me. Sleep well, carry out your business tomorrow, see your patients as usual, and in the evening attend the show at the Oxford. That is all; I am certain you will be quite safe. Thus you will lead Moriarty to me; I will do the rest. As you know, I have a third cage. It will be the indispensable feature of my act. In our brief interview, Wiggins speculated that the cage was a criminal-catching device, a mousetrap for miscreants. I had to laugh, for so it is; both lure and trap in one. Moriarty shall not escape it this time!"

He stirred and rose, looking about him at the interior of the house which was to have been his place of retirement in the England he had grown to love. "And now I see that it grows late. The storm will be upon us soon. Victoria will get us to Willingdon just in time for our train back to London. Let us hope that we shall beat the rain."

20

By the time our train reached Polegate, the Sussex landscape was a green blur behind the flood of rain washing against our carriage windows. The hoot of the train whistle sounded mournful and distant around curves, like a piece of memory broken loose and tossed back by the wind.

Holmes sat across from me smoking his pipe, his expression inscrutable. Though I believed him, my thoughts were in a turmoil of adjustment to the story he had told me. Yet all the pieces fit. There seemed but one chance occurrence in the entire affair, and that was Wiggins' attendance at the Great Escott's performance at the Pavilion Theatre on the very day I showed him the book on stage design which I had saved from Holmes' library.

During our ride to meet the train at Willingdon, Holmes had described the Great Escott's genesis: "Moriarty was in London; I had to remain there too, but I needed an alias. I needed, as well, to lure my enemy to the cage. We had been performers; in fact we were especially skilled in the arts of illusion. Moriarty's particular hatred of me had grown out of the theatrical rivalry his warped brain was pleased to imagine we shared. What better way to rouse him, to make him careless perhaps, than to play upon that? And so I became Escott. I knew sooner or later, when my reputation developed, that Moriarty would come round to see me. He was sure to recognize the cage, and I counted on his acting precipitously. What I did not count on was your leading him to my laboratory. The mechanism he destroyed there was only a prototype; fortunately I had two duplicates in readiness. One he is sure to have demolished at the Pavilion Theatre after our escape yesterday. I ran from that encounter only to keep you from being harmed, Watson. The other I have had transported to the Oxford Theatre, and I shall confront him with it there tonight."

He had raised another subject, an unexpected one, which I had believed long buried: "Does not all this make you wonder about my one-time addiction to cocaine?"

"I have not thought of it at all. Do you mean that the Moriarty affair has something to do with it?"

"In a way. It will appall you to know that the future is given to many diversions, one of them the use of drugs, especially among theatrical people. It was from there that I brought the habit which I satisfied for some years with cocaine. I managed to end it after I believed Moriarty dashed to death on the rocks at Reichenbach, but a good deal of my enemy's changed appearance—his gaunt look and hollow eyes—is due to the fact that he has been ever at the needle. It is a wonder that he has not succumbed to the drug, but he is a creature of astonishing powers."

"Which I hope you will end tomorrow night," I added.

I had few exchanges with Holmes on our way back toward London. As we approached the stop prior to Waterloo Station he took down his carpetbag and opened it to don again Jenkins' dreadful tweed jacket and hat.

"I must leave you here," he told me. "Go on to Waterloo and engage a cab to take you home to Queen Anne Street. You have my instructions from there. Moriarty will play a waiting game. I rather fancy he has learned some respect for you, Watson. You deserve every bit of it."

We had perhaps five minutes before we were to part. One question in particular had been nagging at my brain ever since Moriarty had first hinted that Sherlock Holmes was not the real name of my friend. "Your names, Holmes," I asked him, "yours and Moriarty's—how did you come by them?"

The detective smiled grimly. "My enemy obtained his in characteristically sinister fashion. He murdered the real James Moriarty, a retiring mathematics professor with no connections, because the innocent man was able to provide a useful persona early in Moriarty's career. He kept the name as a convenience and, under it, published two treatises, on the binomial theorem and small planetary bodies, which drew on future knowledge. It was the last time he gave any of that knowledge away freely, and he did it, I think, as a taunt to contemporary science. For myself, I resorted to no such drastic means for my alias; I had no need to. When I wandered into Camford, my first destination was the nearest library. There, examining the books of your time, I chanced upon a volume of essays by the American Oliver Wendell Holmes, a physician like yourself, and I was enchanted by them. I determined then and there to become Holmes."

"And Sherlock?"

Holmes flushed and almost laughed. "Imagine that you could take any name, Watson. What would be your choice? Mine was Shakespeare; I was young, the bard was my god. I could not call myself Shakespeare Holmes; it would have been too conspicuous for one who did not want to draw attention to himself just yet. I saved the Sh and, thinking of the bard's shrewd Jew who yet could bleed, became Sherlock, and so I have remained all these years, and shall until I depart this age."

He rose and gripped my shoulder, squeezing it tightly. Our train screeched to a halt under the sloping station roof from which water cascaded in sheets. "So until tomorrow night and the end of our long road together, farewell."

He fixed a glittering smile upon his countenance and was so completely the commercial traveler Jenkins that I could hardly discover his own features. I watched him stride jauntily down the station platform to disappear in the crowd as my train pulled away toward central London.

Holmes was correct. I saw no trace of Moriarty at Waterloo Station nor during my cab ride home through the rain-swept streets, nor lurking near my house. I had to assume he was correct when he said that Moriarty would be watching nonetheless, waiting, and that he would follow me to the Oxford Theatre on the following evening. I made myself a light supper and retired early after a brandy and soda, over which I ruminated about the day's events. All night long rain beat unremittingly against my windows, and the wind moaned about the eaves. By ten o'clock the next morning I was in my office. I spent an uneventful day with my patients, who gave evidence by their raw complexions, soaking boots and ulsters, and dripping umbrellas that the storm continued unabated. At seven that evening I was in a cab, heading east along Oxford Street. In spite of the rain and lashing wind, the road was crowded with carriages. In one of them behind me, Moriarty followed.

The Oxford Theatre, like so many theatres before the advent of electric lighting, had been the victim of disastrous fires caused by gaslight accidents. It had been partially destroyed twice and, ten years before, demolished and rebuilt on the old site where Oxford Street, Charing Cross Road, and the Tottenham Court Road meet not far from Soho Square. My cab drew up opposite the iron-grated vestibules of the theatre's Oxford Street entrance, and I stepped down upon the glistening pavement, my umbrella raised. A stream of hansoms and four-wheelers came and went, discharging their passengers, and, in spite of the storm, a throng of gaily chattering patrons were streaming through the three arched doorways beneath the bright theatre lights. It was the Christmas season—I had had little time to think of that—and nothing could daunt the spirits of these merry pleasure-seekers.

I did not contemplate pleasure at all. The temptation to look over my shoulder was great, but I suppressed it and pushed straightforward into the throng.

Shortly I was up front in the stalls, with ten minutes to go before the program began.

The house was filling. I allowed myself to look about, not too obviously. I had not been in the Oxford before. It was a small attractive house, not at all in the overblown style of the Pavilion. The dress circle and balcony were supported by graceful cantilevered arcs with no pillars to obscure the view from the lower floor. The upper house was decorated in gold, blue, and pale pink. The plush-covered stalls were a rich shade of green, matching the handsome tableau curtains. The audience was not as boisterous as the Pavilion crowd; they were respectable middle-class patrons dressed in their finest for the evening's entertainment. Nevertheless, George Robey and Marie Lloyd, those institutions of the music hall scene, headed the bill, and excitement ran high.

I had had a night to sleep on Holmes' story, to arrange its details in my mind. As I settled back at last to wait for the overture to begin I thought not about Moriarty lurking behind me nor about the confrontation to come, but about Holmes' being a man from the far future. He would be returning soon, and I would never have the chance to ask him the multitude of questions whirling in my brain. I was filled with regrets about that. What would the future bring? He had already told me some things: there would be flying machines, devices for sending pictures and sound through the air, rocket ships to the moon, the planets, the stars. These intriguing hints had thrilled me; growing identical human beings from cells had frightened me. But still I wanted to know more—about cures for disease, for example, and about other advances in medical science. I had not formulated these questions in time to ask them, but as our train had rushed back toward London through the storm I had described a paradox which struck me.

"I fancy I have helped to make you an international celebrity," I had remarked. "I cannot imagine that the future has forgotten Sherlock Holmes. He must have a footnote at least in your history. Have any of my writings survived? It must be odd to find that you are a famous historical character."

Holmes had answered, "If what you surmise were true, then

I would know the outcome of my meeting with Moriarty to-morrow night. But I do not, for there is no Sherlock Holmes in the history of my time. I can suggest one of two explanations for the anomaly: either I had to be born before history could be altered to include Sherlock Holmes, or, what is more likely, that there are infinite branchings of history, and we, Moriarty and I, were thrown back into but one of them."

I was confused. "Then how can you be certain about the terrible war which you prophesied?"

"I cannot, and that is my hope. If the record of your age has been altered to include me, then perhaps it is possible to change even more of it, to prevent the world war and subsequent wars which were sad signposts of human folly in my time's history. As it stands now, if Moriarty is not stopped, those wars are inevitable."

Thus, the consequences balanced upon the outcome of tonight's confrontation at the Oxford Theatre of Varieties had been made unmistakably clear to me.

At last the house lights dimmed, and Mr. W. G. Eaton's orchestra struck up the overture. Shortly, the acts began parading by. I do not remember one of them except for Marie Lloyd, whose cheerful vulgarity in singing "I Was One of the Ruins Cromwell Knocked About a Bit" roused me to a pained smile. After what seemed hours of acrobats, comic toffs and tramps, simpering soubrettes, and trained animals came the announcement I had awaited: "A welcome addition to our program, ladies and gentlemen! An extra treat for your enjoyment in this season of good will! The mystifying Great Escott!"

And the star-studded scrim and mysterious blue lighting which I had first seen at the Pavilion Theatre were before me again.

I imagined the seething fury which must be boiling in Moriarty's breast. He would be certain now that Escott was Holmes. Would his anger at the detective's audacity make him careless? I shivered at the hatred which might be boring into my back from his eyes.

Holmes' act was much as before, complete with dog, cat,

pigeons, flowers, and five miraculous boxes; the audience response was as effusive as at the Pavilion. At last came the silvery cage, the third cage, the mousetrap for Moriarty. Holmes' introduction to this climactic illusion was changed: "Only one soul on earth other than myself understands the wonder you are about to see, and he cannot perform it!" The words were a taunt, a pointed challenge which Moriarty could not mistake. "Anyone who doubts is welcome to come onstage to examine the apparatus," Holmes concluded.

Did he expect Moriarty to confront him then? If so, he was disappointed, for no one climbed the stage stairs to accept his offer.

And so, entering the cage, he proceeded to vanish.

It was as it had been at the Pavilion. Prepared as I was, the feat still amazed me. Eyes closed in a mock trance, Holmes, wrapped mummylike in his black cloak, began to turn, then to whirl rapidly. The scintillating black space engulfed him as before, disintegrated him into a flare of sparks, and he was gone.

I had to remind myself that this disappearance was an ingeniously contrived illusion. The real mechanism would be engaged only when Holmes lured—or forced—Moriarty into the cage.

The audience thundered its applause. The green tableau curtains swept closed for a change of scene while the chairman dashed out to announce the next act. I experienced a sense of anticlimax. I was not certain what Holmes had intended to happen, but somehow I had thought that whatever it was would occur during his performance as Escott. Had something gone wrong, or had I assumed too much? I glanced as discreetly as possible about the audience. Every face within my view, none identifiable as Moriarty's, gazed with a happy expression upon the stage, where a comic burlesque noisily ensued. There were banjo players, a male quartet, and two or three other turns before the effusive thanks and well wishes of the chairman signaled the end of the evening. The house lights flared; the audience, much pleased except for myself, and presumably one other, began to make its way out.

I rose but stood indecisively while the aisles emptied. What was I to do? Holmes had not prepared me. My task had been to lead his old enemy here; I had done so, I hoped. "Moriarty will play a waiting game," Holmes had predicted. Apparently, he still waited. Was this to be the end for me? Should I go and leave Holmes and Moriarty to do final battle alone?

At the Pavilion I had had clear instructions to stay. Now, lacking them and wishing not to spoil any plan of my friend, I decided that I must withdraw.

The theatre was half empty. I took up my coat, hat, and umbrella, slipped down my row, and proceeded up the aisle. Yet with each step upon the green figured carpet I felt how wrong my leaving was. I had had no proper farewell from Holmes; I could not believe that he had intended to leave me without one. Too, I had spent nearly a quarter of a century at his side in case after case, often in dire circumstances. Now, at the conclusion of his most crucial adventure, was it right to leave him? Was not there one last helping act which I could perform?

I was among the stragglers crowded at the door leading to the foyer. I hesitated. I believe I would have turned back had the choice not been snatched from me. At that moment a steely grip upon my sleeve pulled me toward the shadows below the balcony.

"Watson, this way," whispered the voice of Sherlock Holmes.

But when I turned I saw, not a foot from my face, the leering grimace of James Moriarty. Into my ribs, unseen by the last patrons to pass through the foyer door, he pressed the cold barrel of a pistol.

Rudely he thrust me into a dark alcove, crowding into the narrow space after me. Urgently he continued to force his pistol against my chest, silently warning me that I was not to speak. He gripped my arm fiercely. His ragged breathing close to my ear was fearfully loud. Hidden in the shadows, we watched two pages make their round of the deserted auditorium, checking and locking doors. At last they left together by a side exit, the click of its lock sounding fatefully final. Still holding me tightly, Moriarty neither moved nor spoke for a moment. Desperately I hoped that charwomen would appear as they had at the Pavilion, that one of them would be mad Alice to rescue me from my straits, but none arrived. At last I felt Moriarty relax his hold on my sleeve. Cautiously he drew me out into the back promenade, in the shadow of the balcony.

"A moment more," he said, his eyes glittering in the gloom. He peered upward, waiting. Suddenly the house lights died, shut down by the limes man in his booth high above, and we were left in a dusky light, pierced only by a few electric sconces along the outer aisle of our floor.

I felt Moriarty's hand in my coat pocket, from which he removed my pistol to toss it away among the stalls. "That eliminates your sting." He released me at last and stepped back. He was dressed in evening clothes, as was I, indeed much as I had seen Holmes himself dress for two hours of classical music at some London hall. Moriarty's black silk hat and dark coat made him a sinister figure in the shadows. The whites of his eyes and his teeth flashed triumphantly as he spoke: "You will make the difference, doctor. Holmes and I are equally matched; you must know how equally by now. You will be my hostage. I fancy that will tip the balance my way. Is he waiting backstage? Come, let us not disappoint him." He waved his pistol to urge me down the aisle.

I stood firm. "I will not be your hostage!" I asserted.

His twitching head began to tremble even more, and his brows lowered. The soft voice could not mask his controlled hysteria. "It would be a shame to kill you at once, but I shall not hesitate to do so if necessary," he hissed. "You must have some idea of helping your old friend. Do you think your death will do it? To keep your hopes alive a little longer, doctor, I suggest that you obey me. How can you forego a ringside seat at the conclusion to this bizarre tale? Were I you, I should not be able to resist knowing its outcome. Move along now!" Again he waved the pistol threateningly.

He was right. I could not see how my death would help

Holmes, though I would gladly have given my life for him at that moment. I turned and proceeded down the aisle.

"Onto the stage, now," my captor ordered when we reached the orchestra pit. I climbed the stairs at the side of the stage and pushed my way around the edge of the heavy velvet curtain. Moriarty followed quite close now, and I could feel the pistol barrel pressed between my shoulder blades.

The stage was bare, but lit in ghostly fashion by a single bulb high above its proscenium arch. The backdrop for the last act, a painted scene of a moonlit Venetian villa with gondolas gliding by, was still in place. The cage, Holmes' trap for Moriarty, was nowhere in sight; it was no doubt somewhere below or off in the darkened wings. Like the stage floor of the Pavilion, the Oxford's boards were traversed by cracks which showed where the numerous trapdoors were located.

"Step carefully, Dr. Watson, as shall I," Moriarty warned. "I do not want either of us to disappear suddenly, as you did so neatly when last we met at the Pavilion."

We proceeded cautiously. When we were about halfway across the stage, Moriarty ordered me to stop. I did so and turned to face him. He gazed not at me but up and around the stage area. "Holmes!" he shouted. The hollow spaces echoed with his cry. "I am here, Holmes, as you wished me to be. We have an appointment, I believe; an understanding at which we must arrive. For my part in the argument I bring a loaded pistol with a hair trigger, pointed at Dr. Watson's breast. It would be a shame to allow an innocent man to suffer because we disagree, particularly as he is an old friend of yours, a faithful if foolish servant. Show yourself at once, Holmes, or I shall not hesitate to finish him!"

Moriarty stood about six paces from me. His gun hand did not waver as his hunched torso turned to right and left and his wary eyes roved about into every darkened corner of the stage. I had no doubt that he meant to shoot me if Holmes did not appear, and I was frantically pondering what, if anything, I could do to save myself, when a movement in the floor behind Moriarty caught my eye. Staring at it, I froze.

One of the trapdoors was slowly swinging downward.

Moriarty's eyes were occupied searching the gloom, and he had begun to call out his challenge again; he saw no clue in my surprised expression, nor heard any telltale sound. The rectangular trap opened fully, leaving a gaping hole stretching behind him. From out of the hole, propelled silently upward by some mechanism like those I had seen in Holmes' theatre book, rose the silvery cage, its front side open. Inside the cage was Holmes himself.

The familiar head appeared, the shoulders, the torso. Holmes had removed Escott's cloak and makeup. The contrast between his heroic mien and Moriarty's distorted profile was stunning.

At last I saw them together; the end of the old conflict was near!

But I was the betrayer. Moriarty glimpsed my unguarded look of amazement and joy. The game was up! He started, cried out, whirled before Holmes had fully risen upon the stage. In anticipation Holmes leaped upward out of the cage, lashed out to deflect the gun arm which Moriarty swung upon him. Shaken from the devil's grasp by Holmes' blow, the gun flew high into the air, clattered upon the stage, and skidded away.

The antagonists, both weaponless now except for their physical strength, joined and grappled, grunting loudly, crying out in strangled voices, cursing, falling upon the stage floor to rise and join again. They struck terrible blows, the sound of which was dreadful, but neither man gave way. They tore at one another's faces. Soon both visages were streaked with red, and their hands became like beasts' claws in a frenzy of killing. And yet they fought on. They fell, clattering against the cage. I realized that Holmes was attempting to drag Moriarty into it. Moriarty's only aim was to destroy Holmes. They rolled farther away from me, across the stage floor. I had been frozen in horror, but now I thought of helping my friend. The gun! Might I not retrieve it? But it was too late. The writhing bodies were but a few feet from the fallen weapon. Then an arm reached out to grasp it by the barrel, to strike with it again and again and again . . .

A body lay upon the stage floor. Panting, another figure rose, staggering. It had hunched shoulders and an oscillating head.

A silent cry of despair went up in my soul. Was this the climax—the death of my friend and the triumph of Moriarty? The devil ignored me utterly. He knelt, grasped Holmes' shoulders, and began to drag the limp body toward the cage. When he had deposited it inside, he turned at last to me.

His breathing was still ragged, but a triumphant light gleamed in his eyes. "I have not forgotten you, doctor. I shall do with Holmes as he would have done with me, only I shall not return with him to our time. When he is gone you, and the world, will have to face me without the great detective. I fancy you will all have a hard go of it!" He gave a smug chortle as he turned to complete his task. He was about to swing the cage door closed, when a low moan escaped Holmes' lips.

Hope leaped in my breast. So he was not dead!

Moriarty still had the pistol. He pulled it out and pointed it at Holmes, whose eyelids fluttered, then opened.

"I am heartily glad to see you conscious," Moriarty sneered. "It gives me the opportunity to wish you a formal good-bye. I hope you are alert enough to realize who the victor is in our long campaign. Do not make any foolish moves while I complete my task." He reached out his arm to shut the cage. Simultaneously his gun hand leveled the weapon at Holmes' head.

Only then did I realize that he intended to shoot Holmes before sending him back into the future.

My friend might be helpless, but the campaign which Moriarty was so triumphantly certain of having won was not quite over. Holmes was my nearly defeated general, but as a man of the ranks I could still do something, and I intended to try. Wordlessly I thanked God for the rain, for it had provided me with a weapon: my umbrella. Holmes had said that Moriarty had learned some respect for me; he had not learned quite enough, apparently. He had turned his back upon me, thinking that I would not dare to interfere. Therefore it was with special pleasure that I demonstrated his error to him.

Stealthily I raised my umbrella and brought its bone handle down in a crashing blow upon the back of his skull.

He fell senseless upon the stage floor, the unused gun clattering from his fingers.

Holmes, now fully conscious, stared from me to the fallen form of his old enemy. This thin lips parted upon a smile, and then a huge laugh tore from his throat. With some difficulty he stood. A great bruise and swelling already showed above his left occipital ridge, where Moriarty had struck repeatedly with the gun, and his face was scratched and streaked with blood. His clothes were torn and dusty, and he was obviously exhausted, but he stumbled forward to throw his arms around me in an embrace.

"I never get your limits, Watson," he said as he released me. "You are the best and bravest man I have ever known!"

I shall carry the proud memory of those words with me to my grave.

"And now I must be quick." Holmes bent and dragged the unconscious Moriarty into the cage. He turned to grasp my hand firmly, gazing at me keenly. "The moment has come for parting, old friend. I know that I have sometimes seemed cold and distant, but now you know the reasons and will forgive me, I hope. I go to an uncertain future but before leaving must tell you that I shall think of you always as my one true friend in this or any age."

I was touched by the moisture in Holmes' eyes, but alarmed at his words. "An uncertain future? But you return to your own age; surely it will be capable of dealing with Moriarty."

Holmes released my hand as he stepped back into the cage. "Alas, I cannot be certain of either of those things, Watson. The time mechanism is very delicate, and I can only guess how to set it properly. I do not know how our initial voyage into time may have changed the future. I only know that it is necessary and proper that I remove Moriarty from the world in the same way he arrived."

He reached out and pulled the cage door firmly closed. Its metallic sound echoed over the dimly lit stage. Holmes gave me a brave look from that noble head, bloody but unbowed, and pressed his fingers at two points on the front side of the cage.

"Farewell," I heard his voice as if over a great distance.

Then the cage shimmered and, with a sound like the far-off tinkling of a bell, it, Moriarty, and my dear friend vanished.

On the evening of the following day, Thursday, my wife returned from her holiday to find me napping in my chair in our sitting room. She bent and kissed me on the forehead. My eyelids fluttered open.

"I rang the bell, John, but you did not answer." She busied herself with untying the ribbon of the pretty straw hat which I guessed was a gift from her dear friend in Kent. "I have had a wonderful week. Are not you going to ask me about it?"

I roused myself to glance about. Through the parlor door I saw her portmanteau, valises, and several additional boxes which the carriage driver had no doubt helped her to carry into the entrance hall. Hours of careful unpacking would follow. She walked about the parlor, examining every knick-knack and plant. I smiled lazily at her bustling movements. Her comforting presence already began to fill the house, whose rooms had seemed cold and incomplete in her absence.

I stood and took her hand. "And so, my dear Violet, how was your visit?"

She looked at me closely. "You appear tired, John. Let us talk of how you have spent your time." She drew me to a place close beside her on the settee. "Have you seen Sherlock Holmes?"

"I have," I confessed.

She gave me a shrewd look. "And have you had an adventure?"

"I have indeed, my dear."

"And how is your old friend?"

"He was well when last I saw him."

She seemed satisfied with this. She stood and went to the parlor door. Her figure was plump, but she still walked with girlish, almost coquettish, movements. She frowned at the disorderly pile of luggage. "I shall not be happy until I have put these things away. Will you help me, John?" She picked up a small valise and a gaily wrapped Christmas package. I rose to join her. "And how is your friend's retirement?" she asked suddenly, turning and pausing at the foot of the stairs.

I hesitated, then picked up two suitcases, one in each hand. "He is not retired," I said. "He found that he had some unfinished business."

She arched a brow. "Oh? Well, I expect a man like Sherlock Holmes has much unfinished business." She smiled coyly. "You know, I never believed he had retired, or that he ever will."

Suddenly she put down the valise and box and stepped toward me to fling her arms round my neck. She gave me a mighty hug and a kiss. "I am happy to be back, old dear." She looked at me with a twinkle in her eye. "And if you do not choose to tell me about your last adventure, I shall learn to live with your silence."

The holiday season was past. It was seven days into the new year. The winter was bitterly cold, but before the fire at 221B Baker Street that afternoon it was cozily warm. I sipped a brandy; Wiggins drank a bottle of Piper-Heidsieck in honor of Edward, whose amiable ways he admired and, I thought, rather affectedly imitated. But then, my young friend was an actor.

"Besides comradeship, doctor, which I hope will always be a reason for your presence here," Wiggins was saying, "why else have you come?" He wore his blue-striped caftan and crouched cross-legged on his chair, leaning as eagerly forward as on the evening when I had revealed my dilemma to him. Columbine warbled happily in her cage, and his plants loomed in every corner.

"Do you not have questions?" I replied.

"I am discreet," Wiggins announced placidly.

This was a maddening response for, not having heard from him since the matinee at the Pavilion Theatre, I had come to tell him that I had decided to keep Holmes' secret to myself. I agreed with Holmes that the twentieth century was hardly ready for it.

Wiggins accepted this news with cheerful equanimity.

"I can tell you, however, that in his battle with Moriarty he was the victor," I added.

"I am glad of that. And do I hear a note of special pride in your voice? Were you able to help your old friend?"

I ignored this teasing but to-the-point question. "I have something more to tell you. You know that the cage and the other equipment in Holmes' laboratory were pretty thoroughly destroyed; so too was the cage at the Pavilion— both by Moriarty. But there was a third cage." I hesitated. "It has disappeared. But its mechanisms, which Holmes used at the Oxford Theatre and which were found below stage, have fallen into my hands. They are rather extensive, and since Holmes' bank fund continues to pay for the rental of Mrs. Hudson's basement, I thought that would be the best place to store them. I have prepared her for their arrival tomorrow and have directed that they be set up as they were found below the stage at the Oxford. There are three lorries full. Will you help to direct the workmen should there be any difficulty?"

"I shall. And am I to know no more of the cage?"

I hesitated again. "Only that you were correct: it was a kind of mousetrap, and it fulfilled its end to Holmes' satisfaction."

"Thank you for that, doctor."

We were silent for a moment. The coals hissed upon the grate. Wiggins continued to gaze at me with bright interest.

"And last of all . . . ?" he prompted.

I drank the end of my brandy and soda. I had to tell him: "And last of all, Sherlock Holmes is gone."

"Dead?"

"No, but he is . . . elsewhere, triumphing over evil as ever, I am sure. I do not think he will revisit these shores. England, the world, shall not see his like for a long time. He was the best and wisest man I have ever known."

I took my leave of Wiggins then.

Shortly thereafter I was out upon Baker Street, walking home through a newly fallen snow which muffled every sound.

Epilogue

"**D**R. WATSON?**" I hear Sister Milbank whisper.

The sounds of traffic have died with the light. I have fallen asleep with the tray of papers over which I have labored these several days. My task is done. The Sister's voice wakes me from a dream in which Sherlock Holmes and I trace the spoor of a treacherous criminal along a fog-bound byway of the great city. She, ever industrious, stacks my papers neatly, places my pen by them, and moves my tray aside. I glance out the window. Electric streetlamps make shimmering circlets of light in the frosty night air; the sharp black twigs of the naked plane trees cut across the lonely light like knives.

Alas, the assassin's bullet pierced Archduke Ferdinand's throat at Sarajevo in 1914, and Europe, which had become an armed camp, plunged into the terrible holocaust which Holmes had forecast. His efforts to counteract the effect of Moriarty's evil machinations failed. As he predicted, the United States was drawn into the conflict, and by war's end ten million valiant young men had lost their lives, mowed down by machine gun bullets as they leaped from the filthy trenches to fall upon barbed wire, strangled by poison gas, or hunted down by tanks—all ghastly new weapons of war. Alas too for young Wiggins, who died—I like to think with a smile of bravery upon his lips—at the battle of the Argonne Forest in 1918.

Sister Milbank opens her eyes wide at me, as if at a young child who has just learned successfully to place one building block upon another. "Doctor, I see 'The End' written on this page. You have finished your story!"

"I have."

She beams at me with vicarious pride. "And does Sherlock Holmes triumph in the end?"

I think of the terrible war which he had been unable to avert. "Not completely."

She is surprised and rather disappointed at this. "But I thought your friend was always triumphant."

"Not always. He was human, you see."

The Sister is not quite certain what to make of this. She allows the explanation to dissolve into the air, unexplored. Shortly thereafter, when she has lowered the bed under my shoulders and tucked the blankets firmly round me, she turns down the light and glides out, a wraith in starched white.

I am left to my dreams.

I think again of Wiggins, who did more for England than sacrifice his life. As "Altamont," he, not Holmes, foiled the plans of the German High Command in 1914. (I too had a modest part in that.) It was Wiggins who wrote the narrative of the adventure, calling it "His Last Bow" and substituting Holmes as its hero, partly to protect his own identity (the Foreign Office needed Wiggins' skill at mimicry and disguise), but more as a tribute to his mentor. Never realizing that Holmes had not taken part in it, my agent, Dr. Doyle, published the story in 1917. (It, as well as the "Adventure of the Lion's Mane," helped to sustain the fiction of the detective's retirement.)

Practical considerations intrude on my memories. Tomorrow my solicitor, Murray, the son of the orderly who saved my life at Maiwand, will visit me; it is to be a professional call. Somewhere in the vaults of Cox and Company, Charing Cross, there is a travel-worn tin dispatch box with my name stenciled upon its battered lid. It is crammed with papers, all unpublished, relating to Holmes' cases, and into it I shall direct Murray to place this manuscript. I have no wish to be subjected to men's calumny while I live; I would no doubt be called a liar or a dotard should the story be published now. But I no longer believe passionately that our time is not ready for it. Perhaps there are lessons, not the least of which is vigilance, to be learned therein. And so, to my steadfast and loving wife, or her heirs, shall be left the choice of whether or not the true end of Sherlock Holmes shall be known and the fiction of his retirement upon the Sussex Downs be exploded.

Shadows form upon my wall, shapes of struggle and flight. A lean hawk-nosed profile materializes, and I hear the familiar voice: "Come, Watson, the game is afoot!"

In my dream it is 1895. London is wreathed in a dreadful fog through which a criminal escapes, but Sherlock Holmes is on his trail.

As ever in my dreams, I am by my old friend's side.